COURTING LADY YEARDLY

**Willful Winterbournes
Book Three**

Sandra Sookoo

Dragonblade Publishing, Inc. is an imprint of Kathryn Le Veque Novels, Inc.
P.O. Box 23
Moreno Valley, CA 92556
ceo@dragonbladepublishing.com

Produced in the United States of America

First Edition October 2022
Trade Paperback Edition

ARE YOU SIGNED UP FOR DRAGONBLADE'S BLOG?

You'll get the latest news and information on exclusive giveaways, exclusive excerpts, coming releases, sales, free books, cover reveals and more.

Check out our complete list of authors, too!

No spam, no junk. That's a promise!

Sign Up Here

www.dragonbladepublishing.com

Dearest Reader;

Thank you for your support of a small press. At Dragonblade Publishing, we strive to bring you the highest quality Historical Romance from some of the best authors in the business. Without your support, there is no 'us', so we sincerely hope you adore these stories and find some new favorite authors along the way.

Happy Reading!

CEO, Dragonblade Publishing

Additional Dragonblade books by Author Sandra Sookoo

Willful Winterbournes Series
Romancing Miss Quill (Book 1)
Pursuing Mr. Mattingly (Book 2)
Courting Lady Yeardly (Book 3)
Teasing Miss Atherby (Book 4)

The Storme Brother Series
The Soul of a Storme (Book 1)
The Heart of a Storme (Book 2)
The Look of a Storme (Book 3)
A Storme's Christmas Legacy
A Storme's First Noelle
The Sting of a Storme (Book 4)
The Touch of a Storme (Book 5)
The Fury of a Storme (Book 6)
Much Ado About a Storme (in the *A Duke in Winter* anthology)

Dedication

To Nicole A. Thank you for your everlasting support and encouragement. It means so much to me and thank you for loving my books. You keep reading and I'll keep writing.

CHAPTER ONE

July 26, 1819
Berkshire County, England
Ettesmere Park

W*HAT FRESH HELL is this?*
Gilbert Edmund Winterbourne—Lord Yeardly, a courtesy title of his father's—came awake cognizant of two things. One, his head ached like the very devil, for he'd imbibed heavily the night before after his brother's nuptial ceremony. *Not* because he was celebrating that momentous occasion. And two, there was a woman in his bed, sleeping next to him, and damn his eyes, he had no bloody recollection of who she was.

Slowly so as not to jostle his head or wake the woman, he slipped from the bed and then nearly tumbled onto his arse when his foot caught in the sheet. After righting himself, he frowned as he realized he was still more or less dressed in his evening clothes, but he padded to the other side of the bed in his bare feet. One peek at the woman's sleeping face had his stomach roiling and the urge to retch becoming a very real possibility.

Christ! It wasn't some random doxy. Oh, no. This was his estranged wife, Madelene. He'd recognize that flowing, curly brown hair and the tiny beauty mark over her left eyebrow anywhere.

Damn, damn, damn!

Why was she here at all? To say nothing of how she ended up in his bed. The fact he was still fully clothed meant he hadn't been intimate with her—not that he would have been—but the mystery deepened. Needing answers and copious amounts of tea, Gilbert looked about in dim morning light, for of course it was raining—again—and after he'd located his cane, he quietly let himself out of the bedroom. Once in the corridor beyond, he took a few deep breaths, but the urge to cast up his accounts was still there, thanks to the raging megrim, and it came with a surge of hot anger and bitterness that would soon swallow him whole.

Through the morass of the confusion muddling his head, he remembered Madelene had shown up on their doorstep last night prior to Arthur's ceremony. His sister Sophia had informed him of that fact once his brother had been safely wed. What followed was a bit of a blur, for Gilbert had refused to see his wife until much later in the evening.

She could wallow for all he'd cared—she deserved it after what she'd done—but then he'd belatedly recalled that to the rest of the family, his marriage was still fine on the surface and he couldn't very well turn his own wife away without knowing why the devil she'd come. So, he'd instructed the butler to show her to his rooms, and then he'd taken himself off to drink in one of the village taverns, not returning to the manor until quite late, where he'd tumbled into bed still mostly dressed.

What a damned coil.

Navigating the stairs proved a bit of a challenge with the raging ache in his head and the constant urge to vomit, but he finally managed it, and by the time he'd gained the morning room, he heaved a sigh. The only member of his family there at the early hour was his sister.

"What the devil are you doing here? Don't you have a new husband to bedevil?" Sophia had married a few weeks ago due to thinking she had a heart ailment that would end her life imminently. The news of her engagement had shocked the family. Yet after those events had played out, it was plain to see that she and Mr. Mattingly were well-suited.

And the last thing he wished to discuss this morning was love and romance.

His sister blew out a breath of annoyance as she worried the end of her blonde braid. As of yet, she hadn't dressed for the day, but her trailing morning gown of lace and muslin put him in mind of heroines in the Gothic novels she favored. "There is no need to come the crab, Gil. Rest assured, I am enjoying my husband to the hilt." A faint blush stained her cheeks while he groused to himself. "Soon enough we shall be out of your hair and off to France for a honeymoon trip."

"Well, bully for you." When a footman inquired as to what he wanted, he merely said a pot of strong Assam tea and a cup. "I suppose Arthur already left for his own wedding trip?" How was it that all of a sudden, his siblings were neck-deep into new marriages after years of quiet?

"He and Juliana did indeed leave early this morning for a quick two weeks to London. They don't wish to be too far away in deference to Mr. Quill."

"Ah." Juliana's father was aging and, in the process, his mental faculties were fading. Though the man had attended the wedding yesterday and had been up to Ettesmere Park a few times, rarely did he remember those outings. "Please refrain from telling me how wonderful marriage is. I am not in the mood this morning."

She snorted. "As if you've been congenial about it any other time?"

Gilbert ignored her in favor of pouring tea into the porcelain cup. The strong, rich aroma of the brew teased his nostrils, and he sighed. "This makes me miss India." At least while he'd been there, the fears in his life hadn't been able to touch him.

"I thought you detested living there."

"Oh, I did for a variety of reasons, but when it came to discovering new teas to import back to England, it was amazing."

He pointed to his cup. "This tea is named after the region of its production, Assam, and is apparently indigenous there. I'm told initial efforts to plant Chinese varieties in Assam soil did not succeed."

"Are they not the same plant?"

"Oh, good heavens, no." He grinned as he warmed to his subject, for the study and cultivation of tea was his specialty. "Assam tea is mostly grown near sea level. It's prized for its body, briskness, malty flavor, and strong, bright color." With a slight tip of his cup toward her, he showed her the dark brown liquid. "This tea, or a blend using it, is often sought for breakfast when one doesn't wish for the taste of coffee."

"So, then, it is supposed to help you wake?" She lifted a blonde eyebrow. "Or cure a hangover?"

"Do shut up." He sipped his tea and reveled in the taste of the tannins. "When I think of the two years I spent over there, doing nothing except learning about tea, I realize it was a much simpler time in my life."

At the age of eight and thirty, he never thought he would be living such a half-existence with an estranged wife, no family of his own, and certainly no fidelity in his union. Now that his siblings had found love a second time in their lives, that happiness rankled, for he'd married five years ago next month, and three of those years he'd spent apart from his wife. What had begun with hope, faith, and joy had rapidly descended into grief, bitterness, and anger.

None of which had he been able to let go of in the intervening years.

And when he considered the history he had before he'd met and married Madelene, cold bands of fear gripped him, for it made him think that some of the problems—the very core of why the rift had opened between them in the first place—lay squarely on his shoulders, and since there was nothing he could do about that, there might not be any hope to solve them.

I cannot think about that now.

"Did you talk with Madelene last night?"

What was there to say? "No." He hoped his tone wouldn't invite further discussion.

But when had his sister ever take that hint? "Ah, so then you drank yourself into a stupor and by the time you went upstairs, she was asleep." It wasn't a question. And because it wasn't, he didn't deign to answer. Sophia sailed on as if it didn't matter. "I thought all was well between the two of you."

"How the deuce could you have come to *that* assumption?" Though he rarely spoke about his wife or the state of his marriage, the family assumed they were still happily wed even though he'd made enough sarcastic, bitter comments over the past few weeks to make someone notice if they were paying attention. "I would rather walk across hot coals in my bare feet than have my wife here right now."

At least that was the truth, and he'd had precious little of that in recent years. Regardless, the outburst had caused his head to pound with more authority, so he sipped his tea and hoped his sister would let the matter drop.

She did not. Of course. "What has she done with herself since you were in India?"

"I don't know and neither do I care." He shrugged. "No doubt she has been keeping busy in the London townhouse."

"Oh, Gilbert, have you even written to her?" Distress wove through his sister's tone.

"Occasionally, but in my defense, her letters are few and far between as well." For good reason. He'd simply told her to stop writing him, that he didn't wish to hear from her again after what she'd done.

Sophia eyed him with speculation. She sipped her tea and finally shook her head. "What happened? You have let yourself become jaded and bitter. Frankly, it's not attractive, and even Hannah has noticed you are a grouchy old man."

"I'm hardly old." But it was just a matter of time that his niece would see how unhappy he truly was. "I cannot help what I feel, nor can I go back in time and undo what is broken."

"And that is?"

"There is too much history between Madelene and me now. Hell, it's almost as if my *entire* history is coming back to haunt me." He took a gulp of his tea. Wished he'd had the foresight to bring a flask of brandy downstairs with him. "Suffice it to say, she betrayed me, Sophia." Emotion graveled his voice, and he made a conscious effort to tamp it down. There was no sense in showing his feelings, especially since he didn't intend to let his wife stay at Ettesmere Park. And if he released his control on his emotions, fear would sweep him up and completely upend his life. "She betrayed our wedding vows. With my best friend!" The last words were a touch loud, so he modulated his voice. "How can I forgive that?"

"Madelene took up with Major Pritchard?" Sophia's eyes rounded. "Good heavens. How did that even come about?"

"I don't know." He truly didn't. "But I discovered that fact shortly before I left for India. When I asked her directly if she'd been in Hugh's bed, she didn't give me a straight answer." Another gulp of tea didn't make the telling of the tale any better. "So, I left as scheduled, and I haven't made inroads into repairing that rift. Not that I want to."

If Madelene cared nothing for the sanctity of their vows, why should he?

For long moments, his sister stared at him. "I'm so sorry." She tapped a fingernail on the side of her porcelain teacup. "While you were away from England, did *you* remain true to your vows?"

Heat crept up the back of his neck. "No." At her gasp, he huffed. "It was during a moment of weakness early on in the trip, when I let myself be wracked by emotions. Anger and revenge won out, coupled with loneliness, but it was only one time, and it hasn't happened since." If his wife could seek refuge with someone else, why couldn't he? Hot shame poured into his chest, rising with every breath. How could he remain angry with

Madelene when he'd done the same thing only after the fact? Yet another reason to ignore those emotions lest he do something stupid and become even weaker.

Never again would that happen.

"Does it make a difference that my indiscretion happened during our estrangement, while hers was blatantly done when the marriage might still have been viable?"

"Oh, Gilbert, I'm not certain I have any answers for you on that. It's an ethical issue to be sure." Sophia covered his hand with hers. "What a mess."

"Indeed."

"Mama will be so disappointed. She wants all of her children happy and wed."

He snorted. "Mama can mind her own business. Some matches simply do not take." Especially if it was his fault every pregnancy he'd had a hand in failed. It mattered not that he had been desperately in love with Madelene even before they'd wed. Things had happened over the course of the marriage that had chipped away at those feelings, and love simply hadn't been strong enough to withstand the obstacles.

Compassion clouded Sophia's eyes. "What will you do? Obviously, Madelene wishes to reconcile."

"How can you possibly know that?" His tone was sharper than he'd intended, but he couldn't help it. He didn't want that hope.

She shrugged. "Why else would she have come to Ettesmere Park?"

"Perhaps she is seeking a divorce." Gilbert drained his teacup and then quickly refreshed it. The pounding in his head hadn't lessened with the first.

"An expensive and arduous endeavor at best. Is that something you wish to pursue?"

"I don't know." Though it had been on his mind since returning to England three months prior, he hadn't inquired about the steps needed. Partially out of respect to his mother and her summer entertainment plans and partially due to needing to have one last conversation—or rather argument—with his wife before making such a lasting decision. "It is complicated." To further muck things up, there were still feelings between him and Madelene. Not quite love any longer, but they weren't completely hatred either.

Above all, they both deserved closure before the next step was taken.

"Where is she now?"

"In my bed." No longer was there a thrill when he said that. The first two years of their marriage had been joyful—mostly. But then Madelene had lost a babe near the five-month mark. They'd mourned, of course, and took it in stride. The following year, she had become with child again, except that baby, though it was carried to full term, had been stillborn. After that, the rift between them had occurred, for there had been no words, no way to come to grips with those losses.

His family hadn't known of the first one, and of course, there had been the usual rally about them at the loss of the second. But Madelene hadn't been the same after that. She'd withdrawn into herself; he'd sought comfort in his club, for it simply wasn't done to let all and sundry see a man's pain and disappointment. Then, three months following the stillbirth, he'd indicated a wish to perhaps try again and rebuild their relationship, but his wife had apparently moved on.

With Hugh.

With a wounded pride and a raw, shredded heart, and fear nipping at his heels, Gilbert had taken himself off to India as planned, except he was not accompanied by his wife, and they'd lived apart ever since.

"Did you, ah…" Another blush infused Sophia's cheeks.

"Really? After all the scandalous things you've probably done with Mr. Mattingly, *this* is what has fire in your cheeks?" It was no secret his sister adored everything about the married state, especially the physical. When she merely grinned, he sighed and shook his head. "Of course not. I was drunk and she was asleep by the time I came up. Besides, we haven't seen each other for three years. Those feelings are surely dead."

God, he hoped that was true. If he still felt desire for his wife after all this time, it would surely complicate things further going forward. But a glimpse of her hair and the side of her face in repose had told him nothing.

"I wonder, though."

"Do get off it, Sis." Gilbert waved a hand impatiently in the air. "Mama thinks all is well. What was I supposed to do last night? Dump her into a guest room and let everyone know I have failed as a husband?"

In every way that mattered. If Madelene *did* wish for a divorce, would she marry Hugh? Did she think her own husband's seed was too flawed and that was why they'd had such horrid luck with a baby? If that were the case, how could he, in good conscience, keep her within the bonds of the union?

"I have no answers for you, but you *do* have a mess to sort."

"Agreed, and very little patience to attend to it."

"Perhaps, but your wife is here, and you will need to find out why." Sophia met his gaze. "Don't you think you owe it to yourself to repair what has been broken if the initial feelings are still between the two of you?"

"I don't know."

"Love is the only thing worth fighting for, Gil, and if you still love her—even a little bit—you should do everything you can to bring it back to the forefront no matter what has happened."

He rolled his eyes. "Just because you are happily married again doesn't mean the rest of us want to be." Did he wish to recapture what he and Madelene had in those early days? Was there even enough left to revitalize?

"I understand but please, think long and hard about things before you abandon them." She squeezed his fingers and then released him. "Once you talk to her today, if there is even a tiny little spark still there, chase it. What harm can it do?"

"It could hurt me more than I already am," he admitted in a soft voice. And he would have to come to the realization that everything hinged on him, that it was his fault, and that he should set Madelene free, so she at least had a chance to meet her own dreams.

"But sometimes we need to have the very foundations of ourselves broken before we can rebuild into something better." Sophia gave him a tiny smile. "If nothing else, see what happens once you talk with her this morning. If the two of you end up hating each other, at least you'll know beyond the shadow of a doubt."

"Perhaps." *I'd rather not put myself into that position at all.* The urge to run, and to keep running, took hold until his heart pounded with it.

Sophia rose to her feet. "I shall be available for counsel or commiseration for possibly two weeks, depending on how long it takes Oliver to make travel arrangements."

"As long as you don't push for a repair of the romance, I might take advantage of that."

"Oh, and there is one more thing." One of her eyebrows rose. Mischief twinkled in her eyes. "But I'm not going to tell you, for I rather think the element of surprise will be more entertaining for all of us."

He glared at her. "Go bother your husband. I'm sure he'll be more than receptive to your presence than I am currently."

"Spoilsport."

Once she left, he poured another cup of tea. By the time he'd finished the pot, his head still pounded, and his stomach hadn't settled, but he was in a determined frame of mind. Best to beard the dragon and see where the pieces fell.

Minutes later, he'd entered his bedchamber, and instead of his wife being lost in slumber, she was sitting propped against a mound of pillows. Anxiety and confusion warred for dominance in her hazel eyes that were a tad round with fright. *Bloody hell.* Was she afraid of him? He'd done nothing to warrant such behavior.

Did that mean she had furthered her affair with Hugh and was hesitant to tell him?

His chest tightened with both annoyance and his own suspicion.

Perhaps she thought he would grouse at her. There was plenty to say, after all, for their letters had been few and far between, and even when hers had arrived, they'd been full of nonconsequential things that had nothing to do with her life or his.

Had she made her decision even back then?

He shoved that thought from his mind and once more concentrated on her. The dark waterfall of her hair cascaded over one shoulder, and even though it was an overcast morning, a few threads of silver winked through the mass. Surely, she was too young for that. While she stared warily at him, he continued his perusal. Though she held the bedclothes to her chin, there was no doubt the only garment she'd worn to bed the night before was her shift.

What did her body look like now? When they'd been first married, she had been slender, but with each pregnancy, she'd accumulated womanly curves that had driven him mad.

Damn and blast.

But what caught and held his attention was the large amethyst ring that rested on the fourth finger of her left hand. It was the engagement ring he'd given her when he'd asked for her hand that night of a long-ago ball when he'd thought she would be his everything, the person who would have completed him. When he'd assumed love was all they would need. When he had nothing but silly dreams in his mind and heart.

Except, that had been a foolish notion straight out of a storybook, and he'd been a nodcock to think a happily ever after could have been his.

"Good morning, Lady Yeardly." They were the only words that came to mind, and even then, they sounded rusty as if he hadn't used his voice for years. And because he was probably naught but a cad, he couldn't help adding, "I'm not quite happy to see you again after three years, so perhaps we should get to the point of this visit straightaway."

And he would do his best to harden his heart and lock away any residual feelings for there was no doubt in his mind that their union had already run its course.

CHAPTER TWO

MADELENE WINTERBOURNE—LADY YEARDLY—STARED at her husband, the man she'd been estranged from for nearly three years, the man with whom she would celebrate her sixth year of marriage next month… if they even made it that far. Clad in a rumpled fine lawn shirt that had been rolled up to his elbows and a pair of evening trousers, he appeared as an avenging pirate of old.

A ripple of unexpected need went down her spine, for it had been a long time indeed since she'd seen him. Of course, while he'd been away from her, they hadn't been together intimately, but even before that, while she'd been pregnant, they hadn't done anything carnal either. Physically, she missed him, but what really wrenched at her heart was the absence of support or a gentle touch.

"Good morning, Gilbert." If her voice shook, she couldn't help it, for she hadn't expected him so early in the morning nor looking like a veritable thunderstorm or a man bent on wicked things. "I…" She forced a swallow into her suddenly tight throat. "I suppose you want to know how I came to be here."

"That would be helpful," he all but growled as he stood in the middle of the room. Annoyance flashed in his face, made even more appealing by the trace of dark stubble clinging to his cheeks and jaw. Not once did he approach the bed, and for that she was grateful, but she couldn't stop studying him.

The last time she'd been in her husband's company had been almost three years before when he'd left London to embark upon adventures in India, but he'd changed in the time apart. Bitterness lurked in the depths of his brown eyes; lines of strain framed his mouth and the corners of his eyes. His blond hair, perhaps once set in a popular style, stuck up at all angles. This was a man who had seen far too much disappointment in the world.

And hadn't recovered from it.

"I had grown tired of waiting for you to return to London and me."

He snorted and leaning a silver-headed cane against one leg, he rested his hands on his hips that were as lean as she remembered. But how had he injured himself, and where? "As if it was my responsibility to reconcile when you hadn't written more than a handful of times."

"I wrote, but my heart wasn't in it." A surge of hot anger went through her, and she clutched the bedclothes tighter in her hands. "What was there to say? You certainly told me off before your departure, and nothing I could have added to that conversation would have made a difference. You didn't wish to talk to me of the things that mattered in that moment, and you'd told me not to write besides."

How well she remembered that poignant day. It had been raining, much like it was now, and the morning had been unseasonably warm. She'd been drowning in grief and vulnerability, but he hadn't cared, or if he did, he certainly hadn't shown it. They'd buried their stillborn son not a week earlier, and not once in that time had Gilbert spoken about the death, her feelings on the event, or the disappointment therein.

"Oh, so you have the gall to stand on outraged dignity?" He swept the fingers of one hand through his hair, leaving it in more uneven rows. She well remembered how soft that hair was. A wince crossed his face, for there was no doubt in her mind he was suffering from a megrim brought on by a hangover. The man had positively reeked of brandy last night when he'd come in. Though he'd assumed she'd been asleep, she pretended well. "After what you did?" Her husband shook his head. "Why the hell would I have wanted to stay in London with a wife who had turned a cold shoulder toward me?"

That was outside of enough. As her ire grew, she forgot to hold the bedclothes to her chin, and as they slipped down her torso, he followed their descent with his eyes that were dark with unreadable emotion. "You aren't innocent in this, Gilbert. You *left* me, with nary a word, knowing how much *I* was suffering, struggling. What kind of man does that?" Her voice rose with each inquiry, but she didn't care.

It was long past time to have it out with him.

"What would you have me do, hm?" He took his cane in hand and prowled toward the bed as she sprang out of it. No way would she meet him in a subservient position. "You refused to come with me on the trip, even though it had been planned for nearly a year."

"I had just lost a child. Can you not understand the pain that brought?" To her annoyance, hot tears sprang to her eyes. She rapidly blinked them away, for now was not the time to show him just how low she'd been brought regarding everything in this history. This wasn't the time to let him see her vulnerabilities, her fears, especially because he wasn't ready to talk seriously about them. "Yes, I had promised to go with you to India, but life had other plans. Why couldn't you understand that?"

And where the hell were you when I needed you most?

Shadows scudded through his expression. "It was always my dream to go abroad and learn about tea," he snapped out from around what sounded like clenched teeth. "To bring a new knowledge of various kinds of tea to London, to perhaps open a tea café, or encourage contracts with an importing outfit. At least with that I could have had a tidy income for…"

"Us? Ha!" She crossed her arms beneath her breasts as hot resentment sank into her chest. "I had dreams as well, or don't you consider wanting a family good enough to compete with your dreams?" If she wasn't careful, she'd sound like a shrew.

Something flickered in his dark eyes, but it was gone so quickly she couldn't read it. "Yes, but mine was still very much alive when I left."

A gasp escaped her, and Madelene's lower jaw dropped. "Surely you didn't mean that." She could hardly force the words from her throat due to the tightness there. Hadn't he wished for children when they wed? Was he not devastated when they'd lost those two babes?

"I apologize. That wasn't well done of me." His voice was graveled with emotion that wasn't reflected in his expression. "I refuse to discuss that right now."

"Why?" Fury curled within her, and she advanced upon him. "Why the devil not? Both of us wished to start a nursery soon after marrying since we were both more in advanced in years, after our personal histories and disappointments." Again, tears sprang into her eyes. "And those hopes were dashed, Gilbert. Don't you care?"

"Of course I do—did—but life must move forward. Can *you* not understand that?"

"No, I honestly don't." Her voice rose again, but she didn't care if the rest of the household overheard. "I needed you, but you weren't there for me." She couldn't keep the waver from her tones. "I nearly lost myself after our son was born, and now I feel like I have lost you too."

The admission was surprising, for she hadn't meant to reveal her mindset too soon in the conversation.

"What the hell did you expect?" he hissed with narrowed eyes. Though his eyes were bloodshot and there was pain stamped across his face, he was no less attractive. "Time was of the essence, and I had the one chance to make that journey else I'd need to delay it for months. You were the one who refused to accompany me." He chopped the air with his free hand. "It would have done you good to get away from England for a while, but you proved too stubborn."

"How could I have left him? All alone in that cold ground? Our little son by himself." Her throat constricted. "He wouldn't have known where his mother was." It would have broken her heart all over again to have left her baby so soon after he was laid to rest.

"He wouldn't have been cognizant of the fact. You have to know that." Gilbert's voice was ragged. Grief and agony showed on his face, but he didn't expand his thoughts and neither did he try to relieve those same things that still haunted her.

"That's beside the point!" In her upset, she shoved at his chest. How unfair that he had kept himself in his prime when she looked and felt rundown, ragged, hideous, and very much older than her years. "I had just lost him, Gilbert." She curled her fingers into his shirt, not caring if she caught hair in her fist. "How do you think that made me feel? Any of it!" When she lifted her gaze to his, his eyes were shuttered. Nothing except anger reflected there. "Then when you left, I was alone, surrounded by nothing except confusion and grief and loneliness. And I was so angry with you for apparently having no feelings of your own."

He reeled as if he'd been hit. A muscle in his jaw ticced. "How dare you say that."

"What else was I to think when you never mentioned our little dashed hopes?" She no longer knew how to interact with her husband. There was too much that stretched between them, too many years had passed. Too much emotion had been spilled and the lack of support from the one man who should have been there left her dead inside and alternately furious with him.

Were the feelings that had brought them together still there? Did they have a foundation between them to rebuild upon?

I don't even know that.

For the space of a few heartbeats, he stared at her as if he'd never seen her before, then he wrapped his fingers about her wrist and removed her hand from his person, but he didn't let it go. "There was no time to do anything else."

"Perhaps that was true at the time, but we are still married! You could have delayed your trip for six months, could have written to me with words of comfort and love." Had he forgotten that little tidbit? "Doesn't that mean anything?" The feel of his fingers around her wrist was both troubling and exciting. Despite the heavy subject, faint awareness tingled over her skin.

Yes, she still felt something physical for him. *Drat the man.*

"The bond we share doesn't matter."

A stab of cold disappointment went through her. "How can you say that?" Madelene's chest heaved with her labored breaths.

"How can you think anything remains between us?" The low timbre of his voice sent gooseflesh racing along her back. "We are veritable strangers now."

"I... I..." She tried to tug her hand from his hold, but he tightened it.

Gilbert snorted. "Did you think the second we saw each other again that nothing would have changed?" His eyes were hard like glass, but he tugged her incrementally closer to the hard wall of his chest. "Did you think we would fall into each other's arms and everything that happened in the intervening years would simply vanish?"

"I... I didn't..."

As he stared into her eyes, the animosity in his slowly changed into that familiar desire she'd known in the beginning of their marriage. A shiver moved down her spine. "Did you think I could forget about what happened to put the rifts between us?"

"No, but I thought..." Why was she so breathless? She hadn't seen this man for years. He obviously didn't want her back in his life. "I hadn't thought along those exact lines..."

He released her wrist only to relocate his hand to her waist, slid it to the small of her back. "Did you think I would be so grateful to see you, that you came back to me, that I would fall to my knees and weep in thanksgiving?" His words were a whisper now, the warmth of his breath skating over her cheek.

"I wouldn't want you on your knees." *Don't be an idiot, Madelene. He is baiting you.* "But I *did* think we might be able to sit down and have a civilized conversation regarding our future."

"Our future." A grunt escaped him. His gaze dropped to her mouth. "You were never that reticent before. Didn't care what position I was in as long as I made you fly." For those handful of seconds, the bitterness had left his voice, and in its place came traces of amusement.

Trembles moved down her spine. Waves of remembered sensation washed over her, for in the early months of their marriage, he'd been a vigorous and eager lover. In those days, she'd had the feeling that he was a man who enjoyed the married state and everything it meant. And oh how she'd fallen into scandal and sin with him! How could he have changed? How could she? "Those were the best of days." With each word, her lips brushed his. Would he kiss her? Could he leave those wasted years apart in the past and ask her to start anew with him?

Seconds went by while the pressure of his hand at her back pressed her a tiny bit closer against his body. The clean scent of him, like evergreens and the air just before it snowed, teased her nostrils. Madelene tilted her head back, relaxed her fingers so her hand lay splayed on his chest, and just when she assumed he would finally claim her lips, he stepped backward and put space between them so quickly she stumbled to keep her balance.

Anger wreathed his face. He gripped the silver head of his cane so tightly that his knuckles showed white. "Do you truly think after what happened that I'm going to take up where I left off? That I'm going to invite you into my bed after you betrayed me?"

"Betrayed you how? By refusing to go to India?" Her mind reeled at the change in topic. When he stared at her, she crossed her arms over her breasts to hide her tightened nipples. The last thing she wanted was for him to think she was desperate for him.

"Are you that dense?" Gilbert shoved his free hand through his hair. She couldn't be certain due to his dark trousers, but he wasn't as disinterested in her as he wished her to believe. That gave her a modicum of satisfaction. "Did you think I wouldn't notice?" When she didn't answer, he glared. "You took up with Hugh, Madelene. You went against our wedding vows by having an affair with him."

"What?" Shock ricocheted through her chest. Hugh was her husband's best friend. He was also her best friend's brother. They had all been close over the years, and he had been there acting as support when she'd fallen apart. "I never did such a thing. No matter what you heard, it's a lie."

"Was it?" He thumped the tip of his cane on the floor. "Two people within the *ton* wrote to me shortly after I sailed. The damn letters were waiting for me when I landed in Bombay three months later, the first things I read after I arrived. How the hell did you think that made me feel?"

"Probably as badly as I felt when you left." The words tripped off her tongue before she could recall them. Not that she wanted to. A part of her wanted him to hurt as much as she still did. "I was in agony, Gilbert!"

"That's no excuse!" Anger roiled in his eyes. "Were you or were you not ever in Hugh's bed? It's a simple answer if, as you say, those letters were lies."

Oh, dear God.

In this instance, the truth would *not* set her free. Heat burned through her cheeks. "I was in his bed, yes, but I didn't—"

"Enough!" Gilbert shook his head. Mottled red color crept up his neck and into his face. "Don't disrespect me by telling me more untruths."

"Hugh was there when you weren't! Thanks to him, I am alive today. He stood by me when I contemplated doing harm to myself so I could join our two babes in death. He talked me off that ledge more times than I can count." Would it make her seem weak to mention the depression she'd struggled with after Gilbert had left for India?

"I'm happy for you. Perhaps you should have run off with

him." He strode to the door, but as soon as his hand rested on the latch, she uttered a cry of protest.

"We are married, Gilbert. Doesn't that mean anything to you?"

"It used to before your lover entered the picture." He looked as if he would say more, but merely shook his head. "I am uncertain what it means now."

Why wouldn't he believe her? "Where are you going?"

"That's not your concern."

"It damn well is." Madelene was beyond acting like a lady or being polite. "I am still your wife until such time that isn't true." Perhaps she should tell him to go ahead and seek a divorce—if he could even be granted one. Such things were notoriously difficult to obtain, to say nothing of the reputations a divorce destroyed. She would be forced to leave England permanently. Yet if he hated her so much, couldn't look past her inadequacies enough to wish to salvage their union, he needed to go his own way.

So did she. Regardless of the damage a break would cause.

And perhaps they couldn't put back the pieces of their shattered lives, for they'd been tossed away over the years.

"Ah, yes, my wife because we are still bound together in the eyes of the law." Bitterness dripped from the words. Slowly, he turned to face her. "You realize, of course, that my mother believes all is well in our marriage."

"And the rest of your family?" In the beginning of their union, she hadn't had cause to spend much time with his siblings, for they had been mired in their own forms of grief, and she'd been enjoying her honeymoon period, but she didn't wish them to think poorly of her.

Gilbert shrugged. "Sophia knows there are problems; I didn't specify all of them. Arthur only knows we are no longer close. He wanted me to return to London and work things out. I did not, so we argued a couple of weeks back."

"Yet your brother is no longer in residence, correct?" When she'd arrived the night before, she'd been apprised by Sophia that it was Arthur's wedding day and that she would need to wait until after the festivities ended before having her presence announced.

"He is in London for a short wedding trip."

Madelene nodded. "What now?"

For long moments, her husband glared at her. "I suppose until we can discuss our future, we shall have to pretend we actually like each other."

For the second time that morning, her lower jaw dropped. "Then you wish for a marriage of convenience?" How would that even be possible?

"Apparently so." Gilbert shrugged. "I don't see what else we can do."

"We can talk right now." Daring much, she came across the floor until she'd closed the distance and laid a hand on his arm. "I rather suspect you haven't grieved, and you need to." That's why he'd left so abruptly—he'd been running away.

He snorted. "You no longer have any right to tell me what I need or what I should do."

"Then by that logic, the same applies to you regarding me." If he wanted to play this game, she would too. "So we'll suffer through together."

"No doubt we will." He shook off her hand. "Now, if you will excuse me? There are things I must attend to this morning."

"Such as sobering up?" It wasn't well done of her, but she didn't care. "Is that something new you have indulged in since you ran off to India to have the life you've always wanted?" Where had this penchant for plain-speaking come from? She'd certainly never been that sort of woman when they'd wed. *I'm a missionary's daughter, after all!* There had always been proper decorum and deportment. She'd been the perfect *ton* wife. But there was something about her husband that made her want to pull a reaction from him, make him feel everything she had—still was—so she wouldn't be so alone.

"You have no idea what drives me." His voice was low and almost a growl that sent gooseflesh skittering over her skin.

"That is quite obvious. What else don't I know about you?"

When his face paled, she frowned. What secrets did he keep? "For the time being, I think it best that we sleep in separate rooms. I'll invent some sort of excuse for my mother, but I cannot remain in the same space as you at the moment."

"Fine." Being back in his company had opened wounds she'd thought closed, and though she didn't welcome the emotional quagmire, she needed the healing. "Yet don't shirk your responsibility, Gilbert. The rift in our marriage cannot be ignored any longer. Either we need to start afresh, or we need to make a break of it."

Once more, his hand tightened on the head of his cane. "Do not assume to order me about. I do not belong to you any longer, and perhaps you *are* better off without me," he finished in a soft but choked voice. Before she could ask what that meant, he yanked open the door, stepped into the corridor and then slammed the panel behind him.

"I rather think you haven't belonged to me for a long time." And that added another break to her already abused heart. What sort of demons haunted him? For they had been there long before he and she had wed.

Why did he still harbor secrets that he hadn't trusted her with? Her chin quivered and a tear escaped to her cheek.

How much more can I take before I throw myself into the nearest pond and let fate have at me?

At least then the ever-present grief and pain would cease.

CHAPTER THREE

G ILBERT'S MOOD HADN'T improved as the day marched on, and when teatime rolled around, he'd already cast up his accounts twice due to the deuced pain in his head.

His original plans had been to ignore the customary afternoon gathering of the family, but since he was hungry, he made his way toward the drawing room anyway. He hoped Madelene wouldn't want to socialize with them either. What the hell was the woman thinking wishing to reconcile after what she'd done?

Then his steps faltered, and he paused. After what *he'd* done. A sick feeling began in the pit of his stomach. *Hell's bells.* At some point he would need to admit to his own sins.

Would Madelene even care?

Did he want her to?

His part in betraying their wedding vows, regardless of the fact that she had and then she'd lied about it, didn't exonerate either of them. They were both at fault. Unfortunately, that wasn't the only rift between them, and he suspected a large part of it was laid firmly at his doorstep. Could they all be mended? There was no way of knowing. Neither could he decide if he wished to remain married to her, for the ever-present fear of the past was relentlessly chasing him. Sooner or later, he wouldn't have the strength to outrun it.

Perhaps the better part of valor would be to set her free, let her move on with her life if that's what she truly wanted while he did the same.

If there was nothing between them to redeem. But how could a relationship that had burned so hot and bright simply… die as quickly as it had? The more he thought about it, the more confused he grew.

There were no easy answers. He required more time before he made any sort of decision, for now that his wife had arrived, he couldn't keep dithering about it.

Bloody hell, what a coil. Why did she have to come back?

He rubbed a hand along the side of his face and realized belatedly he hadn't shaved that day even if he had managed to change his clothes into something more presentable. Not that it mattered. She didn't deserve the best of him.

Perhaps no one did if he was the disappointment and failure that he assumed.

Except… when they'd spoken this morning and she'd been clad in naught but her shift, the old familiar desire he had for her came barreling back. And damn his eyes, he'd nearly kissed her. When he'd pulled her close to his body and felt the heat of her— even though it had been done in anger—he'd almost forgiven her everything, for all he'd wished to do was take her to bed, make her remember how good they'd been together, show her how wonderful they'd worked when locked in the throes of physical affection.

Beg her to forgive him.

But then he'd remembered it was *she* who'd broken their relationship in the first place, and he had no interest in taking her back.

Regardless of those perfect moments when they'd actually understood each other.

Damn and blast. What to do? If he chose to pursue his marriage, there *had* to be more between them than merely heat. Perhaps the lack of foundation had gotten them into trouble the last time, for their prior courtship had been quick and short, and he'd been enamored of once more being married, in perhaps having a chance at a family… until that dream had once more come crashing down.

Because of me.

A growl from his stomach recalled him to his original task, and he resumed his trip to the drawing room. The closer he drew, the more the soft drone of conversation reached his ears. Then the sound of masculine laughter grated across his consciousness, and a cold wave of foreboding poured down his spine.

Surely that couldn't be who he thought.

But when he came into the room, it seemed that fate wasn't done smacking him about, for the first person his gaze fell upon was his best friend. Or rather his former best friend—Major Hugh Pritchard. And he was sitting beside Madelene on a low sofa, with a damned teacup in his hand, chuckling at something one of his nieces had said. Madelene laughed along with him as if she were hosting the tea instead of his mother. For that matter, his own parent smiled at the major as if he were the most interesting person she'd seen all month.

Who the hell invited *that man*? A wave of hot anger rolled over him. Knowing his best friend had betrayed him with his own wife and now sat in the midst of his family as if nothing had happened caused something inside him to snap. It all became too much after everything else. As rage came over him and dropped a slight red haze in front of his eyes, Gilbert strode across the room.

"What the devil is *he* doing here?"

Every member of his family jerked their heads in his direction. Madelene's lower jaw dropped.

"Calm yourself, Gilbert. It's not what you think."

"Isn't it?" His free hand curled into a fist. "You dare to trot him out in front of everyone?"

His mother stared with round eyes. "Ah, there you are, Gilbert. I was wondering if you would join us." She rose to her feet with all the elegance of a duchess. Both Sophia's husband—the ambassador—and Gilbert's nephew, John, shot into standing positions as will. Major Pritchard was slower, but he followed suit and set his teacup onto the low table in front of him. "Major Pritchard will be staying with us for a few weeks."

"What the devil for?" He gripped the head of his cane with such force, the imprint of the griffin might be forever stamped on his palm.

Sophia answered in their mother's stead. With twinkling eyes, she stood and drifted closer to the ambassador. "The major arrived yesterday, shortly after your wife did. He said he was worried about you and Madelene, and since he hadn't seen you in an age, asked if we wouldn't mind letting him linger here at Ettesmere Park."

"Why?" It was baffling to him that this traitor was even allowed in the house. Of course, the family didn't know his private annoyances, but that was beside the point.

Had his wife thought to bring her lover along because she couldn't bear to be parted from him for so long?

A pox on them both!

"Why not?" Amusement danced in his sister's eyes. "He is your best friend. I assumed you would be ecstatic to see him again." Even after she knew of his suspicions that he'd shared at the breakfast table just that morning, she was willing to drive the spike deeper into his heart?

"*Former* best friend," Gilbert said beneath his breath, which earned him narrowed eyes from Hugh.

His mother nodded. "It's lovely to catch up with him. His adventures while in the military are simply fascinating."

And the whole time, they glanced at the major as if he were a damned hero instead of the man who'd ripped Gilbert's marriage asunder and then charmed his wife away. "He's a lying sack of rubbish. What sort of man betrays his best friend while he's away? I refuse to have him beneath this roof!" Not able to control the hot anger coursing through his veins, Gilbert tossed his cane away, stumbled the few steps to the man, and then apparently lost his mind as he pounced upon his former best friend.

They tumbled to the carpet in a tangle of limbs.

Shocked screams erupted from his nieces. Emily implored her brother to do something.

"What would you have me do?" John asked. "It looks as if this fight has been brewing for quite some time. Best let them have it out."

"You are the cause of everything!" Gilbert yelled once he'd gained the upper hand and stared down at his friend. He threw a punch that landed square onto Hugh's jaw.

"The devil you say! You were the one who left, and who was there to pick up the pieces?" The major scrambled out from under him, but not before he landed a facer of his own that had pain screaming down the left side of Gilbert's face.

"Gilbert! For shame." Shock radiated from his mother's voice. "Where are your manners?"

"Where are his?" he asked, and threw another punch that the major dodged.

The ambassador quickly sprang into action and helped his nephew wrench him from the major's person. "Perhaps a few moments of calm will help gain perspective."

He didn't want to be calm; he wanted to beat the stuffing out of the man who'd stolen his wife. This perfect specimen of manhood who didn't have the shame of failure hanging over his head, this man who probably had no trouble in fathering living children. The weight of it hung hard about his shoulders. It didn't matter that Gilbert might not love Madelene any longer. She was still legally married to him, and when he'd left for India, he *had* loved her. "I don't require perspective, Ambassador." Tearing from Mr. Mattingly's hold, he faced down Hugh as the other man stood. "You have much to answer for."

"As do you." The major rubbed a hand along the side of his face where a bruise would surely form before the day was out. His black hair was mussed and a shock of it fell over his brow. No doubt that would have Madelene swooning. "But perhaps this isn't the best venue to have that conversation."

"You dare to tell me what to do?" A threat growled through Gilbert's voice. Never had he been as incensed as he was now.

"If it will put some sense into your pickled brain, yes!"

"Pickled last night, yes. Raging megrim now, though." In fact, the pain of it had come rushing back the moment he'd seen Hugh.

"That's enough, Gilbert." Madelene had gained her feet. A flush stained her cheeks while embarrassment flooded her eyes. "How dare you attack him!" She shot a glance to the major and then back to him. "He's only trying to help when we desperately need it."

"Hit him again, Uncle Gilbert!" Hannah, his youngest niece, sat upon the back of a sofa with her eyes bright with excitement. "I don't know what he did, but I rather enjoy seeing men engage in fisticuffs."

Well, damn. No doubt his brother would take him to task once he returned from London for corrupting Sophia's daughter. His breath was labored, and as he curled his right hand into a fist to land his friend another facer—perhaps breaking his nose—his mother came over to him and yanked him aside like she used to do when he and Arthur were younger.

"What has gotten into you?" she hissed in a whisper. "Ever since you arrived at Ettesmere Park, you have been highly unpleasant and full of prickles. I merely thought it was because you missed your wife, but now that she's here, you've taken your foul mood to the next echelon of horrid."

"I have just cause." He hated that he'd disappointed her, but there was nothing for it.

I've disappointed everyone.

"Perhaps you do, but if you still need to vent your spleen, do it outside in the garden. I won't have my drawing room used for such ill-bred antics." She stared him down. "And once you are through, you need to talk to your wife. There has never been a marital problem that couldn't be solved through a serious conversation."

What was this, then? Had she and Papa grown apart during their union? They'd certainly appeared to be a couple deeply in love every time he'd come home. It was something he wished to delve into if given half the chance. "What if those problems are too monstrous to overlook?"

"Only you can decide that, but not if you continue to ignore Madelene." She patted his abused cheek. "I don't know what is happening within your marriage, but I have hope that you can salvage it. Hurt feelings are no excuse to toss away a whole marriage. At least for your own peace of mind do this. Come seek me out later."

"Fine." With a curt nod, he stepped away from his mother with heat creeping up the back of his neck. As he swept his gaze about the room, his focus landed on Sophia.

She shook her head. "I *did* tell you there was more this morning," she said in a quiet voice, but worry had clouded her eyes.

Madelene bounced her gaze between he and Hugh, and damned if he couldn't figure out which one of them she rooted for. It only intensified his dislike.

For them both.

The major tugged on the hem of his sapphire superfine jacket. Annoyance roiled in his blue eyes. "There is much I would say to you, Yeardly. Perhaps we should remove to the gardens."

Without another word, Gilbert retrieved his cane then he marched from the room with as much dignity as he could summon. Hugh could follow or not, but he wouldn't be disrespected in his own house. The gall of the man! He didn't stop walking until he'd reached his mother's beloved gardens behind the manor that were located between the house and the hedge maze.

Fruit trees as well as ornamental trees provided shade over shell-strewn paths. Beds of a variety of flowers—including her prize-winning roses—gave brilliant pops of color to the summer landscape. Bushes, shrubberies, and hedges finished off the gardens. Interspersed within were both wrought-iron and stone benches as well as statuary his grandfather had commissioned and included.

He didn't stop walking until he'd gained the path that featured Greek statues and a stone bench that was one of Sophia's favorites. As if the strength left him, Gilbert sank onto the bench when the muscles in his left thigh screamed from overworking. "Say your piece and then be off."

Hugh shook his head. He looked at the reddening knuckles of his right hand and then sighed. "It's been an age since you and I were so heated we threw punches."

"It has." On this he agreed. They'd been friends since Gilbert's first marriage. But he had no idea at that time that Hugh's sister would become Madelene's best friend and would lead, in a roundabout way, to introducing him to his future wife. "We have been through much over the years."

I don't want to lose a friend and a wife in the same month.

"We have, which is why this current contretemps is stupid." The major held up a hand when Gilbert would have launched into a tirade. "Stop. Let us talk like men, and if you don't like the truths I utter, we will go from there."

Slowly, Gilbert nodded. "Fine."

A long sigh escaped Hugh's throat. He shoved a hand through his hair, further upsetting it. "I never had intercourse with your wife. Despite the rumors and no doubt the tattle-mongers that wrote to you after your departure for India, there was no affair between Madelene and me."

"She admitted she'd been in your bed." The words came out around a growl. "How do you explain that?"

A flush went over Hugh's crushed collar. "Because she told the truth." Again, he held up a hand when Gilbert half-rose from the bench. "She *was* in my bed, but not with me in it. There was a day when I feared for her well-being and her mental state during one of my frequent visits, so I took her home—"

"You bastard." Gilbert scrambled to his feet.

Hugh narrowed his eyes. "I took her home in order to monitor her health. Lord knows there was no one at her own house to do so. When she didn't improve and the depression grew worse over tea one afternoon, I put her to bed following a tearful breakdown on her part."

There was indeed a ring of truth to his words. "And?" He wanted the whole story.

"During her time at my townhouse, I stayed downstairs in my study. I sent for her maid, who then never left your wife's side. Everything was aboveboard, and I put them both into a carriage two mornings later and sent them home."

Gilbert frowned. He wasn't ready to let go of his anger toward his friend, for that would mean a heavier chunk of the blame would fall on his shoulders. And that terrified him. "You left her alone after that, then." It wasn't a question.

"Uh, not quite." Hugh tugged on his loosened cravat.

The hand not holding onto his cane curled again into a fist. "What the hell does that mean?"

"I couldn't leave Madelene to her own devices. She was hurting and in a bad place." Hugh paced a tight line in front of the bench. "I feared she would do herself harm, for she was lost very much in grief."

"She is not your wife, and that is not your responsibility."

Hugh turned abruptly to face him. "But you weren't there when you should have been!" Annoyance rose in his voice and concern clouded his eyes. "She needed someone to believe in her at her lowest point. To assure her that she wasn't the failure she thought. That her damned husband still wanted her after everything." He shook his head. "I stood in the gap, hoping you would come to your senses, return home, and attend to your rapidly crumbling marriage. Help your wife come through her grief."

That answer seemed so simple, and easily Gilbert knew Hugh would do such a thing, for they'd all been close friends years ago. He sat down hard on the bench with his cane between his splayed legs. "I couldn't come home," he admitted in a near whisper.

"Why?" Hugh crossed his arms over his chest, clearly not impressed with the excuse.

"I required a fortune and funds. To keep Madelene in London. To set us up in some semblance of style. Needed to make a name for myself to make her proud." That secret was pulled from a tight throat, and he nearly choked on it. "Beyond that, I had to put distance between me and failure, because what she went through was my fault, I've come to suspect." He met Hugh's gaze. "I am the failure in this relationship. It is my fault she lost those babes." His damned chest hurt so much he could scarcely breathe.

"Why is that a failure? These things happen."

"I know that, but the same outcome occurred in my first marriage." The words were chilling enough, and when Hugh stared at him in open-mouthed shock, he nodded as misery welled to consume him. "Yes, I had been married previously, but no one outside the family knew. It ended in disaster and sadness." He didn't wish to revisit that time, not now. Forcing a hard swallow into his throat, he continued. "I should have told Madelene of both the marriage and the loss of that babe too, especially when *our* difficulties happened, but I couldn't bear to see pity and disappointment in her eyes."

"Bloody hell, man, I had no idea."

Gilbert nodded. "It's a shame I've carried for too long. Having to bury my son with Madelene completely shattered me."

"Why didn't you tell your wife that? Shared grief would have helped you both."

"I couldn't… had no words." The urge to run grew strong again. If he didn't confront any of it, he could ignore it and not feel… He hadn't known what to do, suddenly couldn't relate to his wife, refused to let himself get lost in grief like she had. "I didn't want her to resent me and know that I am responsible for that loss of hope in her eyes."

So he'd left, he'd run, just like he had after his first wife had died, because if he ever stopped running, all of those emotions would catch him, and he wasn't strong enough to survive the deluge.

Hugh dropped a hand on his shoulder, and he nearly cried out with relief from the compassion, perhaps the forgiveness in that one gesture. "Madelene needed you, though. More than ever, she needed your strength, your presence."

"I couldn't. Still cannot, without breaking myself," he whispered. "In this, I'm a failure too." How would his father have acted in the same situation? How would Arthur? Both of those men who he'd looked up to his whole life and strived to imitate. Would they judge him now for his cowardice?

"You'll lose her if you don't make amends with her."

Gilbert shook his head, looked away from his friend. "She is already gone, I'm afraid." He adjusted his grip on the cane's head. "No doubt she wants a divorce, and I'm almost convinced I should try to grant it for her."

"Damn, you're a nodcock." Hugh moved slightly away from him. "Have you ever stopped to think that Madelene might only want you? To hear you say you're sorry? That you don't think *she's* a failure? That you love her still and only wish to be with her?"

Oh, God.

"It is not as simple as that." There was so much beneath the surface.

"Agreed, but your defection wounded her deeply. You abandoned her when she was at her lowest point, and it changed her."

The old bitterness welled through Gilbert's chest. He rounded on his friend. "And you were right there picking up the pieces. You have always been half in love with her."

A flush rose above Hugh's collar once more. "I won't deny that I felt protective regarding her… still do. How could I not? She is my sister's best friend. She was suffering from the dark cloud of depression and was quite vulnerable."

"Ha." Gilbert snorted. "So you comforted her. Did you kiss her?" The man might not have lain with her, but there was certainly affection between them that went beyond friendship.

Heavy silence rolled between them. Hugh hung his head. "Once, but she slapped me directly after and called me out. Said it was wrong and that no matter the state of her union, she was still in love with you."

Does she love me still, though? Instead of the rage Gilbert expected, hot shame welled through his chest, making it ache so fiercely he couldn't take a proper breath. "Oh, God." Had he cocked everything up beyond repair?

"What?" Immediately, Hugh was on the alert. He met Gilbert's gaze. "Madelene and I are close friends. Nothing more."

"I understand that." He'd been an idiot. The weight on his shoulders intensified. "Since I thought she had been unfaithful, one night shortly after I arrived in Bombay, when I was deep into my cups and was in a vulnerable state and randy besides—"

"You bastard!" Hugh took a swing at him, which connected with his jaw.

Pain splintered through his head to collide with the ache already there. Nausea climbed his throat. *I deserve that.* "I know." He sat swiftly back on the bench. "It was one night. She was a society woman—a tempting widow—and I felt horrible immediately afterward. Never saw her again, for I moved deeper into the countryside and made certain I didn't come into contact with almost anyone."

Anger fairly radiated off Hugh. "After everything, your wife was going through—"

"I know." There was no strength left to defend himself. "I deserve your wrath and hers."

For long moments, his friend was silent, then he sat beside Gilbert. "You must tell her, or I will."

Of course he knew the truth of those words, but it rankled that Hugh was suddenly so pious. "I want you out of my marriage." Life was difficult enough without having to fight his best friend for his wife's affections.

Hugh frowned. "Does that mean you wish to repair your

marriage? That you'll fight for Madelene?"

Did he want to? The fear waiting for him if he did so was enormous, for he could conceivably lose her anyway. "It is too early to say."

"Do you have feelings for her?"

Gilbert sighed. He rubbed a hand along the side of his face. Those bruises would have him looking like a dog's breakfast tonight. "I don't know."

"You wouldn't have punched me in the drawing room if you didn't." A chuckle followed his words.

"Perhaps." A sigh seemed to come from his toes. "There are too many obstacles in our path. Perhaps it is best to let her go so she can start over, have her dreams."

A grunt came from the major. "You are naught but a coward."

"The hell I am." Gilbert sprang up from the bench, ready to lay Hugh out for his effrontery.

But the major wasn't cowed. He stared at him with a mix of amusement and concern in his eyes. "The love you shared with Madelene was special. She wrote of it often while I was in Portugal. That gave me hope I would find the same eventually."

He'd known Madelene had written to Hugh, for that was the sort of heart she had, but had they grown too close during that time? "I—"

"At least try, Gil." Hugh stood and once again clapped a hand to his shoulder. "Make an attempt to reconcile for both your sakes, but if you hurt her again, I will shoot you myself." The hard edge to his voice served as a warning.

"You love her." It wasn't a question.

"As I said, we are close, but if she were free, perhaps I would court her, shower her with the affection she should have been receiving from you all along."

"Bugger off." Gilbert threw a punch that caught his friend in the midsection, but then was immediately contrite. "I apologize."

Hugh snorted and sucked in a breath. Amusement danced in

his eyes. "It is time for you to face your demons and sort your life. I won't wait forever, and neither should she." With a hand to his stomach, the major departed the gardens.

With a barely stifled cry, Gilbert once more sat on the bench. How had life come to this pass, and what the hell should he do about it?

CHAPTER FOUR

July 29, 1819

E VERYTHING IS SUCH *a mess!*
Thanks to her coming to Ettesmere Park—even if the dowager countess *had* invited her—Gilbert and Hugh were on the outs and had come to blows.

Madelene rubbed her eyes in an effort to stem the tears that had been all too ready since she'd arrived. She hadn't been able to talk to her husband and broach the subjects they needed to discuss, for he was so angry, and the day he'd attacked Major Pritchard at tea, he'd never returned to the drawing room. Neither had he attended dinner that night, and her belongings had been moved to a different bedchamber.

That had been three days ago. In the intervening time, Gilbert had kept himself scarce. She wasn't certain he was still on Ettesmere Park property, but she hoped he was. Though she'd only interacted with him slightly upon her return, she missed him, missed the vitality he brought to every meeting, missed the heat of him and the tingling sense of adventure she had whenever he came near.

Yes, he held his emotions deep inside, and yes, there was obviously something wrong between them, but if he wasn't willing to open those wounds and clean them, how could anything be solved?

Or healed?

Above everything, though, she didn't want to disappoint Gilbert's mother. The woman had practically taken her in when she'd married Gilbert mere months following the death of his father. Madelene's own family had succumbed to a fever when they'd been in Africa, for her father had been a missionary. How could she tell the dowager countess that her marriage had fallen apart—again—when Lady Ettesmere's had been so lovely and seemingly effortless?

A sigh escaped her before she could recall it, yet the memories poured in despite her wishing to keep them held tightly in the boxes of her mind.

She'd been married at the age of six and twenty to a man of her father's acquaintance, a man of the church, who would someday follow in his footsteps. He had been a minister and she thought she'd wanted that sort of docile, bucolic life.

But such an existence had bored her to tears.

Their first trip to the mission fields was to the jungles of South America, and it hadn't been as successful as they'd both hoped. She had been seasick on the voyage down, but her husband had been full of fervor to spread God's word. Upon arrival, the house they'd been promised had been little more than a hovel that let in all manner of animals and insects. Though not homesick, for she was well-versed in being away from England, it never had that homey feel, but for the love of her husband, she'd made the best of it.

Somehow, they'd made the circumstances work for them, and during the first two years of her marriage, she had miscarried three times.

Stifling a cry, Madeline continued to walk the halls of the manor house. She should have known then that the problem would continue to plague her, but she'd been so hopeful…

Regardless of stopping in the portrait gallery, the paintings couldn't hold her attention, and once more she sank into her thoughts.

Finally, a few months after the last miscarriage, she had been desperate enough to seek advice from the tribal elders of the group of indigenous people they ministered to. Those learned men and women had given her packets of ground herbs for tea and had mixed tinctures from distilled berries and other plants that she should take each night. Most of the treatments had tasted quite foul, but she'd followed the instructions and held out against hope they would work, for she wanted a babe in her arms more than anything in the world. It hadn't helped that her husband had declared her healthy, that going through those trials were God's will for her life, and that she should be grateful to them for it would help her to minister to the women in those tribes they visited.

At the time, she had held her tongue, but now in retrospect, she should have ranted at him and at the very least, argued. How could it have been God's will to make her body defective?

In the end, she had endured long months after that, alternately terrified and elated with each following pregnancy. All of which that ended in heartbreak.

Eight months after she'd started taking the herbal remedies, her husband had been shot in an altercation between warring tribes. She had remained by his side, of course, but the wound had festered in the tropical climate without the benefit of real medical supervision. Infection had set in, eventually raging out of control. Two days after that, her husband had slipped away to the world beyond.

After nearly four years of marriage, she was alone once more.

A portrait of Gilbert caught her eye and temporarily yanked her from her musings. He was perhaps a youth of seventeen, posing in the drawing room with his siblings. The artist had captured that mischievous twinkle in his brown eyes she'd seen many times before. In the rendering, his hair gleamed gold in the sun, that Winterbourne-blond hair they all possessed. Oh, how she'd hoped to have a baby with those golden curls!

But fate, God, or destiny had never aligned with those plans.

As she touched a fingertip to the painting, she escaped into her thoughts again.

Heartsick and lost, Madelene had fled home, and during the grueling sea voyage where she didn't think she would ever stop casting up her accounts, she had met Hugh. Though he'd risen to the ranks of major in the cavalry, he was also a third son of a viscount who had been forced to make something of himself. Thus, the reason for his military career. His commission had ended and was heading to England as well.

They had struck up a friendship, and a few weeks later, he'd introduced her to his sister. She'd become best friends with the woman who was her age, and though she liked and respected Hugh, a romance between them had never bloomed, even if Dinah had championed it. Eventually, Hugh went to work at the Home Office, and her life settled into a pattern of waiting, more or less.

Perhaps a year later, Hugh had introduced her to Gilbert at a society event, and she'd been lost to his charm and wit and the immediate attraction that had sprung between them, for he'd been as different to her first husband as day was to night, as sin was to saint.

And she'd never looked back, yet she was in danger of losing him, just like she'd lost everyone else she'd ever cared about in her life.

"What am I going to do if you decide to pursue a divorce?" she softly asked the Gilbert portrayed in the portrait. "I loved you so much before we lost our son, and you ran. Why did you throw that away like it didn't matter?"

There were no more answers here than there'd been in her bedchamber. Filled with restless energy, Madelene left the gallery with no particular destination in mind. Since she wasn't paying attention, as she rounded a corner, she ran bodily into Mr. Mattingly. "Oh, I am so sorry." She clutched at his arm as she regained her footing. A trace of surprise went down her spine to see she'd nearly reached the drawing room.

"No apologies necessary." The ambassador smiled. His eyes twinkled behind spectacle lenses. "I am often lost in thought. Even more so since I met Sophia. There is much to dream upon, even during my waking moments."

The slightly moony expression on his face pulled a smile from Madelene. "Such is the way of newlyweds." Jealousy speared through her. "I miss that." Those had been lovely days indeed. To cover her confusion, she smoothed her hands down the front of her lavender muslin day dress.

Concern became his primary emotion. "I take it that your situation hasn't improved?"

"Not especially." How much did the family—and the extended family—know of the state of her union? The heat of embarrassment went through her cheeks. "My husband refuses to talk with me. I haven't seen him for three days." The catch in her voice worked to further animate the heat. "It feels terrible, as if I've failed, but I don't know how to approach him when he's essentially sulking."

The ambassador drew her into the drawing room. "It is very likely Lord Yeardly doesn't know how to begin a conversation of any sort with you." He flashed her an encouraging smile. "You see, while you feel awkward and timid in going to him, he might feel the same about you. Being separated for years renders the familiar strange at times."

"I suppose that makes sense." She'd never thought about it in those terms before.

He nodded. "Try not to hold his reticence against him, for it's early days yet."

Thankfully, there was no one in the drawing room at present. Tea wouldn't be served for about an hour. But the ambassador had extended a glimmer of hope, and she wished to chase it. "Do you think there is a chance Lord Yeardly and I can reconcile?" Was she entirely certain that she wished to, though? It would be the height of cruel to remain wed to him when she couldn't fulfil the most basic of roles that a woman could do.

Or rather the expectations that society as well as the church placed upon a woman's head.

"Lady Yeardly, there is *always* hope." Again, his grin was dazzling. "I am living proof that romance can bloom out of nothing, even a bleak outlook."

While she would adore hearing the story of how he courted and then managed to win Sophia's hand, it would need to wait for another day. Right now, her mind was taxed with confusion and disappointment. "Thank you for that."

"Any time." He peered into her eyes with a slight frown. "Is there something I can assist you with? You seem quite scattered and perhaps on the edge of tears." When she would have protested, he held up a hand. "I am not a stranger to those either, for both Sophia and Hannah are ruled by emotions part of the time, so I do my best to mitigate disaster—both real and imagined. As an ambassador, I only want to keep the peace so that we may all work together."

"Truly, they are fortunate to have such an understanding man in their lives." She rather wished Gilbert would learn from this person. Still, this man's words had tears prickling the backs of her eyelids. "Is there somewhere on the property I can go that I might think uninterrupted? At the moment, it feels as if there are people everywhere I turn, and I don't remember enough of the acreage here to find a place."

"That is understandable as well. On both subjects, actually." His even tone of voice worked at bringing her a bit of calm. "It *is* a bit hectic just now what with the earl being on holiday with his new bride." His chuckle cajoled her into a brighter mood, but only temporarily. "I should warn you that the countess's fat beagle is somewhere on the premises. The girls promised to keep him under guard, but he's quite clever in slipping away."

A quick jolt of fear shot down her spine. "Oh, dear. I am afraid of dogs." It stemmed from an incident in her childhood when one of her neighbor's dogs broke away from a hunting pack, jumped on her, and held her to the ground, nipping at her neck, before rescue came.

"I don't know how harmful Regent is, but he'll eventually tire himself out."

She chuckled. "His name is Regent?"

"Oh, yes. You'll understand why once you meet him."

"I'd rather not." Would he laugh at her if he realized the depth of her terror surrounding all canines?

"He is harmless, I can assure you." The ambassador pushed his spectacles back up the bridge of his nose. "Regarding someplace quiet where you can ruminate, I particularly like the heart of the hedge maze. I have been there a few times, and with each visit have found clarity on a variety of subjects." A deep flush crept over his cravat.

Just what, exactly, had he discovered at the heart of that maze?

"Thank you." Despite her own crumbling romance, she gave him a smile, for he was adorable in the new bloom of his. "However, I'm afraid I don't know the directions through the maze. If I find myself lost, rescue won't come."

"Ah, now we have finally arrived at the part where I can assist you."

"How so?"

"I can write down the turns if you'd like."

"There is no need." She laid a hand on his arm. "I shall puzzle it out. Besides, it will offer me some much-needed time alone."

"I wish you good luck, Lady Yeardly. Perhaps today will be the start of a new direction in your life."

"Let us hope so, Ambassador." Because she couldn't continue to exist as she was now, in this netherworld of not knowing. "I cannot contemplate what the future might hold if the tattered edges aren't mended."

A few minutes later, she glanced at the sky when she gained the back lawn. Fat, dark gray clouds loomed and stacked on the horizon. It would rain soon, and she didn't particularly like being wet, but for the time being, the air was close and stifling, the temperature hot. Barely had she taken the first turn in the hedge maze than she was beset by an overweight beagle who barked joyfully the moment he saw her.

"Get away!" A scream of terror released from her throat, but of course the dog didn't obey the command. As he bounded after her, Madelene pelted along the paths as if her life depended upon it.

The baying of the hound continued unabated behind her.

"Help!" She tore down each path, and the crushed shells ground beneath the soles of her slippers. Blindly, she took the next few turns, but the dog thought the chase was a game. He barked and followed her. Once he nipped at the hem of her dress. The sound of fabric tearing reached her ears, but she didn't halt. "Help me!"

Her forward trajectory was suddenly halted when she ran bodily into yet another man.

"Madelene?" Gilbert's arms went immediately around her. His cane thudded against her backside. "What the devil is going on?"

Relief slammed down her spine so she couldn't properly enjoy the solid feel of being held by him. "Oh, hurry. Save me from the hound from hell." When the dog darted forward with a joyful bark of welcome, she scuttled behind her husband. "Get him away!"

"Calm yourself." He chuckled but left her behind him. "It's just Regent. He's my sister-in-law's dog and truly harmless." Amusement threaded through his voice, but he didn't grin.

As if to reassure her, the dog barked again.

Madelene squealed. "He's going to bite me!" Terror clung to those words, but she didn't care if her husband heard that weakness. "Oh, please, get him away." If her heart pounded any harder, it would leap out of her chest.

"Doubtful." He took her hand with his free one. "Come with me."

"Where?"

"Does it matter?" Her husband tugged her down the path, made a couple of turns, and soon enough they entered the heart of the maze. Of course, Regent followed after them, all waving ears, wagging tail, and exuberant barking. When she yelped in pure fright, Gilbert put his hands on either side of her waist and hoisted her up so that she could stand atop one of the stone benches near a pretty grouping of rose bushes. In the process, his cane tumbled to the grass.

Regent was immediately there and attempting to take the object into his jaws.

"Do something!" She held her skirts away when the beagle put his front paws on the edge of the bench and tried to get at her. Apparently, the cane was not as fun as she.

"Relax, Madelene. It's a dog, not a monster. This corpulent canine is not a threat unless you are a rabbit or squirrel." Amusement threaded with annoyance in his voice, but he kneeled next to the beagle and scratched behind his brown ears. "Regent, go find Sophia." The dog barked. His tail wagged furiously, but it appeared he might understand what Gilbert told him. "Go find Emily. She has treats."

Regent barked. He turned about and then ran off in the opposite direction with a long, soulful bay that only a beagle could make.

"Thank goodness." Madelene shook with both relief and shock. "Dogs terrify me."

"I know." Gilbert turned around and faced her. The bruising on his face did nothing for his looks. "That dog from your childhood."

"Yes." Trembles moved through her heart. "You remembered."

"I'm not an ogre. Of course I remembered. Haven't I kept you safe from all canines since the time you told me?"

"Yes." Except for the three years they'd been apart, but she didn't mention that. When he put his hands on either side of her waist, her heart beat a little faster, and as he swung her to the ground, she stifled a sigh. How had she forgotten how strong he was? "Thank you."

"You are welcome."

"That's something about you I've always admired." At the cock of his eyebrow, she hurried onward. "You have the knack of rescuing me from various situations others would consider trivial but are truly frightening to me."

"We all have fears and demons that haunt us," Gilbert said softly. "Who am I to judge another when I am not perfect?" He sounded congenial enough, and that was a vast improvement from when they were last together, but he eyed her with wariness.

Had he thought of her over the years they were separated? Did he still harbor a shred of interest for her beneath that reserve and carefully cultivate mask?

"In any event, I'm glad I came here. This is a beautiful area that promotes calm. I especially enjoy the statues."

He nodded. "This is one of my mother's favorite places on the property. Sophia's as well. They have both done an admirable job in cultivating the roses." His eyes slightly narrowed. The breeze that accompanied the rain clouds ruffled through his blond hair. "What are you doing out here? It will rain soon."

"I'm afraid of that, but it couldn't be helped." She shrugged. Oh, he was so handsome today in a brown tweed waistcoat that drew her attention to his flat abdomen. His shirtsleeves had been rolled up to his elbows and the buff-colored breeches hugged his legs to the point where she could easily be jealous of the garment. In short, he was the very picture of an English gentleman at leisure, despite the bruises on his face and knuckles from his fight with Hugh the other day. "My thoughts are too consuming, and I couldn't concentrate inside the house, so I thought by coming outside, they might sort themselves."

He retrieved his cane. "Did they?"

"Unfortunately, no." There was so much she wished to say to

him that the words crowded her throat and stuck there. "I was also hoping that I might run into you so we could talk."

A grunt came from him. "Then we are doing this now?"

"We ought to, don't you think? You have avoided me for the last three days. Delaying it won't help."

For long moments, he regarded her. Finally, he nodded. "Perhaps you have the right of it. We should face things head on."

"And you promise to have a civilized conversation?" She didn't want more trouble along the lines of what she'd witnessed between him and Hugh the other day.

"Yes." The word was clipped, short. "Neither of us can move forward without coming to a bit of common ground first."

"Good." Though her throat was tight with unshed tears, she drifted toward the rose bushes as the gray rain clouds moved over the area and hid the sun. "I appreciate the courtesy."

Now, what to say to him that would remove both of them from this horrid mess they'd fallen into?

CHAPTER FIVE

"I T's HARDLY COURTESY. You are owed my time and attention for the very fact that you are my wife." Gilbert shook his head, knowing all along that he hadn't treated her as such. "By all means, let us open Pandora's box." He wished he could say he was beyond caring, but that would be a flat out lie.

Three days ago, he'd had it out with Hugh, had been forced to acknowledge some of his own failings and insecurities. He hadn't yet confronted them, but that day was coming; he could feel it in his bones, and quite frankly, he didn't much care for that much introspection, for that would lead to other things and then the flood gates holding back his emotions would slam open.

And he'd be lost.

To say nothing of the threat Hugh had issued when he'd more or less said that he would try for a relationship with Madelene if Gilbert ultimately set her free.

Did he want to give her up to another man? Even if she would probably have better chances of meeting her dreams?

I simply don't know.

It was a coil. Especially when he'd been all too amused when he'd come upon his wife literally running from the most docile beagle in all of England. It was one of those adorable tidbits he remembered about her, and if he wasn't careful, he'd find himself trapped back within her pull.

Madelene touched a fingertip to one of the rose blooms, and he was struck again with how delicate she was, how haunted she looked with the slight dark circles beneath her eyes and that trace of a frown tugging at the corners of her rose-hued lips. "Does your mother still tend to the roses? I remember she has won awards at country fairs for these roses."

"Oh, of course she does. Though I think Sophia has taken over that task presently. It is their goal of coddling a grafting to force a new variety of rose that will give Mother the edge during a show next year." A pair of gardening sheers lay near one of the bushes along with a few cut roses that were wilting and dying. Perhaps his sister had been here recently. "No doubt Mama will resume her reign once Sophia moves to London with the ambassador."

For the first time since his sister had wed Gilbert realized everyone's lives were changing. Arthur had married and so had Sophia. No longer would either of them have extra time to just pop out to Ettesmere Park, and in his sister's case, she would no doubt become quite the world traveler.

"I'm going to miss my siblings." He hadn't realized he'd spoke the thought aloud until Madelene looked at him a frown.

"You act as if they are going away permanently just because they have wed."

It was uncanny how well she still knew him. "I feel as if everyone is moving in directions opposite of me." It was more of a truth than he'd uttered in a while. "Arthur and Sophia have once more found love and romance. It will serve as steppingstones for their lives."

"Is that something you are interested in finding again?" The question, couched in a soft voice, sent awareness over his skin.

"I don't know." Letting himself love someone—her—made him vulnerable and open to the horrors that existing brought. How long would it be before those things broke him, perhaps beyond fixing?

"That's understandable." She moved her attention to another

rose bush and again, traced the petals of a flower with her fingertip. "I envy your mother this hobby."

What an odd thing to say, but it drew him closer to her. "You never found one?" Truly, he didn't know much about the woman he'd taken to wife now that years had separated them.

"I tried thinking it would help ease my mind and distract me, but in the end, I could only concentrate on walking, either through Mayfair or Hyde Park."

His chest tightened, for her life sounded all too lonely, and that fault fell exclusively on him, but he wasn't ready to own that responsibility. So he summoned his ire and the familiar bitterness, because he had already become accustomed to them. "Did Hugh accompany you during those times?" It wasn't well done of him, but it stuck in his craw that she had spent many of her days with him.

That Hugh had sought her out to give her the companionship she lacked.

Because of me.

Madelene sighed. Her shoulders dropped a bit. "At times he did."

Annoyance speared through his chest. If he didn't feel for her any longer, why was there a wild swing of emotion? "How much were you in his company?"

"Enough that we grew close," she said as she turned about to face him.

The hand on the head of his cane tightened. The silver bit into his palm. "Yet you couldn't bring yourself to accompany me to India."

She blew out a breath of frustration. "You left me, remember." In her agitation, she curled a hand into her lavender skirting. Belatedly he recalled she adored any shade of purple and it brought life to her skin, worked with the high color in her cheeks and stole away some of the sadness in her eyes. "How could I be close with my husband when *you* walked out on our marriage?"

"You know exactly why I did." Though, after that talk with

Hugh, after discovering from his best friend that Madelene did not indeed take the major as a lover, it was still the easy excuse. If he told her the real reason he'd fled, she would hate him. How could she not? When a man couldn't sort through his own emotions, couldn't find the words to talk about his disappointments, what good was he?

"Oh, Gilbert." The sadness had returned to her hazel eyes that were more green than brown at the moment. But the longer he regarded her, the more shadows haunted those depths that had nothing to do with the threatening rain clouds. "I don't wish to fight with you. I am done with that, and it serves no purpose." She shook her head. "Additionally, I simply have no strength to keep on that path."

Alarm wormed its way into his chest and tightened it by increments. "Are you well?"

"I don't know." Madelene wandered around the heart of the maze. He declined to follow, for every time he came near, he wanted to kiss her, tell her with actions how sorry he was he'd been away, but that would lead to disaster. "However, I *do* know I am not the same woman I was when you went to India. Or before that, if you wish to know the truth."

"Fair enough." He wasn't the same man. They had both grown, and unfortunately, that had been apart. But none of this was moving them closer to a goal. Slowly, he trailed after her. The relatively cool breeze blew over his skin like a refreshing whisper. "What do you want from me, Madelene?" Perhaps he didn't wish to fight either.

As she turned, muscles worked in her throat. "I either want you to make amends in this union or try to grant me a divorce regardless of the scandal, but we both cannot remain stuck, trapped in the marriage that might have been ill-advised since it fell apart so quickly."

Hot anger stabbed through him. "*You* want a divorce?" As if she had grounds, for he still hadn't found the courage to tell her of his indiscretion. "So you can finally marry Hugh?"

God, how could he see her around London on *his* arm and know that he didn't try hard enough to save what he'd had?

"No, of course not." Another sigh escaped her. The breeze flirted with tendrils of her dark hair that had escaped their pins. It was something he'd always remembered about her, and he also knew those strands would be soft and if he was fortunate, would curl about his finger. "But—"

"—but he *is* available—"

"—he was there when you weren't," she continued as if he hadn't interrupted her. "Hugh offered support, kept me from losing myself to grief, to the darkness that wished to bury me after we lost our son."

"I'm glad you are *so* happy with him." Not matter how hard he tried, he couldn't stop the hurtful words from pouring from his mouth, but perhaps it was better than yelling his ire to the heavens.

"Gilbert, please listen to what I need to tell you." She came close with a hand extended. The faint scent of lilies of the valley wafted to his nose, and again, that awareness for her danced over his skin. "I never had intercourse with Hugh; I never betrayed our marriage vows."

Hot shame and guilt slammed into his chest with such force that he gasped for breath as the first few raindrops flew onto his cheeks. He hadn't been as respectful. He shook his head while his jaw worked. "I know. Hugh told me," he finally admitted in a choked voice.

"Oh, good." Madelene visibly relaxed. "I was prepared to tell you that my history has been sterling, that you had no cause to doubt my fidelity."

"I know it now." And the dagger of guilt kept twisting inside his chest. What should he do since he was the one who had obviously been in the wrong?

Apparently unaware of his internal struggle, she continued and tucked her hands behind her back. "I was in a dark place and desperately needed comfort and support. Hugh gave it willingly and I let him because I didn't want to be alone. I needed the company, the feel of a man's arms around me." She held up a hand when he would have protested. "For support only."

"I'm sure you were both quite happy." He couldn't keep the bitterness from his voice, especially when he was lower than scum.

Anger leaped into her eyes. They glittered in the gloom from the oncoming rain. "Why are you acting like an arse? I am telling you how I coped during that dreadful time when I didn't think there was any way out."

"You could have written, told me you were coming out to India to join me, let me be *that* to you." Would he have welcomed her with open arms at the time? There was no way to know, except every moment he stood here with her ramped his need to feel her body against his, to reassure himself that he wasn't as horrid as he thought.

"Except you withdrew from me long before our son was stillborn." A half-stifled sob followed the accusation, and the sound went straight to his bruised heart. "I grappled with depression and wanting to end everything so I could be with our son." Another sob escaped. "I still do at times."

"What?" That whispered confession had shock plowing through him with the force of a blow. "Things are that bad even now, three years later?" Good Lord, he had no idea, but he didn't want her to kill herself. Despite the confusion he held for her and their marriage, a wave of protection welled within him.

"Grief doesn't take a holiday." She wiped at a few raindrops on her cheeks. "I need to talk about that time in our life with you—my husband, the baby's father—need to hear you say you forgive me that disappointment. That none of it matters…"

Oh, God.

Gilbert battled with his emotions as they pummeled him one after the other—shame, guilt, grief, compassion—and since he hadn't properly let himself feel these in the past three years or so, he had no idea what to do, didn't want to show weakness or lose himself as she had. Eventually, he ruthlessly shoved them all down and clung to annoyance. "Who do you prefer? Him or me?" Lingering reaction graveled his voice. His muscles tensed and he wished to run, to flee far away from this garden where everything was slowly working toward the surface.

The place where fear cooled his blood.

When she looked at him, met his gaze, blatant need blazed in her eyes. Desire fairly crackled between them. "I don't ever put him in such an equation."

He snorted. "Seems like you do, for he's already halfway smitten."

"I cannot help that." Emotion flitted over her face he couldn't read in the overcast light and the increasing rain. "Perhaps if you are worried, you should give me something to compare him to."

"Well, damn." Gilbert stared at her, shocked that those words had even come from her. "It seems you've acquired some cheek while we've been apart." Desire jumped into his brain to take over. With a growl he tossed away his cane, closed the distance, and caught her up into his arms. For the moment, she was still his wife. Then he claimed her lips in a hard kiss designed to tell her in no uncertain terms that she belonged to him.

In *this* moment.

He couldn't allow himself to think beyond the present.

Madelene struggled. She wrenched away, her chest heaving. "What are you doing?"

"Without putting that great an emphasis on it, but before I left, we *were* newlyweds and there is no scandal in it if we were to indulge now." That brief kiss hadn't been nearly enough. No matter the rain, no matter that they were at the heart of the maze where anyone could come upon them, he wanted this woman.

"I suppose you are correct." Her gaze landed on his mouth, and he tried—unsuccessfully—to tamp down a groan. "There is no harm, and it has been a long time…"

Unable to wait any longer, Gilbert curled a hand about her nape and dragged her against his body. As she rested her palms on his chest, he claimed her mouth again. Over and over and *over* again, he kissed her, drank from her, reintroduced himself to her.

The heat of her invited further exploration while the gentle rain did little to cool his ardor, and each time she returned his kisses, the petal-softness of her lips tugged him closer to the edge of reality. Years ago, they'd thoroughly enjoyed each other's bodies once they'd wed, to the point where Arthur made jest of them, especially since they'd married a mere six months after the death of his father.

But Madelene had been increasing and they couldn't wait for the mourning period to expire else scandal would come knocking at the door. He should have known then, when she'd lost that pregnancy early on, that it was just the beginning of the hardships they would encounter during their union.

But he'd been so damned happy to have her in his life, to be married again after his first one had ended so horrifically. He'd wanted to share the world with her, to have her as a partner in everything he undertook…

Yet it hadn't happened exactly as he'd hoped.

Not wanting those maudlin memories to intrude and steal the moment, Gilbert growled as he broke the embrace. When she uttered a protest, he grinned. "We are only relocating," he said by way of explanation. Strain graveled his voice. Then he took her hand and pulled her off to one side of the maze's heart where the ruins of a stone wall stood as a testament to an outbuilding that used to occupy the space before his grandfather had designed and ordered the building of the hedge maze. The slight overhang from a few fruit trees would provide protection from the desultory rain.

"Perhaps we should head back to the house—"

"No!" Seconds later they reached the stone wall, and they trampled around the bushes containing apricot-colored roses. "I need you now, here." The moment would lose its appeal if they left the maze, and the fear that she wouldn't want him after they left this place guided his decision.

"I like this impromptu side of you."

He kissed her again, hoping to prevent more words, for they weren't needed. Perhaps the only thing that could help heal them both was the simple act of being together. Then he was adrift on reacquainting himself with her body, of ferreting out those secrets he'd long since forgotten, and she had the power to take away some of his fears.

At least in this moment.

Madelene, to her credit, wasn't passive in the quest for physical repletion. She pulled his shirttails from his breeches, and the second her hands slid over his skin, shivers of need careened down his spine to lodge in his stones. Soft sounds of encouragement left her throat. And when she nipped at a spot below his jaw, urgency surged through his shaft.

"I'm not going to last long today."

"I don't care." With a tug to his cravat, she brought him closer, and he came willingly, trapping her between the stone wall and his body. "I only want you."

Truly, there was no time to finesse the coupling, for he hadn't been with a woman for well over two years, not since his indiscretion in Bombay, but there was something about having Madelene back in his arms that made him creep closer to insanity.

As the patter of rain increased its intensity, Gilbert worried her nipples with the pads of his thumbs though the lightweight fabric. Her swift inhalation and subsequent groan pulled a grin from him, so he bent his head and took one of the hard buds into his mouth to a squeal of approval from her. That he remembered, and it spurred him onward.

With more haste than honor, he wrenched her skirting upward and encouraged one of her legs upward to curl about his hip. She clung to his shoulders, and with each passing moment, the rain dampened their clothes. It seeped into her hair, catching on a few strands like tiny, glittering diamonds. As he fumbled with the buttons of his front falls, she sucked in a breath, tried to put a hand beneath his shirt again, but he kissed her for a distraction. If she continued to touch him, he'd spend all over himself.

Finally, the damned buttons were finished, and the panel fell down. As his engorged length sprang out, his tip glanced along her flesh since she was still opened to him.

A sigh shuddered from her throat. She held his gaze. Blatant need shadowed those depths. The trembles that racked her body transferred to him. "It's been so long—"

"Shh." Gilbert cut off anything else she would have said with a searing kiss and not able to wait, with a flex of his hips, he penetrated her, not stopping until he'd fully impaled her.

"Oh!" Madelene clutched at his shoulders. Her eyes briefly rolled back in the way he remembered when something felt extraordinarily wonderful. "This moment has always been a favorite…"

With a hand beneath her thigh to keep her leg up, he planted the palm of his other on the wall beside her head. "Agreed." Slowly, he withdrew sheerly for the pleasure of stroking back into her honeyed heat. As her body quivered around him, the hold on his control snapped. "This will go quick."

"It matters not." While she looped her arms about his shoulders, she layered her body closer to his. "Make me fly," she whispered into his ear. "Make me forget."

In this, they were of one accord. Right now, there was only her and him.

There was nothing romantic about this coupling. It was merely the mutual sharing of bodies in a quest to gain carnal satisfaction. Again and again, he stroked into her. Deeper and deeper he drove until the only thing he could think about was how the heat of her body felt around him, how the scent of lilies of the valley reminded him of happier times, how each sound she made as he claimed her tugged him back to the past when things had been good, and he hadn't felt like as big a failure as he did now.

She moved her hips, met him thrust for thrust, their bodies

gliding seamlessly against each other in a dance as old as time. There was no time to finesse the coupling or make it more pleasurable for her; he wouldn't last long. Already, tingling moved through his stones as they tightened and drew close to his body.

"Oh, God." He barely felt the rain on the back of his neck or seeping through his fine lawn shirt. All too soon, urgency took control, raced through his shaft. He stroked once, twice more, but he was done. A wave of bliss engulfed him as he exploded into his release. Though she'd made all the appropriate sounds of enjoyment, she hadn't hit that all-important pinnacle with him; how could she? He hadn't made certain to put in the time to bring her to that peak.

Perhaps it didn't matter. The act was more symbolic than anything.

For long moments, he leaned into her as his breathing regulated, but she wrapped her arms about his shoulders and held him close.

"I'm sorry it was lackluster for you," he said against the shell of her ear.

"Hush, Gilbert." She pressed a kiss to the side of his neck, just above his cravat. "There is more to a coupling than a release."

He didn't know if that was true, but the air between them had been cleared and they once more stood on even ground, but he remained confused about what to do regarding their union. "This doesn't mean we have reconciled." Yet he wanted to think there was a glimmer of hope in the mess that hadn't been there before.

"I understand and agree." She let her leg slide back down. "But I want to say that I missed you like this. Missed the intimacy we used to have. Missed being in your arms, knowing your kisses, being close."

Emotion rose up his throat and threatened to choke him. "I missed you, too." With the remainder of his strength, he tamped down those feelings. Now was not the time to let them out. This coupling was only acting on mutual need.

Yet, still he held her tightly to him, and when he realized she was softly crying in his arms, he tried to comfort her as best he could, held her much longer than he ought, for he very nearly fell victim to the grief he'd buried and ignored years ago.

I cannot let her see how broken I truly am.

Abruptly, he pulled away, not looking at her as he stuffed his flaccid length into his breeches and did up his front falls. "I must go, but we will talk again later. I promise."

Then he ran like the coward that he was and didn't stop running until he gained an empty room inside the manor house where no one could bear witness to the emotions battering him.

One thing was certain: he'd enjoyed that coupling more than he should, even if it had been a poor showing. *Now what the hell do I do?*

CHAPTER SIX

July 30, 1819

MADELENE HAD CHOSEN the library to hide from the Winterbourne family merely so she wouldn't need to answer questions or run the risk that someone might look at her and see—or suspect—that she'd come together intimately yesterday with Gilbert.

A soft smile tugged at the corners of her mouth. As couplings went, it wasn't the best; but then perhaps that was something else they had to learn all over again after being apart for three years. Despite that, it had been lovely to have been in his arms, to feel his body against her, have him filling her as completely as she'd remembered.

And the kisses he'd imparted had made her head spin, for in that, he was the man she'd married when there had been so much hope.

As she attempted to read, her concentration kept wandering, for all she could think about was her husband and what yesterday had meant for their relationship, especially after he'd run from her as if the hounds of hell were after him.

Why?

Stop wondering, Madelene. He is obviously struggling. And he chose to do so silently. The realization that he probably didn't have anyone to talk about his grief with smacked into her, so much so she set aside her book. Then why did he refuse to do so with her?

Before she could become too lost in her thoughts, the man himself came into the room. He was halfway across the floor before he spotted her and then stopped abruptly with his hand tight upon the head of his cane. The bruises on his face left the once-handsome visage an ugly mess of blue, purple, and green. "Ah, I didn't know the room was occupied." He cleared his throat. "I shall leave you to it."

"Please stay." She rose to her feet while a silly little tremor moved through her lower belly. "I would like your company."

For long moments, he pondered, his body taut as if he wished to run. Finally, he nodded. "All right. I needed to speak with you in any event. Especially after having thought about certain… things… over the past few days." He made his way to the sofa she'd previously occupied, and when he sat down, he glanced at the book she'd abandoned. "Fairy stories still hold your interest?"

"Of course." Madelene smiled. She regained her spot on the sofa. So close to him that his heat beckoned, she didn't dare to do anything that might spook him into running. "Those stories are full of hope and the hint of romance. Tell me it's a bad thing."

"It is not." But the expression on his face suggested otherwise. "Don't you find that some of those tales are contrived and not a true representation of life?"

"Not at all. Even beyond fairytales, in any book which promises a happy ending, I believe such stories are timely, for there are always challenges we all must grapple with." She offered a smile. "You don't agree?"

He relaxed his grip on the head of his cane. "I do, actually."

"Truly?" That was a surprise. He used to laugh at her love of fairy stories and books which contained romance.

"Yes." Gilbert shifted on his cushion, turned toward her, and for the first time since she'd come back into his company, the anger had cleared in his eyes. In its place was confusion and perhaps a tiny bit of longing. For what she couldn't dare to speculate. "From my understanding and my own research, every fairy story is full of obstacles the couple needs to surmount in or to have the chance for love and a decent life, yes?"

"Yes." She nodded. "You have read them? Since when?"

A trace of a flush rose above his cravat. "I was able to procure a few books while on the passage over to India from a rather well-read gentleman. Much of those long days at sea were passed with reading."

"Why?" She was agog with surprise.

He shrugged. "I was curious, and they, perhaps, reminded me of you."

"Oh." Another round of tingles moved through her belly. "How sweet." Surely, this was odd behavior for him, but it rather tickled her that she'd made such an impression. "Do you think there is a correlation between such stories and what we are facing?"

"Perhaps."

Now was as good a time as any to broach the subjects they should discuss. "I feel what you and I must overcome is so daunting, though." She clasped her hands in her lap. "There is so much history there..." A sigh escaped even as knots of worry pulled in her belly. "Perhaps we weren't meant to be together after all."

Shadows scudded through his eyes. "Do you love me, Madelene?"

The question was so unexpected, she gasped. She hadn't counted on needing to answer this inquiry so soon in their reconciliation. "I honestly don't know, but I would like to think that in spending more time with you, those feelings might return or be enhanced." For neither of them was the same person they'd been three years before. "Love is more than physical intercourse. It is respect and attention; it is forgiveness and compassion. It is the will to face unpleasant things together."

"Fair enough." Slowly, he nodded. "Would you rather give

up on us right now due to the amount of work there is between us instead of discovering if we can go the distance and see those obstacles through?"

The fact he was offering such a thing caused her lower jaw to drop. "At what price, though? Is it too steep?" For if an attempt at a reconciliation didn't work, it would be twice as devastating to lose him.

"Does the cost matter?" Gilbert shrugged. "At the end, we might have a second chance at romance. Knowing my siblings have both found the same has made me think that perhaps you and I might have a chance…" That longing flashed across his face once more. "And perhaps we might have the knowledge that even though the both of us have made mistakes—"

"—you more than me—" she couldn't help but interrupting.

"—regardless, we need a healthy dose of forgiveness before we go forward," he ended with a tight grin.

Unexpected tears sprang to her eyes. It was the closest he'd come to an honest talk, and she appreciated his willingness so much. "If you need to hear me say it, then I will." Daring much, Madelene took his hand. "I forgive you for leaving me at my lowest point and going to India. That is in the past, for you are here now."

He nodded. "Thank you." The words were graveled by emotion she couldn't clearly read on his face. "I don't deserve it, though."

"Oh, Gilbert, of course you do. Everyone does." She moved the book out of the way and then scooted across the cushion to sit next to him. "I'm glad you are open to moving forward together. I feared…" Her words trailed off, for the next admission would leave her vulnerable. "I feared you hated me for my failures."

A startled look came over his face. "Why do you think I'd hate you?"

"I cannot carry a child full term let alone birth one alive." A waver set up in her voice, and when she would have returned to her seat, he stayed her flight by grabbing her hand. "It's the sole reason I came here to perhaps request a divorce, if such a thing can be procured. You don't deserve to live with such disappointment—"

"Stop." A muscle ticced in his cheek, and his eyes were haunted. By what she could only guess at. "That is not your fault." His hand shook in hers. "There is something I should have made you aware of before we wed. It might have swayed your decision."

"What is it?" The knots in her stomach grew.

"Years before I'd ever met you, I was married to someone else."

Another wave of shock plowed into her. "Why did you not tell me?"

"I didn't think it pertinent. And quite frankly, when I met you, you proved such a distraction, everything else slipped my mind." A tiny grin accompanied the words. "It was my past history and had no bearing on my future."

"Of course it did! That is something that would have helped make you into the man you are now. It gave depth to your character." She reeled from that missing information. "How long was the union?"

"Three years." He avoided her gaze and focus his attention on something just past her right shoulder. "It matters not how we met or how long we'd known each other prior to that. The important part here is that she had trouble conceiving like you." A choked sound came from him. "She did manage to have a full-term pregnancy, but when it came time for the babe to be born, disaster followed."

The words were so raw she felt them deep in her own chest. "What happened?" It simply boggled her mind he'd been married, but to discover his wife had been increasing? There was no response she could formulate right now.

"There were complications." He shook his head; his gaze was far away, lost to the annals of time. "The delivery seemed to take an eternity. The wait was unbearable. She suffered so much during the labor." Incrementally, his fingers tightened on hers. "When the infant finally arrived a few weeks early, they were both in trauma. The baby couldn't take in air; my wife was hemorrhaging."

"Oh, Gilbert." The tears in her eyes spilled onto her cheeks.

He didn't appear to have heard her, for he was still lost in the past. "In the end, my wife lost too much blood, went unconscious. She died later that night never having woken. The baby—a girl—preceded her into death by a few hours. From what the midwife said, her little lungs were perhaps malformed. It was unlikely she wouldn't have survived anyway." A half-stifled sob left his throat. "I never had the chance to say goodbye or to hold either of them."

The wealth of emotion he struggled with was staggering. It fairly rolled off him in waves. How could he openly mourn the loss of that woman and that babe without ever having shed a tear for their own? Threads of hot anger wound through her chest, but then she tempered it with understanding. Perhaps he didn't know how to express those feelings, and this was only the beginning. "I'm so sorry." Not knowing what else to do, Madelene slipped her arms around him and simply held him. It would be slow going.

"I am too."

"Death is an exacting mistress." The grief he was caught in resurrected her own, but she fought it off by swallowing and breathing deeply. Right now, she wasn't in the right mood to allow those emotions to well.

"Yes." Tremors shook his body, and for a wild second, she thought he might shed a tear or finally open up about everything he held inside, but he remained stoic. For long moments, he leaned on her with one arm about her waist. Eventually, he sighed and pulled out of her arms, peering into her eyes. "Which leads me to where we are now. It is my belief you haven't failed as a woman, for that is my cross alone to bear. I should have told you of my history before we wed, so you might have had a chance, so you could have chosen another…"

"Oh, please don't think that." She had been remiss in sharing her own past, but now wasn't the time, not when it was crucial he tap into his own pain. "I will never regret having married you. Even now."

"Perhaps you should. I am far from perfect." His voice broke. "It's why I have struggled with the decision to either remain married to you or go through the rigorous steps to seek a divorce." Once more his gaze swung to her, and there was such pain reflected in those dark depths that it stole her breath. "You deserve a chance with a man who doesn't have the apparent health issues I do. If you were to marry Hugh, you could—"

"—no." As her heart trembled, she laid a palm on either side of his face, wouldn't let him pull away. "Hugh is a close friend only. I have no romantic feelings for him, and besides, I am married to *you* and no longer wish for a divorce or even a separation." It was apparently the day for shocking revelations, for as she spoke those words, she realized they were true.

"You don't." It wasn't a question.

"No." Carefully, she touched her lips to his. "I want to try and reconcile with you, for I don't believe our story is done just yet."

A slow grin curved his mouth and some of the shadows left his eyes. "Neither do I."

"Good." Feeling all too reckless and a tad bit wicked, Madelene kissed him. Never would she have enough of the press of her lips to his or how he tasted slightly of mint. As she pulled away, she gently sucked at that upper piece of flesh. It wouldn't do to continue on and give desire a foothold, for they still had much to talk about. "I am glad we have reached a tentative understanding." Then giving into the impulse she'd had since yesterday, she brushed the shock of blond hair from his forehead.

"So am I." He looked as stunned as she felt.

"If you don't mind me asking, what has caused this sudden change in your attitude? Two days ago, you acted as if you hated the sight of me. Now you are willing to work through our issues. Why?"

The flush over his cravat deepened into a mottled red as a sheepish expression crept over his face. "Certain things have changed between us."

Good heavens. "If it is because we had intercourse, just stop. You could have done that with anyone, and it wasn't satisfying besides." *Well, drat.* Perhaps she shouldn't have mentioned that bit.

The flush on his neck intensified. "It wasn't that." Gilbert took her hands in his. "I simply thought since my mother assumes our marriage is healthy, and since you and I are both here, we should see if there is enough left to revive our union."

Confusion clouded her brain. "Why?" Then she gasped. "Quite simply, you are jealous of Hugh." As far as she knew, he and the major hadn't talked to each other since that scuffle at tea.

"Perhaps." He offered a wry grin, and she remembered why she'd fallen for him in the first place. "I won't give you up to him, Madelene. Surely you know that."

"I am beginning to see it, but you needn't worry in that quarter."

"It doesn't matter." A warning growled through his tones.

She tamped the urge to sigh. Such responses were from young men who hadn't matured. Had her husband learned nothing in the years apart? "I don't know that I want our old relationship revived," she said in a quiet voice. "Don't you think we owe it to ourselves to start afresh?"

"I do, which is why I came seeking you out today." Taking hold of his cane, he heaved himself to his feet and brought her into a standing position as well. "So, does that mean you agree to reconcile?"

"For how long? There must be a deadline in place, else we'll never make progress."

"Agreed." He nodded. "Perhaps we should start small. Two weeks? After that, we can reassess how things are going. Besides,

Mama will probably wish to return to Town by the end of August, so that gives us a month."

"It sounds reasonable." But a frown tugged at the corners of her lips. "Only if you promise to talk with me—really talk—in order to work through the things that loom between us. You need to acknowledge your grief, Gilbert, and everything else you have been avoiding over the years." Never once had he told her about his previous marriage or the heartbreak that had brought. It had to be festering.

He tugged at the knot of his cravat and took a step away from her. "I promise." The words sounded wrenched from a tight throat.

"And you won't keep bringing up the lies that I had an affair with Hugh?"

A muscle in his jaw ticced. "I will not. There is more than enough evidence presented to assure me you didn't cheat."

"Good." She remained wary but hopeful. That ever-present pull of desire between them refused to stay buried. "Then I agree, but I am not moving back into your bedchamber. I need time to readjust to having you in my life despite what your mother believes."

"That's understandable." Something—disappointment, annoyance?—flickered in his eyes, gone so fast she didn't catch it.

It was lovely, this being with him, but he looked all to ready to run from her. Again. "Do you plan to court me?" It had been an age since she'd been with him in any capacity beyond arguing or avoidance.

"Is that what you want from me?" He eyed her with a mix of speculation and hope.

"That might prove best, and would reassure your mother. We cannot go forward as we are now." She paused in order to think over her next words. "We both need to learn about each other in light of certain new revelations, and trust between us needs rebuilt."

"Agreed." His voice was ragged. "Shall we begin by going for a walk? I could use the fresh air."

No doubt he didn't like being confined.

"That would be lovely. Let me run upstairs and change into something more appropriate." She laid a hand on his arm as she passed. "You *will* wait for me, won't you?"

"Yes, of course." The grin he offered was faint. "Don't dawdle. I'd rather not have anyone else try to join our walking party."

With a nod, Madelene left the room. Perhaps the rainclouds in her life were finally clearing.

CHAPTER SEVEN

August 1, 1819

FOR THE FIRST time in his life, Gilbert was at sixes and sevens. How the hell did a man woo a woman to whom he was already married?

Two days ago, he and Madelene had come to an agreement. They would enter into a courtship that would hopefully result in them learning about each other now that life's difficulties had torn them apart. Aside from the walk they'd taken over the property, he had no idea what else to do.

"What the devil is wrong with me?" he asked a vase of flowers as he passed it in the corridor. "I already did this, but it feels different this time," he said to an oil painting that depicted a field of wildflowers.

I'll need to work harder to win her heart a second time.

The moment he reached the door to the drawing room, he was hailed.

"Uncle Gilbert!"

He tamped the urge to groan. That was Hannah's voice, but he couldn't ignore his youngest niece no matter how he wished to in the moment. After a couple of deep breaths, he turned about and entered the room, where both Hannah and Emily—his oldest niece—were seated side by side on a low sofa with several books scattered about the immediate area. At their feet, the fat beagle slept, and every so often his paws would move as if he were chasing a rabbit.

"What did you need, Hannah?"

"I merely thought to talk with you since I haven't seen you much these past handful of days." She gestured him further into the room. "Please, sit with us."

Emily giggled. She pushed a lock of blonde hair behind her ear. "He looks rather lost, don't you think?" she asked Hannah, who nodded. "Courting must not be going well."

"Truer words, girls." With a nod, Gilbert dropped heavily into a chair near their location.

"Tell us the truth, Uncle, are you truly so dismal at romance that you haven't managed to secure Aunt Madelene's heart?" There was no malice in Emily's expression, but suddenly he felt as if it might be an attack.

He tugged at his cravat. "What do you mean?"

Hannah rolled her eyes as only a twelve-year-old could. "Are you in love with her?"

Heat crept up the back of his neck. "I am not certain."

She huffed. "Does she love you?"

"I don't know that either."

"Then that is why you need us."

A frown tugged at the corners of his mouth. "How so?"

Emily snorted. "We will give you advice." She shrugged as if the answer was obvious, and he was the world's biggest nodcock for *not* knowing that.

As uncomfortable as it made him, the idea held merit. He adjusted his grip on the head of his cane. "Perhaps you have the right of it." As he bounced his gaze between his nieces, he sighed. "Since the two of you had a hand—I'm assuming—in finding your parents' matches, perhaps I should listen to your counsel."

"I'm glad you've come to your senses, Uncle Gilbert." Hannah's expression was so serious that he wanted to laugh, but he bit the inside of his cheek to prevent it lest she think he made jest of her.

"Very well. Let's begin." He rested an ankle on a knee and peered at them with speculation. "It is no secret I am attempting to court my wife. Since I've been away, we have grown apart." The girls didn't need to know of the other complications that had sprung between them. "Though I won her years ago, we have drifted away from each other, but I am encountering difficulties in drawing close to her again."

Would they laugh at him?

Emily's smile could rival the sun. "I think it's quite admirable and romantic that you wish to woo your wife."

"Exactly," Hannah was quick to add. "You are noble and clever, so why are you having such difficulties?"

Oh, let me count the ways.

"I am feeling much like a stranger around her." To say nothing of the fact that he was the one who broke their nuptial vows, for she certainly hadn't. Hot guilt circled through his gut as he stared at his nieces. When he eventually confessed all to his wife, how could she ever forgive him after he'd acted so poorly toward her in the same situation? Her alleged infidelity notwithstanding, he would have left for India anyway, for the memories—the ghosts—contained in London would have haunted him until he broke.

"The trick is to discover what Aunt Madelene likes now and then go do those things with her," Emily said. "Take my father for example. When he was certain he would never marry again, the moment he met Julianna, he wished to know everything about her, and once he knew what she liked, he put himself into her path."

Hannah snorted. Amusement danced in her eyes. "Except, you and John were heavy-handed in pushing him into those meetings."

"Yes, we were, but eventually Papa figured it out." There was absolutely no apology in Emily's expression. Oh, she would be trouble once she had her come out.

He didn't envy Arthur that responsibility. "That is perhaps one of the problems I'm facing." Gilbert struggled to his feet. Needing to burn off restless energy, he strolled to one of the windows, but as soon as he glanced out, annoyance lanced through his chest. Madelene was walking the lawn with Hugh, and her hand rested in the crook of his bent elbow. "What the devil?"

Both girls sprang off the sofa and rushed to the window.

"Oh, Major Pritchard is so handsome," Emily breathed. Clearly, she was enamored with the man. "I wish I was older and have already had my come out, for I would surely flirt with him."

Good Lord.

Gilbert huffed his annoyance. "I rather think he's not the man for you."

"But look how considerate and caring he is toward Aunt Madelene," Hannah pointed out as she pressed a palm to the window glass. "The way he's holding his head near hers so he can hear what she's saying." A sigh escaped her. "To have the attention of such a man! Additionally, I'll wager he is handsome in his military uniform."

"Absolutely," Emily was quick to agree. "There is something about a man wearing a uniform that tickles my belly." She clutched at Hannah's hand. "Do you think we can persuade Grandmama to throw another ball? And would she invite some of the area's eligible men who were in the military?"

"We can certainly ask."

"Girls, enough." He shook his head. How much trouble would he land in once Arthur and Sophia figured out their children were plotting to gawk at men when he was supposed to be looking after them? "I don't wish to talk about Hugh, especially when he's currently in my wife's company when she's supposed to be letting *me* court her." He couldn't quite keep the annoyance from his voice. Did she not think him serious, or did she just not wish to try to save their marriage as she'd said the other day in the library?

"Put away your growls and claws, Uncle Gilbert." Emily patted his arm. "Aunt Madelene and Major Pritchard are merely close friends." She peered up at him and held his gaze with hers. "He is much too honorable to steal her away from you."

Ha! She obviously didn't know the man well. Then her words sank into the confusion swirling through his brain. "How do you know?" Did *he* want to know?

Emily's grin was on this side of charming. "He and I have talked."

"The devil you say." Poor Arthur was going to have his hands full. He fervently hoped that Julianna would prove a guiding force in the girl's life.

Hannah huffed. "Language, Uncle Gilbert."

"My apologies." He peeked outside once more. Madelene and Hugh had stopped strolling and were now talking on one of the garden paths, partially obscured by an ornamental tree. "Why would you have had cause to talk with the major, Emily?"

"He is a guest here, after all, and I didn't wish to be rude." She tossed her head and moved the blonde waterfall of her hair over one shoulder. "Besides, Hannah and I aren't full of anger and bitterness like you, so the conversation therein was quite pleasant."

"Yes, exactly," Hannah said with a nod. "Despite what you might think of the major, he has nothing but good things to say about you."

Bloody hell. These two were a handful, and he really needed to do a better job of keeping an eye on them. Perhaps it was a good thing Hannah would accompany her mother to France when she left for her wedding trip. "Regardless, your admiration for the major doesn't negate the fact that he is with her right now and from the looks of it, he's easily charming her when I am struggling with the same."

Did he sound as pathetic as he felt?

Emily glanced out the window once more then slanted her gaze back to him. "I wouldn't worry, Uncle. Major Pritchard is very much Aunt Madelene's best friend." She shrugged. "They have been close for a long time, from what I understand. He only wants her happy."

"As if I don't want the same?"

She pointed her gaze to the ceiling. "I didn't say that."

"Perhaps it was implied." He frowned at the window. Why did Madelene prefer to spend time in Hugh's company instead of his? Had he not done enough in the way of sharing, of understanding? "Do you think the major will succeed in stealing her from me?" That fear was uppermost in his mind, and it sent icy chills of terror down his spine.

"You poor confused thing." Hannah closed the distance between them and gave him an impromptu hug. Not knowing what else to do, he awkwardly patted her back with his free hand. "That largely depends on how obstinate you continue to be toward them both."

That was a fair point. "I suppose I *have* been angry for a long time." And sometimes the fear he battled with manifested itself in ire and bitterness.

Hannah nodded as she stepped away. "You have, and it is *not* attractive."

"Oh, I quite agree." Emily nodded. She pushed open the window panels. Immediately, the summer breeze came into the room, and she lifted her face. Blonde tendrils danced on the air currents. "A reconciliation won't magically happen. You need to make an effort with her. Give Aunt Madelene flowers and chocolate. Take her shopping in the village or have tea in that adorable little café." She was nothing but honest as she looked at him. "But you *must* spend time with her, else the major will fill in those gaps."

"Perhaps you are right." Outside, Hugh and Madelene had continued their walk, and their rambles took them out of his sight line. Would Hugh try to steal a kiss? Was he even now telling her the dark secrets Gilbert kept hidden in a bid to pit her against him? His chest tightened. Surely not.

"Those are all good ideas," Hannah said, and the sound of her voice yanked him out of his thoughts. "Tell her you love her no matter what has happened."

"I thought I've tried to reassure her."

"But have you *said* the words?" Hannah pressed.

"Not those exactly." How could he when he didn't know *how* he felt about her?

Emily sighed. "I want a man who will do all of those things for me. It sounds so romantic to be wooed."

That struck Gilbert as funny, so he chuckled. Both girls frowned at him. "Why not choose a man like your uncle?"

Both of the girls laughed.

"With *you* as the example?" Emily roved her gaze up and down his person. "No, thank you."

He frowned. "Why not?" Was he no longer a catch?

Hannah huffed out a breath, and he once more felt like a nodcock. "Perhaps a man more like Uncle Arthur. He is ever so romantic. Or a man like Mr. Mattingly. He made a terrific effort when he won my mother." She eyed him askance. "Can you come up to that mark, Uncle Gilbert?"

"I… uh…" Could he expend that sort of effort to reap that reward? But he didn't want to hear all the ways he'd failed. He tugged on the knot of his cravat, for he was desperate to try something. There was every possibility Hugh would be true to his word—in all things—and that would spell disaster for winning Madelene's affections. "I'm not certain, but I don't wish to lose my wife again."

It was perhaps the most honest thing he'd said to any of his family members in recent days.

"At least there is that," Emily said softly to Hannah.

The younger girl nodded. "We can work with it."

He readjusted his hold on the head of his cane. "What do you suggest I do in order to win Madelene? When I met her—through Hugh—it was rather a quick courtship and subsequent engagement due to circumstances surrounding my father's death. But it was easy with her, and we didn't properly do the sorts of things I probably should have to make her feel special and wanted."

I cannot believe I am telling them this.

The girls looked at each other and shared a speaking glance as well as grins that bordered on mischief.

"What will make her weak at the knees?" Emily asked. "What does she swoon over?"

"I honestly have no idea." Outside of physical connection, he'd not take the time to discover. "She likes reading, and fairy stories." Another frown tugged at the corners of his mouth. "I feel as if I don't know her that well at all since so much has changed between us." He shoved his hand through his hair. "We were still newlyweds when I left for India, but certain… difficulties arose and I…"

Well, they didn't need to be privy to all of that.

Hannah bounced up and down in apparent excitement. That didn't bode well for him. "Well, you are not exactly a dashing hero in your current state, but we can start with your appearance."

He touched his fingers to the bruises on his cheek. "That cannot be helped." Yes, he wasn't as brave as Hugh or as handsome as the ambassador, so where did that leave him?

"It's all right, Uncle Gilbert. We shall help you." She stepped into his space, and with a quick tousle of her fingers, had a few bits of hair falling over his forehead. "That's better. It gives you a mysterious air." Then she loosened his cravat. "And don't always try for formal. Ladies adore seeing a man in disarray, especially when the hint of skin is teased."

Oh, bother. Heat crept up the back of his neck.

"Ooh, and be sure to roll your shirtsleeves up. Show your forearms. That is quite attractive," Hannah was quick to add. "And find a waistcoat in her favorite color. I would adore that, myself."

I am going to hell if I stand here and listen to any more of this.

"Yes, and don't shave one time when you meet her. Sometimes women like to see their men a tiny bit rugged and unkempt." Emily smiled as she stepped away to study him. "I would imagine any woman wishes undivided attention from her suitors. At all times." She winked. "When you are together, listen to what she says, really listen. It means so much."

"Yes." Hannah nodded. She fussed with the chain of his pocket watch. "And you will need to smile more, Uncle Gilbert. Honestly, you are much too grouchy at present. Ladies don't enjoy that, and there is no need for doom and gloom." Her expression brightened. "She is here now. That is half the battle."

"Noted." He cleared his throat when a ball of emotion rose into it. "What else?" Now that some of his previous bitterness had faded, he would work at being happy for himself.

Hannah's eyes twinkled. "What about dancing? Women adore that. Mama does especially."

"Dancing might prove problematic with the limp, but I'll try."

Emily nodded. "It is especially delicious when you are alone and can hold your lady close."

He did *not* wish to know how she had experience in that.

"Oh, you can take Aunt Madelene on long walks," Hannah said with a nod. "There are plenty of pretty areas around Ettesmere Park."

"Yes, and Julianna likes Otis Hill," Emily added with a grin of her own.

"Ooh, I'd forgotten about that," Hannah said as she twirled about the space. "I've heard it's especially romantic at night under the stars."

Emily's eyes twinkled. "And if you cannot figure out how to kiss her when the chance arises, there is no hope."

For the first time in a long while, Gilbert allowed a genuine grin. He chuckled, and it felt so good to do so he did it again. "These are all good ideas. I appreciate that."

"I should hope so." Then Emily sobered. "You *will* win her heart again, won't you, Uncle Gilbert?" A frown took possession of her lips. "Aunt Madelene is ever so nice, and if she marries the major, we shall never see her again."

Knots of worry pulled in his gut while cold fingers of fear played his spine. "I will do my level best, but I must warn you that a courtship is no guarantee romance will follow."

Again, both girls shared a glance.

Then Emily shook her head. "You have much to learn about women, Uncle Gilbert. Romance is found in *everything*, and it helps tremendously. You only need to believe."

"So I am beginning to believe." He heaved a sigh. "I suppose I should formulate a plan and begin it immediately."

"Yes!" Hannah shoved at his shoulder. "Go! And remember what we've told you. In the end, sometimes the best thing you can do is let her into your heart even if it *is* a mess. At least she will know you are real."

"Truly," Emily agreed with a nod. "It is good to find out you are not alone in the world or in how you feel. Just be honest. That will go a long way into winning her back."

He was more confused than ever. "What if, when I lay bare my soul, she doesn't like what she sees?" That had been the driving force behind why he'd run from everything.

Emily's eyes were kind as she shuttled him toward the door. "Then you will know the truth and can make your next decision. If Aunt Madelene cannot accept you at your worst even knowing that you are trying to change, then you shouldn't be with her at all."

It all sounded so simple coming from these young people. Could being himself unlock the walls they'd both thrown up around their hearts? Suddenly, he felt older than his years. "I shall do my best."

Hannah patted his hand. "That is all anyone can do, but we shall help if needed."

"Thank you. If you'll excuse me? I'd rather like to find my wife now."

And he hoped to God these fanciful measures worked.

CHAPTER EIGHT

August 3, 1819

"U H, MADELENE?"

She swung about from her contemplation of the front lawn from the morning room windows at the sound of Gilbert's voice. "Yes?" Then, as she took in his appearance, she gasped. "Merciful heavens! What happened to you?"

A grass stain decorated one knee of his buff-colored breeches while a button had gone missing on his tweed waistcoat. The sleeves of his fine lawn shirt had been rolled up, but there were red welts on each forearm as well as his forehead and neck. The shirttails hung haphazardly out of the waist of his breeches.

"I was out gathering wildflowers to give you in a bouquet." He thrust the floral tribute toward her, and once she took it, he came deeper into the room, his limp more pronounced. "However, the bees took great exception to such an activity. I was stung more than a few times, and it would seem my body doesn't do well with that."

The riot of colors in the bouquet were pretty indeed, but she quickly laid the offering onto a nearby occasional table as she rushed to his side. "You poor thing. Do they itch? Are you having difficulty breathing? Feel feverish?" She'd never known anyone to have a violent reaction to a bee sting, but then, he'd been stung multiple times.

"At the moment, they hurt like the devil." He tugged on his cravat, eventually loosening it so that the length of fabric hung down his chest like a lifeless snake. "And..." A red flush covered his face.

"And what?" She brushed a shock of hair from his forehead. He truly did look uncomfortable.

"One of those buggers went beneath my shirt and stung me on the back. Took forever to beat it out of my clothes. When I tried to outrun the bees, I tripped on a tree root and wrenched my knee. My old injury now throbs as well."

"I am so sorry." Though he was truly a pathetic sight, she lost a piece of her heart to him in that moment. The poor man was trying to conduct a proper courtship, and it was beyond endearing. Sympathy filled her chest. Madelene took the opposite arm from his cane. "Let's remove to the servants' hall. Perhaps the housekeeper has a salve we can put on those stings."

"I had envisioned the afternoon ending much differently than current circumstances." A hint of embarrassment threaded through his voice as he hobbled in pace with her.

"It matters not. You brought the flowers anyway, and the thought is what was sweeter." Her mind reeled to know that he'd done something so romantic. For the past two days, he'd been a more congenial version of himself, and that was pleasant enough, but they hadn't had a moment alone together, for the dowager countess had kept them all busy with the news she would throw one last ball for the summer in a week's time. While they slowly made their way downstairs toward the servants' hall, she asked, "How did you come by the limp?"

"A stupid accident on my part." He huffed out a breath. "Six months into my time in India I was touring a tea field in the hill country. A snake came out from hiding and startled me. I lost my footing and took a tumble—a rather long, bumpy tumble—down the hillside, crashing through tea bushes as I went." He glanced at her. "My ankle was broken and though it was set by a physician at the nearest fort, the medical facilities and expertise weren't up to typical British standards. The bones didn't heal properly, which left me with a limp and pain in the joint when it rains or grows cold."

"You really have had a tough time, haven't you?" Knowing that little tidbit about him made him more endearing.

"I have."

"I should have been there with you. Perhaps you wouldn't have fallen down the hillside." It was a risk mentioning her absence while he was in India, but it couldn't be helped.

Where she expected anger or even annoyance, he only held tighter to her hand. "That would have been lovely. There are so many beautiful places in India you would have adored seeing, Mad. Such wonderful people there."

A tiny thrill twisted down her spine at his use of the old nickname. "Perhaps we will have the opportunity to go yet," she said in a soft voice as they descended a narrow wooden staircase at the back of the manor that led directly to the servants' hall.

"Please don't give me false hope when things aren't nearly settled between us." The words came out on a choked whisper, and once they reached the housekeeper's room, he put a bit of distance between them.

"Oh." Quick tears jumped into her eyes. She blinked them away and peeked around the doorframe. "Mrs. Ardmore? Perhaps you could help us?"

The older woman with graying black hair glanced up from the table at which she worked, and when she saw Gilbert, she gasped and pushed to her feet with alacrity. "Oh, dear heavens, what have you done to yourself, Lord Yeardly?"

Madelene glanced at her husband. "Perhaps you have a salve or balm that will take the pain from the stings?"

He shrugged and gave the housekeeper a wry grin. "I believe bees don't care for me, Mrs. Ardmore."

"Of course. You may make use of my office." She waved them both inside. "I'll go hunt down the salve and perhaps a cold compress." With another glance at Gilbert's injuries, she shuddered. "You poor thing. I've never seen the like of this before."

Perhaps a minute later, the housekeeper returned along with two kitchen maids. Everyone buzzed about Gilbert as he sat on the chair Mrs. Ardmore had recently vacated. A wet, folded rag was pressed into his hand by a pretty maid who kept tittering at him as she dabbed at his face. The housekeeper gave her a small pot with a yellow-hued salve inside while a maid dabbed at the welts on his face with another cloth.

"Once Ellie is finished cleaning the stings, you can apply the salve. The herbs will take away some of the pain while the honey will keep away infection and make certain you remove any stingers that may be embedded," Mrs. Ardmore advised. "Should I help? Would you prefer tea?" Clearly, she wasn't used to the upper class visiting her domain in search of assistance.

"This is fine," Madelene assured her. "Once I have taken care of him, perhaps some lemonade? We shall go to the kitchens and pick up it. Lord Yeardly might prefer sitting docilely in the gardens after this."

"Away from bees, though," he added and then winced when the maid touched her cloth to one of the welts on his arm.

The maid, Ellie, giggled.

"Of course, Lady Yeardly." The housekeeper attempted to hide her smile. "Come, girls. I'm sure my lady can take care of the rest."

"Thank you, Mrs. Ardmore." Madelene waited until the room had cleared before turning to her husband. "It seems you haven't lost your charm."

"What are you talking about?" He held the cold compress to the side of his face.

"The maids think you are quite handsome." Gently, she removed the cravat from around his neck. "In that, they are correct."

A mottled red flush slipped up his neck. "Such gammon."

"The truth. I have always thought so." She kept her voice vow and steady in the hopes of conveying calm. As she talked, she dipped two fingers into the small pot of salve and then rubbed the thick goop into the bee stings. Only twice did she find bee stingers, which she promptly removed and flicked away.

He tilted his head up and met her gaze. His was inscrutable. "I appreciate that."

"No doubt you charmed your way through India, hmm?" The welts, combined with the greenish purple bruises that were just beginning to fade, took away from his good looks, but it didn't bother her. He still retained that same cheeky smile.

"I don't know about that." His gaze jogged away from hers as she worked. "Most of the time, I was by myself, unless I had a guide to navigate through the jungles between tea fields."

The words he spoke conjured images of adventures in faraway places, where the sun would shine, and the air had probably been redolent with foreign spice. They recalled her time in both Africa and South America, and though she'd long ago broken with the edicts and fervor of the missionary portion of her life, she missed the days of traveling.

"Were you lonely?" Perhaps he would talk about his time there and whether he grieved while away.

"More often than not, but I kept busy learning about tea every waking hour." He snapped his gaze back to her as she rubbed salve on his forearms. "I am good at what I do, Madelene, and have no regrets in going."

"I never said you did." Perhaps that had been his way of coping. Though removing himself from the difficulties in their marriage wouldn't solve the problems, she could see why running would have an appeal. She'd been left behind with nothing but grief at every turn. Did it make her stronger for this moment when she didn't know if she wished to win back her husband's affections?

That wasn't something easily answered.

"Perhaps you should stand and remove your shirt."

He frowned. "Why?"

"You mentioned a bee stung you on the back. I cannot put this salve on it if you won't give me access."

"Right." Slowly, he rose to his feet, leaned his cane against the table's edge, and then fumbled at the ties of his waistcoat.

She batted his hands away. "Let me." In another lifetime, one of her favorite things had been to help him undress, for there had always been the thrill of intercourse that followed. Oh, they had been such a good fit back in those days! Desire had been explosive and undeniable; he'd coupled with her every chance they had… until the rift between them had happened and he'd started spending more time at his club or buried in researching tea.

Yet, those feelings were still there on her part, and every time she saw him, they raged within her, calling out to him.

Could he feel it?

Once his waistcoat fell to the floor, Madelene eased the fine lawn shirt up and off his body. Her breath caught and she couldn't help but explore the plains of his back with the fingertips of her free hand. Yes, he was as gorgeous now as he had been then, and there, in the small indentation at his waist just over the edge of his breeches, was an angry red welt of the bee sting. "Give me the compress. This one is a bit bigger than the others."

"It does carry more of an ache." Gilbert handed her the folded cloth.

As she dabbed the fabric over the welt, he winced and glanced at her from over his shoulder. "Is it terrible, then?"

"Not very. Hopefully, it will calm like the others, but it's probably worse because the bee was trapped inside your shirt." After she had cleaned the area, she couldn't help rubbing the cloth up and down his back. His skin retained a hint of a golden tan. Perhaps he enjoyed spending leisure time in the out of doors here on the family property. With every stroke, heat slapped at her cheeks. It was quite illicit standing here in an unfamiliar room with her husband half-naked but also quite thrilling, and it had been so long since she'd been given such a boon.

"Madelene?"

"Hmm?" Up and down, she moved the rag, tracing it along his muscles, following the line of his spine down to the small of his back where the red welt rested.

"What are you doing?" His voice was graveled with the same building need coiling through her lower belly.

"Searching for other injuries." After tossing the rag to the corner of the table, she rubbed the salve over the welt. There was no stinger there either. "How do you feel?"

"Marginally better. How long do you suppose I'll look like a hideous monster?"

"That depends on how long it takes for you to heal." Once she put the pot of salve on the table, she spread her palms over the breadth of his back. Had his shoulders always been that broad? Had his skin always been so inviting? "It would also be helpful if you wouldn't antagonize any other living beings for a while," she whispered, for the moment seemed all too sacred.

Gilbert chuckled, and the rich sound reverberated in her chest. "That is something I need to work on." He lowered his voice. "For far too long I've taken refuge in anger and bitterness, and in many ways, I think that has hindered my ability to move forward in many avenues."

"At least you have acknowledged you are a part of the problem. In that you can chase a solution." It was more than they'd had days ago. Trembles danced down her spine. He was slowly learning. Did that mean they would grow close again?

"It certainly puts a dent into a man's ego." Gooseflesh rippled over his skin. Was it from her touch or her proximity?

At this point, Madelene didn't care. She continued to smooth her palms over his back. The scent of him teased her nose; the heat of his body seeped into hers. Daring much, she pressed her lips to the middle of his back. A swift inhalation of breath escaped him, and she smiled. He wasn't immune to her.

And if she didn't stop her ministrations, she would embarrass herself.

"Your ego perhaps needed deflating." Drat if she couldn't cease touching him. He was a gorgeous man. Unable to tear herself away, she slipped her hands around to his abdomen. Muscles tightened and flexed beneath her fingertips. The sprinkling of coarse hair there rasped against her palms and worked to further increase her need. Nearly lost, Madelene dared to drag her lips between his shoulder blades as she moved her hands upward to stroke along his chest. "When you were in India, did you think of me fondly at all?"

It might be vain of her, but she had to know.

For the space of a few heartbeats, he remained quiet. "There were moments when I did, of course, and no matter that I hated you for what I thought you'd done—erroneously, I now know—I did miss you fiercely at times." His swallow was audible as he held her hands away from his body, and when she assumed he would remove himself from her embrace, he merely turned about and put his hands at her waist. The depths of his eyes were dark with emotions she couldn't read, for he'd long ago learned the skill of hiding them, but the fact he was feeling them was a good sign.

"Oh?" She rested her palms on his chest and slowly inched her way upward. "Why didn't you write to me, tell me what you were going through? It would certainly have helped me to feel not so alone in the world."

He clinched his jaw. A muscle twitched in his cheek, but with a sigh, he brought her closer to his body. "I couldn't, for if I allowed my thoughts, my emotions, to spill out onto paper, I doubted I'd be able to stop. You didn't need the additional anxiety of knowing I was falling apart after... everything." The raw emotion in his voice connected her more to him than anything ever could. "And I didn't have the words in any event. After all, what could I say that would make things better?"

It comforted her to know she hadn't been far from his thoughts. "It would have simply because we could have been united in grief." That pain was never far from her heart, and sometimes waves of it would crash against her to steal her breath. "It is not too late to share those thoughts now."

"Perhaps." Gilbert edged his hands up her sides, and she shivered. "Or I could do this." Slowly, ever so slowly, he lowered his head and claimed her lips in a tender kiss that had shivers of need falling down her spine.

She twined her hands about his neck and applied herself to kissing him back. In this one moment, they understood each other perfectly. There were no obstacles between them, no misunderstandings, no secrets, no grief. There was just her and him and the chance for healing.

Just as he drew the tip of his tongue along the seam of her lips, and she moaned her approval, the sound of rustling fabric at the door had her springing away from him. A glance at the doorway revealed Mrs. Ardmore, who stared at them with round eyes.

"I beg your pardon, Lord Yeardly, Lady Yeardly. I just wished to check on you…"

Gilbert grabbed his abandoned shirt from the table. Embarrassment threaded through his chuckle. "Think nothing of it. We were merely carried away by the moment."

The housekeeper glanced away with red cheeks. "Cook has set out glasses of lemonade for you both, and a small plate of the cakes you particularly favor, my lord."

"I'll be certain to thank her." He sent her that charming grin. "I apologize for taking such liberties in your office." Once he'd smoothed his shirt over his torso, he took his waistcoat and cravat in hand. "However, we shall return this room to you." Gilbert winked as he passed her at the doorway. "Thank you for the salve. It has quite helped."

"You are most welcome, Lord Yeardly." She cast a look of confusion to Madelene, who shrugged.

"I took advantage of the situation," she mumbled as heat infused her cheeks. Unfortunately, the break meant the momentum she'd gained in having him open up to her was lost. "Our union is still quite vulnerable." And why she felt the need to ramble and explain only God knew.

"There is no crime in it, Lady Yeardly." The woman touched her arm as she, too, went into the corridor. "I wish you luck," she said in a low voice, but Gilbert had already passed into the kitchen. "You are good for each other, I think."

"Thank you." She gave the housekeeper a smile before hurrying after her husband. Would he regret how much he'd already betrayed? Only time would tell.

CHAPTER NINE

ONCE MORE, HER husband managed to surprise her, for when she expected he would make excuses and go back to the house to nurse his wounds—both physical and emotional—Gilbert thrust the plate of treats into her hand, took the two glasses of lemonade, tucked his cane beneath his arm, and then led the way slowly out of the kitchens and then around the house to the gardens.

By the time they'd settled onto a stone bench, she glanced at him with sudden shyness. Why was there this awkwardness between them after the closeness they'd enjoyed in the house-keeper's office? Did they truly have nothing in common any longer except the simmering heat between them and the grief that he may or may not share?

"I can hear you thinking," he said as he gave her one of the glasses of lemonade.

"Is it any wonder? I have questions." She sipped at the refreshing liquid. The tart-sweet flavor danced on her palate.

"There will always be questions." Gilbert took the plate of teacakes from her and then ate two of the tiny treats with gusto. After washing them down with a gulp of lemonade, he sighed. "I haven't had these cakes since I was a youth and we visited here in the summer months."

"The staff dotes on you." That had been readily obvious.

"Tell that to Hannah and Emily. Not only do they not think I'm attractive, but they say I'm too grouchy to be around ladies."

Madelene chuckled. "Perhaps they only wish for you to do better." Curiosity ran rampant in her mind to know just why the girls had said that.

"Then it's good they are bedeviling me, for I *want* to do better." He ate another cake and then followed it with a few gulps of his lemonade, which emptied the glass. "It's been nice, these past few days, having you about. I never realized how much I'd taken that for granted when I was away."

Had he taken that for granted? Her cheeks warmed. "I'm glad you have realized it though," she said softly. A companionable silence brewed between them. It was one of those quiet stretches that was comfortable enough that she didn't feel the need to immediately fill it with conversation. Intermittently, she sipped her lemonade. "I wonder what dear Hannah will say when she sees what the bees have done to you." She couldn't keep the humor from her voice.

Gilbert snorted with laughter. "She'll either lecture me or ring a peal over my head for being such a nodcock."

"I don't think that's necessarily true." When she smiled at him, he returned the gesture, and it caused her heartbeat to kick up. Wanting to listen to the sound of his voice a bit longer, she rushed on. "Tell me why you are so passionate about tea."

Surprise flickered over his poor, abused face. "No one has ever asked me that before."

"Well, I am now." Truly, she was interested in what he spent his time doing.

"Oh, there is so much to learn about tea, and so many varieties! China was the country of origin of the vast majority of the tea imported to Britain, but the end of its monopoly stimulated the East India Company to consider growing tea in India."

"Which those people had no doubt been doing for years before the British made their presence known."

"No doubt. India had always been hub of the East India

Company, where it played a leading role in the government. They were quite powerful at the time. This led to the increased cultivation of tea in India, beginning in Assam, which is one of my favorite varieties."

As he talked, he ate steadily at the remaining cakes on the plate. "India and China are, of course, the primary growing regions, and one day I would like to travel to both places merely for the joy of discovery, but so many people believe that black tea is the only one worth of being in their cup." As he warmed to his subject, years seemed to fall from his face until he once more resembled the man she'd fallen in love with years ago.

"How interesting. I'll confess, I've never truly thought about where tea comes from."

He nodded. "When tea came to Britain, it was heavily taxed. One unforeseen consequence of the taxation was the growth of methods to avoid having coin taken out of the public's pockets. So, smuggling and adulteration hit the market."

"I would adore knowing a smuggler." That would be the height of excitement.

"I never knew you had such a scandalous nature." Admiration twinkled in his eyes.

She shrugged. "What can I say? A lady worth her salt needn't be entirely proper all the time."

"Indeed." Gilbert took her glass and sipped at her beverage. "By the eighteenth century many Brits wanted to drink tea but only the upper class could afford the high prices. Of course, the *ton* doesn't part willingly with their coin, and they are quite perverse, which meant there was a certain enthusiasm for smugglers."

"I can understand that." Madelene couldn't help her smirk. "I'm surprised you didn't turn to such an occupation."

"Perhaps I would have in another life." His chuckle tickled through her insides. "Regardless, some of their methods were brutal, but since millions of British tea drinkers supported them for a chance at having tea whenever they desired, the practices continued. I would imagine the illegal activity grew over the years. No doubt over a million pounds of tea were imported to England by nefarious means."

"I cannot imagine that tea would have become so popular." The history of the beverage was fascinating.

"Oh yes. The people of England are crazy for it and have been for quite some time. Yet, part of the taxation of the tea meant that since everyone wanted to make coin on the trade, much of the smuggled tea was adulteration. Simply put, some of the smugglers put leaves from other plants into the brew. The colors therein were not convincing to a tea connoisseur, of course, so anything from sheep's dung to poisonous plants were added to make it look more like tea."

"Poison?"

"I am afraid so. Tea is a big business, and over the years, the lower classes caught onto it, so that is where the inferior smuggled tea usually landed."

"That's horrible!" She had no idea bringing tea to England was so fraught with danger.

"Sad but true." He nodded in agreement. "By 1784, the government realized the problem needed solving. Prime Minister, William Pitt the Younger, cut the tax from one-hundred and nineteen percent to twelve and a half percent, which made *legal* tea affordable."

"I would imagine the smuggling stopped."

"Almost overnight." A grin tugged at the corners of his mouth. "It boggles the mind that tea literally began as a tempest in a teapot and then grew into a hurricane of supply and demand."

"Well, it does solve every problem."

"True. Over the years, debate grew about whether tea drinking was good or bad for the health. Wealthy philanthropists theorized that excessive tea drinking among the working classes would lead to weakness and melancholy."

"Of course they did." Madelene shook her head. "No one

ever wishes for the lower classes to actually enjoy their life or do something the upper classes do."

"Exactly. The rich were not concerned with the continuing popularity of tea among the wealthy classes, for whom strength to labor was of less importance." He snickered. "I wonder how the debate will grow as the years go on."

"No doubt they will maintain that tea is an alternative to consuming liquor."

"That very well could be an argument." Her husband nodded with approval. "I can say with a positive guarantee that tea will become a lucrative business in the future and will be enjoyed all over the world in all walks of life."

And he would be part of that push. Her respect for his acumen rose.

"Beyond Assam, do you like any other varieties?"

"I do, and there are so many I haven't yet tried. Oolongs from all over Asia. Darjeeling from India. Oh, and I want to explore blending teas to see what happens, perhaps even use bits of dried fruits." His eyes shone with the fervor. "There was a specific drink I had while I was gone, called chai, wherein milk was added to the tea with spices. I would adore finding a shop that sells it so you could sample that."

"From what you have told me, it rather sounds like your days of traveling are definitely not over."

"I hope not." Gilbert finished off her lemonade. "I would like to go again to India, visit China, continue on through the far east, perhaps reach Nepal. Imagine the knowledge to had! However, I won't make that decision until things here are settled." A somberness took hold of his expression as he once more looked at her.

Knots of worry made themselves known in her belly. "If the truth be known, I miss traveling as well."

His eyebrows soared in surprise. "Oh, right! That slipped my mind. Your father was a missionary. In Africa, correct?"

"Yes. Those countries were beautiful. But again, as anywhere, the contrast between rich and poor was staggering. Then I went deep into the jungles of South America with my first husband. Again, beautiful, but rampant poverty. Just as dangerous between people, animals, and the land itself." A sigh escaped her. "Though rigorous and hard work, I liked being away from England and learning about other cultures."

"Ah." A certain sadness drifted over his features. "I had also forgotten you were married before," he said in such a low voice that she had to lean closer to hear.

"I never spent much time talking about that time in my life." Some of her own gaiety faded. "That marriage ended in heart-ache, much like ours did, except my husband died of an infected gunshot wound."

Shock rounded his eyes. "You lost a child at that time?"

"Yes." For long moments, she remained quiet as she stared at the plate in her hands. "Eventually, I asked the village elders for assistance, but all the teas and tinctures they gave me, all the sacred waters they told me to bathe in ultimately failed." Her voice wavered. "My difficulties with conception continued, made worse by the fact my husband maintained it was God's will, and that I should concentrate on other things."

"That's an arrogant and ignorant way of looking at it, and it's insensitive besides." Annoyance wove through his voice. "He should not have said that to you. But then, I didn't really expect a man of the church to be understanding. If you are not furthering the dictates of religion, you have no value."

Her heart trembled at his defense of her. A wave of sadness came around her all the same. "Perhaps, but the failures on my part persisted, which is why marrying again—should our union not prove viable—will make no difference." She found his gaze with hers. It was vital he knew this to make his ultimate choice. "*I am the broken one.*"

"Ah, Madelene, I am so sorry for what you've been through, but equally sorry you think that of yourself." Gilbert rested the glasses as well as the plate on the grass beside the bench. Then he gathered her close and simply held her. "Your self-worth is not tied to your ability to bear children."

Ready tears sprang to her eyes. "On some level I know that, but I have failed so many people…"

"You have *not*." He drew a hand up and down her back, no doubt hoping to calm her. "Disabuse yourself of those notions this instant." The rumble of his voice in her ear both gave her a sense of peace but quickened her heartbeat. "You are a wonderful, caring woman with a heart full of compassion and—"

"—and love," she interrupted as she wrapped her arms around his middle. "But I have nowhere to give it." Would they ever be in a place where love would be enough between them? Where they could simply enjoy each being married with no expectations? Would she ever come to that sort of peace?

"Don't say that. You have me, don't you?"

I don't know. He hadn't told her how he felt about her now, and neither did she suspect he forgave her for not giving him a child. Not having the answers, she allowed herself to luxuriate in the strength of his arms, in the heat of him, of listening to the beat of his heart beneath her ear.

"By the by, I named our son." Would he take violent exception to the decision?

He pulled slightly back. "I never knew that."

"How could you?" She peered into the dark depths of his brown eyes and wished she could lose herself there. "You were in your cups when we buried him and absent most of the time after his birth." The words were said mostly on rote, for she'd had years to think about this very conversation.

"I know." Gilbert tensed. Would he run again? "Those days were trying." A muscle in his cheek worked. "I had hoped to be strong for you, to hold back my emotions—"

"—which you did and are still doing," she gently reminded him.

"But our son's death wrenched up memories of the past…"

If he would only talk about those things! "So you ran away

instead of letting yourself feel those emotions, confront them." His behavior made sense in retrospect, but there was more work to accomplish.

"I told you I am not perfect." His voice was graveled, and for one moment, she thought he might give into a sob, but then he fought his way back to control. "Perhaps I am too broken, as well, to rebuild our pieces."

"No." Madelene shook her head. They were closer than he realized. "This is why we have each other, Gilbert, to help through the valleys. If we don't learn to lean on each other, we'll never have a chance at repairing what we used to have." As she held his gaze, she laid a palm to his cheek. Briefly, his eyes shuttered closed, and he shivered. From her touch or the subject matter? "Our son's name was Edmund."

Awe lined his face. "My middle name."

"And your father's name as well." She blinked back lingering tears lest she become a watering pot again. "I would like to think our son would have taken after you."

He glanced away. "A coward and a liar?"

What did he have to lie about? "No. A man willing to grow and learn. A man who is doing his best to navigate a life that has been more difficult than most. A man with potential if he would just realize it."

His Adam's apple bobbed with a hard swallow. "I was so looking forward to that babe, Mad. Please don't think I wasn't due to my behavior during the time." The words sailed out on a choked whisper. "I had always wanted a family, and when that kept crumbling time and again…"

"I know." It was more of an admission than she'd ever had from him before.

"I couldn't bear it. Those disappointments. Thinking they were my fault. Watching you go through such pain and devastation." He shook his head, and his face was haunted. "I didn't know what to do, how to help. Words felt ineffectual. There was nothing I could do."

Her heart squeezed. "I would have welcomed them, though, for we could have grieved together."

"Again, I'm sorry."

It was enough, and he was entirely too genuine. "Each time is no less heartbreaking, yet part of me, perhaps stupidly, wishes to continue to try. Even though I know what will happen. Even though I'll soon be too old."

When he looked at her, hope lit his eyes. "That is largely your decision. I won't put you through that gauntlet unless you are entirely certain, and we have come to some sort of understanding."

That same hope began to bloom deep in her soul. "Perhaps it is something we can continue to discuss in the coming days but thank you for sticking by me right now." She blinked back another few sneaky tears. "It means so much to have you believe in me."

"Oh, Mad." He tucked a tendril of escaped hair behind her ear. "I don't deserve you."

Needing to dispel some of the tension, Madelene nodded. "Agreed, but here we are." When she grinned, he did too. She patted his cheek. "No one ever said that two broken people couldn't go on to live extraordinary lives together. There is much ahead that can become your—our—legacy if we wish it."

"I sincerely hope that is true, because I am not yet ready to give up—on anything." Slowly, as if he were unsure of his welcome, Gilbert slipped a hand about her nape and then dragged her to him. With a tiny sigh, he kissed her, and the instant their lips touched, that same familiar desire sprang between them.

For several moments, they were the only two that existed, and she kissed him back with as much spirit as he gave her. Heat wrapped around her while the insane idea to straddle him on that bench took hold. Perhaps it was time to throw caution to the wind and court him as he was attempting to do with her.

Then the insistent barking of the rotund beagle broke through her passion-fogged brain. With a gasp, she pulled out of

Gilbert's embrace and sprang to her feet. "Oh, no." He laughed at her while she darted behind him in an effort to put a barrier between her and Regent. Seconds later, the dog rounded a corner and pelted down the crushed shell path that would lead to their bench. "Keep him away."

Her husband snorted in amusement. As he stood, the evident of his desire and carnal interest was evident at the front of his breeches. She ignored it and so did he. "You are going to have to confront your fear soon, sweeting."

Was he aware that he'd used an endearment? "Only when you do as well."

Then Regent was upon them, cavorting about Gilbert's boots with such jolly energy that his ears flapped and his tail wagged. "Touché," he said softly with a smile as he kneeled to give the beagle the pets he demanded. But he tilted his head and met her gaze. "I am trying."

"So am I." But now the outlook wasn't so bleak, and if she wasn't careful, she'd tumble back into love with her husband.

CHAPTER TEN

August 6, 1819

GILBERT HUMMED TO himself as he walked over the lawn of Ettesmere Park. He had a bouquet of flowers in his hand—that he bought from a seller in the village—and a tin of biscuits tucked under his arm. For the past few days, really longer, he and Madelene had been getting along extremely well. It was the closest he'd felt to her since the early days of their marriage, and while he was heartily enjoying their time, there was also an edge of worry that underlay everything.

"Yeardly!"

The hail yanked him from his ruminations. He glanced up to find Hugh crossing the lawn toward him. "Damn." There was no time for a confrontation right now, but he waited patiently until his friend reached him. "How are you this afternoon?" The man looked like the typical gentleman at leisure in the country, and Gilbert envied him the dark hair and fit figure.

"I am well." As always, the major was the picture of health even at the age of nine and thirty, much better than Gilbert himself. Granted, Hugh had the full use of his limbs, and he certainly wasn't wracked with bitterness and guilt. "On your way to see Madelene?"

"Did you think I would carry around a bouquet of flowers for my health?" He couldn't quite keep the sarcasm from his voice. One thing he despised about the mess of his marriage was the shifting of the relationship with his best friend. "I apologize. That wasn't well done of me."

"Think nothing of it." Hugh tugged at the bottom of his navy tweed waistcoat. "I have found there are many places on this property if a man requires a ramble away from everyone else. I spend much of my time in contemplation at one of the ponds."

Gilbert frowned. "Is all well with you?" He hadn't really inquired about the major's health since he had arrived at Ettesmere Park.

"As far as I know. Occasionally, I am tired, but mostly I am bored or consumed with ennui. Most of the time, I don't understand the point of cooling my heels and having no purpose."

"I understand that." The man had been out of the military for more than a few years. "Do you miss London and the Home Office?"

"That depends." He shrugged then pushed up his top hat in order to wipe his sweating brow with the back of his gloved hand. "I don't miss the politics involved but having a specific mission or a set of hours sometimes brings comfort to my days."

"I can imagine that rankles." Gilbert shifted his weight and readjusted his hold on the offerings he'd gotten for his wife. "How long did you plan to stay here?"

"As long as it takes to see Madelene happy."

Immediately, Gilbert bristled. "Are you implying I cannot manage the task?"

"The fact you consider making your wife happy a task is concerning." Hugh looked him up and down. "Quite frankly, I'm not certain you can." He crossed his arms at his chest. "Perhaps you should give me a status update on your relationship."

The gall of this man! Threads of hot anger wrapped about him, but he tempered the reaction with a few deep breaths. "We are making progress. It is rather slow, but progress, nonetheless. I'm pleased with it."

It wasn't any of the major's business.

Hugh nodded. "Good. Have you talked of your grief with her, or of your other concerns?"

"Up until this point, our discussions have varied. However, we have touched on the loss of our babe and grief from our pasts." Gilbert tightened his grip on the head of his cane. "As for actually allowing myself to grieve, to bring up the emotions I've denied over the years, no. I haven't, for I don't wish to break in front of her."

"Why?" A frown marred Hugh's features. "Shared grief leads to shared understanding. That is what married people do. Quite frankly, that is something you owe her after everything."

"Perhaps." But he wouldn't do so merely because this man demanded he should. "Honestly? Fear holds me back. I don't want her to think less of me when we are tentatively growing closer." Why did he admit that? In doing so, would Hugh find him weak?

"While that is understandable, Madelene deserves to know, deserves to see the same emotions in you that she has struggled with for the past three years. She needs to feel that support from you, needs to see you were as broken about losing those babes as she was, lest she think you don't care."

Another stab of anger went through Gilbert's chest. "What do you know of it?"

"I know that she's been hurt by your actions, that she's still vulnerable due to her losses, that all she wants is support and encouragement, to be loved despite what she considers failure."

"I am well aware of that," he snapped. "And I am trying, believe it or not."

"Perhaps." Hugh held his gaze. "Have you told her of your indiscretion?"

"No." Knots of worry pulled in his belly. "And you don't have that right. I do not want to ruin what I am rebuilding with Madelene, so under no circumstances are you to tell her." He blew out a breath. "Please, for the sake of our friendship. Let me do this in my own time."

For long moments, Hugh regarded him with speculation. "You owe her the confession if you even hope to move forward with her."

"Don't you think I don't know that? Don't you think it's not ever present in my mind at all times?" Gilbert hissed. "It is terrifying to contemplate." For, after everything, she might demand a separation or even a divorce. Had it been a mistake neither of them could overcome? "Don't you think I don't regret every moment of every day what I did, especially now?" The longer he talked about it, the more his unease grew. Emotions climbed his throat, tightening it.

Hugh unbent enough to rest a hand on his shoulder. "Breathe, Gil." Concern lined his expression. "If you are this upset about it then you are nearing the critical point of your marriage. While that is encouraging, it's also concerning. If you prove too unstable, prove a danger to her, I must demand you set her free. It is only kind."

"The fate of our union is not your business!" Ire burned hot through his chest. Of course Hugh would be there to pick up the pieces, for hadn't he hinted at the fact that he was sweet on Madelene?

I refuse to have my damned best friend steal her out from under my nose.

"Believe it or, I am championing for you to win her back."

"Ha! That's doubtful."

"It's true." The major squeezed his fingers on Gilbert's shoulder. "If Madelene is the woman I believe her to be, she will take what you'll say into consideration. After all, she is strong, and if she loves you, this obstacle can be overcome by you both."

"I hope you're right."

"She only wishes to be loved. In fact, she's desperate for it."

Gilbert snorted. "And you want to be the man to give her that when I fail."

"*If* you fail." For long moments Hugh stared at him with speculation in his eyes. "However, if she cannot forgive you for the indiscretion and she pushes for a divorce, and if by some reason it is granted, I vow I will be there for her, to love her where you couldn't. In this I refuse to lie and pretend I won't."

"Well, damn." It was another worry to add to the pile. After the way he'd behaved toward her over the same situation, of course he had doubts she would forgive him. "I will tell her in my own way and my own time. You owe me that latitude."

"Of course I do, but your time is running out, and I swear, if you hurt her, I will take her away from you to save her the additional grief."

This was outside of enough. "If you don't mind, I'm going to see my wife now. We have planned to swim this afternoon."

"Very well. Do have a marvelous day, and I wish you good luck. Madelene is a wonderful person." A trace of shadows entered his eyes. "If she were mine—"

"But she isn't, and I will do everything in my power to make certain she isn't," Gilbert was quick to interrupt. How the hell could he return to London knowing his wife was living with another man, and his best friend at that? It would completely break him. "Perhaps you would do well to find your own woman and forget about the ones who are not available." Unable to linger in the major's company without growing more annoyed, he nodded and then took his leave.

Truly, Hugh needed to leave Ettesmere Park and allow him to court Madelene properly without the constant threat of exposure or betrayal hanging over his head.

Yet it put a fire beneath him, made him rise to the occasion and do better.

Damn the man's eyes.

WHEN HE GAINED the entry hall of the manor, he was surprised to see Julianna's elderly father being escorted by a woman he didn't recognize. He frowned at them, for this was highly irregular. Usually, Mr. Quill was accompanied by Sophia or his nieces.

"Mr. Quill, is everything all right?" Who the devil was this woman?

The older man focused his faded gaze on Gilbert, but there was no recognition there. "I am going out for a walk, young man, and do not think to tell me otherwise."

His frown deepened. "I beg your pardon." He flicked his regard to the woman holding Mr. Quill's arm. "Who are you?" No one had informed him that a nurse had been hired to look after Mr. Quill.

"You don't know?" Her blue eyes twinkled with merriment.

"If I did, do you think I'd be asking the question?" Truly, was everyone hellbent on being obstinate today?

"You cannot pull me from your childhood memories? I certainly remember you," she continued on with a smile that said the whole conversation was naught but a big joke.

Annoyance stabbed through his chest. "I'm afraid not. Perhaps we can stop wasting time. Tell me who you are."

"You are absolutely no fun, Lord Yeardly." The woman chuckled. "I am Miss Louisa Atherby. Your cousin in a roundabout way."

"What?" He stared with more authority. Perhaps in her early thirties, Louisa was a second cousin once removed of his father's. Due to odd circumstances that had taken her to America and the Continent, she'd more or less grown up without steadying influences in her life, which had meant she was often in residence at Ettesmere Park in the early years of their childhood, but he hadn't seen her since going to school at Cambridge. From all accounts, she'd been a hoyden and hadn't managed to pull out of her penchant for chasing scandal. Her wheat-blonde hair was also familiar, as were the deep blue, almost violet eyes. "Surely not."

"Why not? I'm standing here, so it's not out of the realm of possibility that it's true." She regarded him as if everything he said was humorous.

"I have no time for your riddles and foolishness." He shifted the flowers and tin of biscuits in his hold. "Why are you here? And after such a long absence?"

Her shrug was an elegant affair as Mr. Quill fidgeted. Clearly, he was anxious to be off. "Lady Ettesmere invited me."

"The new Lady Ettesmere or my mother?"

She frowned. "Oh, did Arthur marry again?"

"Yes, just recently, in fact."

"I see." Surprise flickered over her face. "The dowager invited me."

"Then you are over two months tardy to her midsummer ball."

"It couldn't be helped. Now I'm here and find that many things regarding the Winterbourne family have changed."

Gilbert snorted. "You have no idea."

"Come along, young woman. The fish won't wait all day," Mr. Quill said as he scratched the gray whiskers on his chin.

"Of course." Miss Atherby glanced again at Gilbert. "In any event, I found this gentleman wandering the halls upon my arrival, so I thought I would accompany him to a pond, since he was determined to head out anyway." She smiled at Mr. Quill. "I could use the exercise, and your mother encouraged it since everyone else is out."

That was interesting "Oh? Where is the family?"

She shrugged. "Errands? Shopping? Chasing entertainment or fellowship? It is rather dull here just now, regardless."

"I see." Conceivably, the house was empty. Could he use that to his advantage? "Where is my mother?"

"The last I saw, she was in the morning room writing letters. She told me she had quite a bit of correspondence to attend to and afterward will talk with Cook and the housekeeper about the possibility of hosting a ball soon."

"Damn, Mama does like to entertain, but another ball?" He

shook his head. "I don't suppose you have seen Lady Yeardly in your rambles through the house?"

His cousin screwed up her face much like she'd done in childhood. "Short lady, dark hair, wearing a purple dress?"

"Yes." At least he thought that's what Madelene had been wearing when he'd left earlier to procure her gifts.

"Ah. I passed her on the stairs not long ago. She was quite distraught, though, and I think she headed upstairs."

Mr. Quill took a few steps forward. "By the time we get to the pond, the fish will be dead, young woman."

She grinned. "We are going, Mr. Quill, I promise. I didn't anticipate being waylaid by my cousin." To Gilbert, she said, "We shall catch up soon. Then you can tell me all about that strikingly handsome major I saw walking the grounds not ten minutes past."

Oh, bother. Why the hell was every female beneath Ettesmere Park's roof so taken with Hugh? There *were* other men in the area.

Then she was gone, leaving him frowning at the butler, who shrugged as if he couldn't puzzle out the tempest that was Miss Atherby.

After readjusting his hold on his gifts, Gilbert made his way upstairs. Time was of the essence now to confess everything to his wife, for he didn't wish for Hugh to get the march on him, and he wanted Madelene to hear of the indiscretion from him, so he could explain, and hopefully mitigate any damage that might occur. At the door to her bedchamber, he paused. The sound of sobbing met his ears, and he frowned as his chest tightened. "Madelene?" What the devil had occurred to send her into such distress? Never did he like knowing she was in tears, for he felt ineffectual.

When she didn't answer, he awkwardly pressed the door latch while his hands were full and then pushed the panel open, pushing it closed behind him with a foot. "Madelene?" She had thrown herself over the foot of the bed, crying on her folded arms. Her purple dress was hopelessly wrinkled and rucked up to reveal her stocking-covered legs to the knee. And dear God, she made a mouth-watering picture. "What has occurred? Are you well?" His chest constricted. Had she already discovered his terrible secret? Had Hugh betrayed that information.

Or was it something else entirely that she'd found him lacking in?

"Oh, Gilbert." She lifted her head. Tears streaked her face, but it was the fathomless despair in her watery eyes that had his heart squeezing. "I received proof that a dream has completely no hope of coming true." Then she erupted into another series of sobs that left him even more confused than before. "And I don't wish to believe it just yet," she said with a wail.

"What do you mean?" Carefully, he set the tin of biscuits on the bureau top and rested the bouquet of flowers next to it. As far as he knew, she hadn't had any callers who might have upset her.

"Here." She drew a crinkled sheet of stationery from beneath her and shoved it in his direction over the bed. "I saw a physician in London before coming here. He has finally written with the results and his prognosis from that examination."

Leaving his cane leaning against the bureau, Gilbert approached the bed. With a shaking hand, he took up the paper and smoothed out the letter. Heavy writing filled the page, but the contents itself were shocking at best.

Dear Lady Yeardly,

I am writing today with the results of your examination from two months prior. Unfortunately, in my professional opinion, you will never be able to carry a baby to full term. Any pregnancy you experience will no doubt end with disastrous results. After hearing the details of your reproductive history and based on my own findings when I examined you, I am of the belief that your body is somehow defective and am advising you to do everything in your power to see you don't increase again.

That, combined with your advanced age, has rendered you essentially an unfit candidate to ever have children. In regard to the concern you mentioned at the time of your exam, it would be kinder of you to let Lord Yeardly try to procure a divorce, for many men will desire to have issue and further their lines, especially as they progress in age. In this way, you will not need to live with regret or the worry that you can never provide him with an heir. Find solace in the childless life you shall need to live. Many women in these same circumstances go on to fill their days perhaps as a companion or a governess if you feel you must be around children. In this, you will undoubtedly feel a sense of worth.

I suggest you make peace with this diagnosis for the sake of your well-being, for if your depressive attitude persists, we might need to discuss the possibility of either daily dosing with laudanum or an institution for your future. Insanity is not out of the question for women who have failed to bear children. It is the opinion of the medical establishment that pregnancy and madness go hand in hand. You should do all you can to keep both at bay.

If you should require further clarification or a recommenda-tion for institutional care, please do make an appointment at my London offices.

Respectfully,
Doctor Abrams

"Dear God. This is horrific," he whispered into the room at large, and when his gaze landed on Madelene, she once more buried her face into her arms. "The gall and arrogance of the man!" How dare this physician tell her she would never bear children, that she should avoid any circumstances which might see her pregnant, without telling her exactly what was wrong with her. "I rather doubt from the vagueness of this letter he understands how the female body works."

"Yet shouldn't he know? He is a physician!" The words were muffled by her arms, but there was no mistaking the despair in her voice.

"Bah!" Did anyone within the medical establishment have

knowledge regarding a woman's fragile health? How much strain and strength it took for them to do the miracles that were thrust upon them? With each question, the annoyance for this so-called doctor grew. The fairer sex had always been relegated to the shadows and treated much like chattel, but this was outside of enough. "Because of the misinformation and the decided lack of authority regarding a woman's body and anything regarding pregnancy specifically, there might *not* be anything wrong with you, Mad, and you could very well still bear a child. It perhaps will take longer than most."

"I'm not so certain." She raised her head and once more looked at him with a tear-stained face. "You know my history more than everyone. I don't know that I have the strength to go through another failed pregnancy."

"I understand." In some annoyance, he balled up the letter and threw it into a corner of the room. "Hell, I rather doubt this doctor knows enough to give a woman pleasure. His wife must live in constant disappointment, for I'll wager he's never even found her pearl."

The words had the desired effect. A tiny giggle escaped Madelene. "How unfortunate for her. That is a vital component of coupling."

"Agreed, but there are many men out there who don't think so." He shook his head as the shock and anger at the doctor's letter still circled through him. "Under no circumstances will I allow you to be put into an institution if the sadness you're struggling with grows overwhelming."

"Truly?"

"Of course. Yet if you feel the need for laudanum, I won't dissuade you, though I would question the intelligence of wishing to live in a drugged haze."

"I don't want that."

"Good." He perched on the side of the bed as she turned over onto her back with her head close to him. In this he was quite honest. "For that matter, what sort of man would I be if I sought a divorce for no other reason than my wife couldn't bear children?" With a faint smile, Gilbert brushed a lock of her hair from her forehead. "After all, a man doesn't marry a woman exclusively for the offspring she could potentially give him. He weds her because he loves her, because he wants her at his side, and that is enough."

Suddenly, he wanted to be that man on whom she could rely and go to for the support she needed. He wished to protect her, keep her from the ills of the world, fight back everything that made her sad. When they'd wed, he only wished for a companion to go through life beside. Children would have been lovely, but they weren't necessary to fulfill him. Now, more than ever, he suspected he only needed her.

Would he have that chance to show her that they hadn't wed in error, that the feelings they used to hold for each other were still present?

She laid a hand on his knee. "I appreciate that, but he said that I am too old and I—"

"Hush." Leaning over her, he cupped her cheek, slid his fingers into her disheveled hair, and lowered his head. "What does the doctor know? Whatever happens is between you and me. No one else can offer an opinion or an order, and I refuse to abandon hope on all fronts." Then, because there was such trust and sadness clouding in her brown eyes, and her chin quivered in adorable vulnerability, Gilbert brushed his lips over hers.

When she made a soft sound of acceptance or encouragement, he was lost. Even more so as she tightened her fingers on his knee.

No matter the outcome of this afternoon, he would strive to show her that she wasn't worthless and that he did still care for her.

CHAPTER ELEVEN

MADELENE LIFTED A hand, slipped it about his nape, and urged him closer. The words he'd said to her sent a few pieces of her heart back into his keeping. Had he realized he'd shared so much in that short conversation? Then, it didn't matter, because he was hers. Gilbert was her anchor in a world that seemed flooded with horrible news and impossible odds. In him there was a familiarity that she appreciated as well as an edge of excitement she craved.

She returned his kisses and, in the process, forgot about her tears and her earlier upset. In this man's arms, those disappointments didn't sting as much even though they'd yet to talk about their shared grief. It would come. Hadn't the closeness and intimacy returned in their marriage after the years apart?

Shifting her body so she could loop her arms about the breadth of his shoulders, Madelene applied herself with every ounce of feeling into that embrace. He cradled her head with one and while he slipped the other to her hip and pulled her closer as he deepened the kiss. After nibbling the corners of her lips, he teased their seam until she opened to him, and the moment his tongue touched hers, heat flooded her.

Over and over, they parried, and satin slid against silk, and still, she couldn't have enough of him. When she desired him absolutely, she plucked at his cravat. "If I am not able to feel your skin against mine, I shall go mad." And that was a different sort of insanity than she felt most days when grief and loneliness stalked her. The last time they'd come together for the purposes of intercourse, they'd both been fully clothed in the maze and the coupling had been all too fast and largely unsatisfying.

Tremors of anticipation danced down her spine, for this time would be different. Already, she could feel it.

"That can be arranged." The emotions filling his eyes were so warm and inviting, she wanted to dive in and drown in those dark pools, and with a parting kiss, he slid off the bed. "I don't wish to assume, but I need to hear that you indeed wish to do this," he said as he struggled out of his jacket, that sapphire one she adored. "I need this coming together to be much different than the previous time we came together."

So did she. "Oh, yes. There is nothing I would rather do just now." Not willing to remain parted from him, Madelene left the bed and crossed to his location. She removed his waistcoat while he made short work of his cuffs, collar, and cravat. The undressing of a man was every bit as delicious as it had always been. As various bits of clothing littered the floor, she yanked the tails of his fine lawn shirt from his breeches then impatiently pulled and tugged it up and off his torso. "I have long waited to see you nude."

His chuckle sent threads of need through her chest. "I am not that yet."

"No, but this is a lovely start." The second she rested her palms on his chest, slid her fingers through the crisp, coarse hair there, his muscles contracted, and he sucked in a breath. "There is so much I want to do to you." Heat slapped at her cheeks. Was that too forward of her to say? Even as a married woman? "So much I want to experience."

"I don't believe I've told you nay." Gilbert framed her head between his hands and kissed her with what felt like all the pent-up emotions she had within her as well.

This was the man she remembered from the early days of

their marriage; this was the man with the air of mystery and excitement that she'd pledged to spend the remainder of her life with, and now it seemed that those promises would indeed still come to fruition despite their separation. It was quite heady indeed.

"Rogue." But she slid her hands over the breadth of his chest, her fingers dancing along the planes of his torso. He'd kept fairly fit in her absence, and to her eyes he was perfection. Everywhere she touched provoked either a half-stifled groan or the flinch of muscle. Never could she have enough of him. Down, down, down she went in her exploration until she teased at the waist of his breeches. Then, daring much, Madelene eased her hand downward as she held his gaze, and as she stroked her fingers along his erection through the fabric, his whole body shuddered.

"If I am a rogue, you are surely a minx, or perhaps a temptress of old." Gently, he urged her hand away, brought it to his lips, and kissed the back. "Never think that during the time we were apart, I didn't want you. Even when I was out of sorts with you. I felt the loss of you acutely."

Her heart trembled. "It was a misunderstanding. Surely, I don't hold that against you."

Shadows clouded his eyes. "I wish I had been as understanding as you are, as you will perhaps need to be."

What did that mean? When he didn't comment further, she continued her ministrations. Where their previous coupling had been frantic and hurried, there was no such energy this time. While she pressed kisses to the side of his neck and upper chest, intent to explore as much of him as he would grant, her husband methodically worked the short line of buttons at the back of her dress from their holes. Once the garment gaped, he tugged it down her shoulders. When it pooled and hung at her elbows and waist, he cupped her breasts, worried the nipples through the fine lawn of her chemise, and she was once more lost upon a sea of heated, familiar sensation.

"Gilbert..." Madelene's head lolled onto her shoulder. So

long she'd dreamed about his touch, of having him all to herself, to reconnect with him in this way. His second courtship had been sweet and lovely up to this point, but there were times in a woman's life when she wanted that physical contact. "Take me to bed."

He lifted his head from where he'd been teasing a nipple with his lips, and the smile he gave sent shivers of need careening down her spine. "I have waited to hear those words."

"Good." She stepped away from him in order to let the dress fall completely from her frame. As he watched, those dark eyes roving up and down her form, she removed her petticoat and then her chemise until she stood naked before him with the exception of her slippers and stockings. For the space of far too many heartbeats, he said nothing, and insecurities came pouring in. Would he no longer prefer her over someone perhaps slimmer, younger, prettier? "Uh, I have perhaps gained some weight over the years due to not taking care of myself as I ought after the loss—"

"Hush." Gilbert quickly closed the distance. He claimed her lips in such a searing kiss that she felt the heat of it all the way to her toes. "You are ravishing. Tempting. Perfect." Slipping his hands around her waist, he drew them down to cup her buttocks and bring her flush to his body. The undeniable evidence of his desire pressed with insistence against her hip. "The new curves are beyond distracting, and I cannot wait to explore each one."

"Oh!" She threw herself into his arms with such forward momentum that he teetered backward. They both toppled onto the edge of the bed in a tangle of limbs. "You have never ceased to be charming."

"I don't know about that." Before she could move into the middle of the mattress, he slid from the bed, tugged her more flush to the edge so that her legs dangled over the side, and then with a grin that promised wicked things, he kneeled, encouraging her thighs apart as he went. "However, I do know I have waited what seems like an eternity to taste you."

Madelene clambered to an elbow. "Surely you don't intend to—Oh!" Her husband had indeed meant exactly what he said, for he buried his head between her thighs and licked at her flesh while she squirmed in both surprise and delight. It had been an age since he'd treated her to that sort of carnal play. "Gilbert, stop, I want to…" But her words died in her throat as he spread her open with his fingers and then touched his tongue to that tiny, swollen button at her center while she dug the heels of her slippers into his shoulders to pull him closer.

Merciful heavens!

Since he wasn't inclined to let her go, there was nothing to do but enjoy everything he did to her. Around and around, he circled that nubbin with the tip of his tongue, and just when she'd become accustomed to that feeling, he suckled that dynamic piece of flesh. Mad streaks of pleasure shot through her being. She clutched the bedding in one hand while hanging onto the side of the mattress with the other.

"Please, more," she asked in a barely audible whisper, and there was no shame in the begging, for they were married, and this bonding was long overdue.

The cheeky man was quite skilled in his craft, and before she was ready, the pressure that had built low in her belly broke. Falling over the edge into bliss surprised her, for it had been quite some time indeed since she'd last experienced it. With a cry that she didn't care who heard, Madelene temporarily lost the ability to breathe as the gentle wave of intense sensation washed over her.

Gilbert chuckled against her flesh but pulled away with a grin. "Merely the first course."

Even though a pleasant sort of lethargy weighted her limbs, Madelene pushed herself onto her elbows merely to watch him as he removed first one of her slippers and then the other. Slowly, oh so slowly, he released one beribboned garter and then rolled the stocking down her leg. Residual tremors deep in her core were enhanced by the feel of his fingertips on her skin, caressing, teasing, urging her up that hill again where another release would surely wait.

Only when she was completely naked and almost panting with pure desire did he stand and attend to the rest of his undressing. With a dry throat yet a watering mouth, she crawled up the bed to recline amidst the pillows while Gilbert removed his boots. The dull thuds of them hitting the carpet seemed to echo in the room. Then, he wriggled out of the breeches and was unashamedly nude in all his glory.

"My goodness." She couldn't help but stare and quite frankly didn't know where to look, for every part of him was wonderful. From his belly that was a tad less taut than it had been when they were newly wed, to the curve of his pale backside, to his erect member, he was exactly the man of her dreams. "I had forgotten what a memorable picture you made."

"Such gammon. I am the same as I have always been." When he joined her on the bed, he layered himself over her and settled between her splayed legs that were bent at the knee.

"Except that is not true." She ran a hand up his spine. The weight of him pressing her into the pillows was quite lovely. "You *have* changed. Incrementally, and have again since we first began to repair our relationship." As she furrowed her fingers into the hair at his nape, she smiled. "As a matter of fact, I adore the man you are becoming."

The shadows in his eyes returned but were gone at his next blink. Emotions she couldn't read battled for dominance in his expression, and in the end, he simply kissed her, whether to show her his devotion or to hide, she had no idea.

With a happy sigh, Madelene looped her arms about his shoulders and applied herself to kissing him back, completely lost in the wonder that was her husband. The longer they communed without words, the harder the hot length of him against her thigh grew.

Eventually, the restlessness that circled through her insides was impossible to ignore. She slid a hand down his back, and at his buttock, squeezed a cheek. A groan escaped him.

"It's a slippery slope when you think to tease, madam," he whispered against the side of her neck. At the same time, Gilbert put a hand between her thighs, and the second his fingers found that button which throbbed with renewed need, she loosed a sound of excited anticipation.

"Then show me why I shouldn't continue in the same vein." Oh, it was such a lovely thing to have her husband back, for she'd missed the banter, joking, and teasing.

Of course, he didn't answer verbally, the cheeky man. Instead, he rubbed that nubbin with varying degrees of friction while taking a hardened nipple deep into the warmth of his mouth. Her back arched of its own accord, for the dual threads of pleasure he invoked were enough to threaten to tear her apart. Yet there was nowhere else she wished to be than at his mercy, and she encouraged him onward with the touch of her hand to his, pressing him closer to where she needed him to be the most.

Once again, the rush of release caught her unawares. Madelene cried out with surprise and complete abandon as wave after wave of intense sensation crashed into her. Need throbbed through her core, caught her up in that tide, and she bucked her body into his while heat flooded her system.

There was no time to catch her breath, to retaliate with pleasure of her to him, to move, for Gilbert slid the wide head of his member along her sensitive flesh to pause at her entrance. When she assumed he would spear into her, he merely teased, paused just inside her passage, and then kissed her as if he had all the leisure time in the world. Just when she thought she might go insane from the delicious anticipation, he withdrew and then thrust back into her body without stopping until he was fully sheathed.

Her moan blended with his, and as he encouraged her knees closer to her chest, he went ever deeper, and he moaned again. "I had forgotten how lovely this feels, how you fill me, how we fit so well." When she peered into his eyes, *something* passed between them. An almost sacred promise was exchanged, as if she'd given him pieces of her soul and he had returned the favor. The fractured pieces of her didn't matter in that moment because he was there to seal them with the jagged shards of himself.

Gilbert kissed her with such tenderness that tears sprang to her eyes, and it was then that he began to move within her. Gentle strokes left her gasping for more than he was giving, teasing little pushes that left her hovering on the edge and chasing that glimmering bliss once more. But she wanted all of him, more of him, to feel the raw need that bound them both together.

She canted her hips to better receive him, wrapped one leg around his waist and moved in time to his thrusts. This coupling had been a long time coming, and by far it was more special than the last one in which they'd indulged. For long moments, she existed in a world made only of hot feeling and pleasure that splintered through her body at each stroke. As best she could, Madelene held him close, whispered scattered endearments into his ear as he worked her over.

Then everything subtly shifted.

Frantic need hurtled down her spine and through her core. Her breathing became more erratic to match his. The heat of the summer's afternoon bore down on her, leaving her sweaty and sticky, but still their bodies moved together in a beautiful dance as old as time.

"Oh, God, Mad, I am losing control." His words were ragged with strain as he clutched at her hip, holding her steady and bringing her impossibly close to his body.

"I am losing…" That quickening of her pulse, the crawling insanity that came just before she was hurtled over the edge teased her. While Gilbert's strokes went ever deeper, ever faster, she touched a hand to her breast, rolled the nipple, plucked at it in an effort to enhance the sensations he already provided. That little bit of added stimulation proved her undoing. "I… oh! Gilbert!" Her body stiffened as release roared through every pore and nerve ending, setting her on fire as she crashed, fell, tumbled into that white light where only pleasure existed.

For long moments as her core contracted, she floated on a sea of lovely feeling, then as he pushed into her once more, he shouted her name, joined her in that place where only lovers knew the way into, and he ground his hips into hers before collapsing on top of her.

Madelene snaked her arms about his waist and held him close. His pulse thundered, his breath sounded ragged in her ear, sweat dampened his back beneath her fingers as her body shook with residual tremors. In this one moment, she was content, almost happy. "That was amazing." It was how things had been between them in the first year of their marriage, before life's disappointments tore them apart as well as misunderstandings and accusations.

"Agreed." He nuzzled the crook of her shoulder and then rolled onto his side. "I had forgotten how well we work together, and it's rather lovely to know our bodies remember."

She curled against him with a hand to his chest. "We were rather carried away in those days."

"We are that now, but can you blame us?" When he sighed, it ruffled the curls on her forehead. "We are rather good together… or we were."

"Of course we still are." Madelene pressed her lips to his chest. How much did she adore the tactile feel of him? It was one of the things she'd missed when they'd been separated. "Can you not feel it?"

And what was more, after this coupling, he hadn't made excuses for it or told her it had meant nothing for the relationship. They had connected on a deeper level than they had before; that had to mean they'd only strengthened the relationship.

"I hope you believe that, for there is something I need to tell you, and any woman worth her salt would be furious to learn." He sounded so forlorn that her chest tightened.

"Whatever it is, we can work through it, just as we have with everything else." Didn't he realize they were stronger together than they were apart? Lifting up on an elbow, she peered into his face, holding his gaze. "Is this why you've been so distant sometimes since I came back?"

"A bit, but truly I have been battling through a range of emotions that stem back to the losses we've experienced, to the dreams we haven't realized, to the challenges we are encountering." Genuine honesty lined his face. "I'm afraid, Madelene. Afraid of hurting you, afraid of ruining everything, afraid of being naught but a disappointment without leaving a legacy or even an impression on this world. Afraid there is nothing left for me in this life, and I have made too many mistakes to render anything right again."

"Oh." Never before had he opened himself up to her so acutely than he was now. She must tread carefully. Her throat constricted. "Perhaps you should tell me instead of giving whatever it is more power. Let *me* decide what to do with the news." But knots of worry pulled in her belly. Had he made up his mind that he wished to pursue a divorce after everything?

Please God, let me meet this obstacle with strength and grace.

Chapter Twelve

*D*AMN, *DAMN, DAMN.*

The time had come for him to confess his indiscretion to his wife, the woman he'd spent the past week or so courting, the woman to whom he was rapidly losing his heart.

Again.

Which meant he was vulnerable and would feel hurt.

Again.

Not knowing how to begin—why the hell had he chosen this moment when everything was perfect after a coupling?—Gilbert buried his nose into her hair and breathed in the faint scent of lilies of the valley. "When I left for India, I was in a temper with you."

"Oh, I remember." A trace of humor wove through her voice. "You assumed Hugh charmed me away from you."

Out of instinct, his body went taut with jealousy. Only after she caressed a hand down his back did he slowly relax as well as he could knowing he would need to shatter this peaceful moment they were enjoying. "I did, and the gossipmongers didn't help in that regard." How had he been stupid enough to believe what those letters had said? Why couldn't he have trusted her? "However, he *did* kiss you."

A tiny gasp betrayed her confusion. "How did you discover that?"

"He told me the afternoon we started a brawl in the drawing room."

"It's true. Hugh kissed me, and in that moment, I had a choice to make, for it wasn't unwelcome."

His heart squeezed. "At least you're honest." Keeping the growl from his voice proved quite the chore.

"How can I not be, when everything keeping you and I apart are lies?" She pulled back in order to peer into his face. "But in the end, I couldn't betray our union even if you *were* away, and I had no idea if I would ever see you again." Her chin quivered. "You should know I slapped him and told him that could never happen again."

"Hugh told me that as well." None of this made his looming confession easier; it was only postponing the inevitable.

"I didn't initiate the embrace."

"That was readily obvious." While he searched for the words he needed to say, Gilbert plucked the pins and a pair of tortoise-shell combs from her hair. They fell to the bedclothes, but he desperately wished to see her dark brown hair down about her shoulders. With a tiny sigh, he encouraged a strand to curl about his finger. "I was wrong to accuse you of having an affair with him like I did, and I should have believed in you because you are my wife."

"I won't disagree with you." She looked at him with specula-tion. "What is troubling you? I don't understand why you feel you need to stall."

Because I don't want to ruin what we have by a stupid indiscretion from my past.

For a conversation of this magnitude, he didn't wish to ap-pear vulnerable. Nor did he want to sully the intimacy they'd just shared. "Ah, Madelene, how did life prove so complicated?" He rolled away from her and then slipped from the bed. "How did we go from a happy couple with the world at our feet to estranged without trust and far too many secrets?"

"We have evolved as a couple. Don't you feel that?" She

watched him with eyes that were more green than brown. From the flush on her cheeks and chest, to the sparkle in those eyes, to the satiated smile curving her kissable lips, never had he seen her more content.

And he was about to destroy that, perhaps already had.

"Yes, but…" Was it worth the argument?

"Secrets have no authority if you don't let them have it." As he retrieved his breeches from the floor and yanked them on, she continued. "I would like to believe that love has more power than that, and that fate isn't quite done with our story yet."

Oh, of that I'm fairly certain. He turned away to hide his trembling chin. *I'm sure fate wants nothing more than to tear us apart once more. And this time it's clearly my fault.*

He paced the space between the bureau and the bed, postponing the inevitable. A silver, ivory-handled vanity set rested on top of the bureau. So easily could he imagine her brushing out her hair each night before she laid down and every morning before she dressed it. When she glanced in the hand mirror, did she still see the woman in her youth, or did she see the woman he was coming to adore? The woman with a will of iron and the capacity to continue caring despite the horrid things she'd been dealt?

"Gilbert? Please talk to me." Fabric rustled indicating she'd left the bed. Seconds later, she touched a palm to his naked back, and he flinched. He didn't deserve any sort of consideration from her. "I would like to think you trust me enough with everything that bothers you." She slipped her arms around his waist and pressed her body against his. "I trust you."

Well, damn.

Unexpected tears sprang to his eyes, but he rapidly blinked them away lest she saw them. He shoved at the thoughts of how good her breasts felt on the skin of his back, how much he appreciated the heat of her, how he wished he could take refuge in her body and forget about the words he must say. But he couldn't do this while she was so near. Turning, he gathered her hands in his and gently set her from him.

"I *do* trust you." Now. After he had no choice but to unravel the lies and innuendos surrounding what he'd thought he knew, she had proved to be nothing except honest with him. "However, when I tell you this secret, you perhaps won't trust me."

"What do you mean?" With a frown, Madelene backed away, found her chemise, and then quickly donned it.

A sigh of relief left his throat, for since she was somewhat clothed, he was able to more fully concentrate on getting through this. "After the sea voyage to India and after I finally made it to Bombay to settle, I was excited to start my adventure with tea."

"I don't blame you. It was always your dream to study there."

"Yes." Why did she have to be so congenial? "I spent six months in Bombay, merely to find my bearings, study tea estates, and to secure lodging as well as travel plans into the places of the country where tea is grown." Filled with restless energy, Gilbert resumed pacing. He shoved a hand through his hair. "I had hired a guide who agreed to take me through the tea fields and would introduce me to the people who owned the plantations. The night before I left for that tour, I hit the lowest point I'd experienced since the death of our son."

Madelene drifted to the trunk resting at the foot of the bed. She perched upon it with compassion etched on her face. "That's understandable. Grief hits people in different ways and sometimes when it's least expected."

"It happened exactly like that. I couldn't imagine how difficult it was for you to have carried that child for nearly a year, and then in that pinnacle moment when you expected to hold the child in your arms, there was simply... nothing." His throat was tight with unshed tears. No amount of clearing it alleviated the problem. "That led me to thinking about my own history. Then guilt swept in, for I thought this was all my fault. That there was something wrong with my health which caused the termination of pregnancies." The force of the emotions he was rapidly losing control over left his voice graveled. "It laid me low."

She's going to hate me.

"Of course it's not your fault." Worry clouded those pretty hazel eyes. "Surely you realize this." She shrugged. "Perhaps the parts of us that are responsible for creating children don't mix well, and we will probably never know why that is."

"But we shouldn't have to worry about such things! We shouldn't need to brace ourselves to mourn each time you find yourself increasing." Hell, after their two couplings this month, it was entirely possible Madelene was even now pregnant. Would that end as all the rest had?

I cannot bear another disappointment.

"Don't you think I'm not already aware of all those things?" she asked in a soft voice. "A part of my heart breaks each time a pregnancy is lost, and I imagine if there comes a time that I should deliver another stillborn child, I will once more land in a pit of darkness and despair."

"Then why do we keep repeating this pattern, keep coming together intimately, if a doomed pregnancy is always a risk?" It was maddening, insanity really, when the cost was so high. Eventually, neither of them would be able to pay it.

"Because I refuse to give up hope, even if what's offered to me—to us—is slim at best." A waver set up in her voice. "To have a baby in my arms, a child that is from both you and I…" She shook her head, and he admired the hell out of her tenacity, her determination in the face of heartbreak. "Perhaps it's a foolish dream, but I won't give up. The possibility of having another stillborn or miscarried child is there, and compromised well-being is not a place I wish to visit again, but they seem to go hand in hand. Please promise me that if I do, you won't run away this time."

Heat crept up the back of his neck. "I promise, but perhaps you will break your own once you hear the remainder of my story."

She nodded. "Very well. Please continue."

"In any event, I was laid low that night when I attended a ball thrown by a wealthy member of the *ton* who lived in Bombay due to her brother being involved with the East India Company." *Dear God*, he'd arrived at the defining moment where he would confess to his indiscretion. Would he lose what he was just beginning to find again? There was nothing for it; he had to proceed lest the sin eat away at his soul. "I was in my cups by the end of the evening. However, brandy removes the sting of grief only so much."

"That is why it's essential you talk about all of it, to get it out so you can confront it and then move past it." Once more, Madelene gained her feet. When she came toward him, he held out a hand and shook his head.

"Please, Mad, stay over there else you'll distract me, and I refuse to have this looming between us as an added barrier." His chest was so tight, he feared that his heart would simply pop right out of it and shatter upon the floor. "Regardless, I had drunk copious amounts that evening, and it made me melancholy and lonely." Not wishing to watch the reactions play across her face, Gilbert moved to the window and looked down into the gardens. "I had intended to remove myself from the ballroom in favor of hiding in a card room, but I was waylaid by the hostess."

"Oh, no." The words were low but filled with enough denial that his chest seized again.

"Yes." He nodded and wished he were anywhere but here. "We strolled through an impressive garden, and it was pleasant to have the company." With a palm pressed to the window glass, he concentrated his gaze on two maids were whispered together while their arms were filled with bed linens. "When she initiated a kiss, I didn't dissuade her."

The muffled sound of dismay that came from his wife sliced right through his heart. If he looked, would she be standing there with her fingers pressed to her lips? With tears of dismay in her eyes?

In order to continue the confession, he had to shove that reaction from his mind else he'd throw himself onto his knees and beg her forgiveness before the fact. "You must understand that I assumed you had already betrayed me with Hugh, that you had thrown me over for him." Not that it mattered. This wasn't a game of tit for tat. "So, with that anger still simmering and combined with loneliness and grief, I was vulnerable and not thinking clearly."

"Please tell me you didn't…"

"I did." He hated every word of this, knew it would cause her pain. "When she suggested I accompany her back into the house and led the way to her bedchamber, I followed."

"Oh, Gilbert." Such disappointment rode on those two words that they could have been poison-tipped arrows.

"I'm not proud of what I did." He swung around to face her as she stood in the middle of the room with a pale face and large eyes clouded with confusion and hurt. "But I wanted to make you hurt like I was." A muscle in his cheek twitched, and he despised himself all over again. "I broke our wedding vows six months after I left you with a stupid decision to bed a woman I didn't know and never saw again."

Madelene pressed her hands to her reddening cheeks as her eyes rounded and shock filled her expression. "You betrayed our marriage bond," she whispered and then quickly sank into a nearby chair. "As a form of revenge against me because you thought I'd done the same with Hugh." It wasn't a question. "How could you? After everything you knew about me, after I had just buried your son before you fled to India? After we should have been pulled closer together in mutual grief?" Her voice rose with each inquiry.

"I did, and I'm not proud of it." Needing her assurance that she didn't hate him, he took a few steps toward her, but she vehemently shook her head. "It meant nothing."

"That's not true! You shared your body with another woman. You had the greatest intimacy with someone who wasn't *me*, your wife." She wrapped her arms about her middle and seemed to shrink into herself. "How could you?"

"I hadn't planned on it, but I was so angry—"

"—and drunk—"

"—there was that." He shook his head and tried to force moisture into his suddenly dry throat. "I've hated myself every damned day since the incident, knew that if you and I would ever attempt to reconcile, I would have to face this demon, and it has left me terrified to face you with each passing minute." Since the damage had already been done, he decided to confess more of what sat on his heart. "I feared this moment since the moment you walked into Ettesmere Park."

"Ha! You hated me then."

At least if she was arguing, there was a chance to fix this. "True, but when we decided to repair our damaged union, that fear sat heavy on my chest and shoulders. I knew with every day that we drew closer together, I would have to make this confession."

"Why did you choose to do so now?" Confusion warred with annoyance in her eyes.

Well, damn. This next bit would make him look even more the cad. "The day I fought with Hugh, I accidentally confessed my indiscretion to him. Basically, he told me that if I didn't tell you, he would, because you deserved the truth and didn't deserve a man who had indulged in the sin I did." Although, his friend hadn't said that last bit aloud, it had been implied.

Slowly, Madelene rose to her feet, and she had never looked more like an avenging fury than she did at that moment, clad in her ivory shift and her dark hair wild and unbound. She only needed wings and a sword to vanquish her enemy—him. "Then you had no intention of telling me of your affair until Hugh was involved."

"No!" How to convince her that what he'd done was an aberration. "Truly, I *had* meant to tell you, but each time I tried to put the words down into a letter, it seemed cold and impersonal, somehow." Would he lose her after all? Retreating to the window once more, Gilbert rested his fist on the glass and then laid his forehead on his hand. "Then, once I'd returned to England, I proved I was again a coward. Instead of going to London and seeing you, I came here, to hide, to perhaps lick my wounds because I couldn't face you."

"And once more, you ran, but you couldn't outrun those fears," she said in a low voice.

"No." Beyond the inability to perhaps father a child, he had failed in a myriad of other ways, but the most significant was betraying what he'd had with his wife. It didn't matter what he'd believed of her at the time or how angry he'd been or how inebriated he'd been, there was no excuse. This one thing had the ability to destroy the tentative trust and love he might have built between them since her return. "I went on a hunting trip shortly before my mother's midsummer ball because I couldn't bear to surround myself with my family and run the risk they would see through the wavering façade I'd put up for defense."

"And when you came back, it was to the knowledge that I had arrived."

"But the urge to run hasn't gone away." With cold dread dripping down his spine and knots of worry pulling in his belly, Gilbert turned to face her. Shock slammed through him to see understanding reflected in her eyes. "After that, it was only a matter of time before I would have to talk with you, admit to my shame."

"Why didn't you just tell me and spare yourself the agony over the years?"

"How could I?" He shoved both hands through his hair. "You've suffered through so much already, and if you looked at me in the way I look at myself in the mirror, I would have put a ball through my brain years ago." A half-stifled cry escaped him. "But then, I suppose this unrelenting pain and grief and anger would finally go away."

Understanding dawned in her expression. "I *have* struggled with those sentiments but have never fully reached the point where I wished to have it all end and actually go through with it."

Tears welled in her eyes. For herself or for the situation? "Why didn't you do it?"

Is that what she wanted, then? To finally be free of him? Gilbert shoved the thought away. "Because… because… You came back, and we talked…" He swallowed around the ball of emotion wadded in his throat. "I never thought I would actually start to care for you again," he said in a choked whisper. "How could I continue to court you if I were dead?"

Would she think him beyond weak?

A tear fell to her cheek, and that silver track took years from his life. "How can you continue to do so now after what you've told me?" She scrubbed at the moisture. "This is a rather large revelation. It has the power to wrench away the trust we have just extended to each other, and I don't know how I feel about that."

Fair enough. Infidelity wasn't something that would vanish in a fifteen-minute admission and conversation. Another wall of hot guilt slammed into him, but this time, he feared it would take away everything he wanted. "It was two and a half years ago, and I haven't done it since. I kept myself away from people most of the time I was in India because I was so appalled at my behavior." The breath he drew in was ragged. "You have my word and my promise that I will never stray again."

For long moments she stared at him with her arms wrapped tightly about her middle. Emotions danced over her face—shock, disgust, sadness—and each one pierced his heart because he was solely responsible for putting them there.

And she said nothing.

If she were to yell at him, throw something at his head, offer to talk to him about the indiscretion, he could have coped, but the silence was horrible. "You won't forgive me this one thing?" So much rode upon her reaction that he could scarcely breathe.

Slowly, some of the light faded from her eyes. "Would you have forgiven me if I had truly bedded Hugh?"

"Damn." Gilbert put a hand to his chest where his heart

ached so acutely, he could hardly breathe. "At the time, no, I wouldn't have, but—"

"You cannot have it both ways." With a huff of frustration, Madelene retrieved her clothing from the floor. "Don't think to hold me to a different standard than you hold yourself." As she struggled into the petticoat and tied the garment about her waist, she glared at him. "I want to understand you, Gil, I truly do, but if you remain stubborn, if you are unwilling to embrace *everything* about this life—both good and bad—then we are both stuck, and what will that eventually mean for the future?"

Say something, you great nodcock, else she'll leave!

"If I do that, who will I be once I don't have the anger, the grief, any longer?" he asked in a barely audible voice. "I have carried this around for so long…"

After donning her dress without doing up the buttons, she shrugged. "I couldn't begin to say, but that is something only you can puzzle out." Once she'd scooped up her slippers, she headed to the door. "I have been patient with you, but don't think that will last forever. For the sake of this marriage, you will need to make a change. Not for me; I have already accepted you as you are, but for yourself. For your own peace of mind."

Bloody hell, I'm losing her. "Where are you going?"

"Somewhere I can think. I need to decide how I feel about this, about you, and whether or not I can live with what you've done… if it's something I can easily forget and forgive."

Then she was gone, and the door slammed behind her with a resounding sound of finality.

"Oh, God." Gilbert staggered over to the chair she'd recently vacated and dropped into it. "What I am to do now?" For this could very well be the gulf in the union he wouldn't be able to bridge.

All thanks to one stupid, drunken night when he'd thought his marriage had already ended.

CHAPTER THIRTEEN

WHAT DO I do now?

Madelene reeled after Gilbert's revelation. Her breath came in rapid pants. She didn't even care that her gown gaped about her bosom. Clutching the fabric to her body, she pelted for the stairs. He'd bedded a woman in India. He'd broken his marriage vows to her. He'd left her grieving in England and then found solace in some other woman's arms.

How could he do that?

Despite what he'd told her, had he seen that woman again? Or worse yet, had he done the same with someone else? Would this always be something she'd need to worry about in the future going forward? It didn't matter that he was now wracked by guilt or that he'd been genuinely upset when he'd told her. Just knowing he'd done that—when she had *not*—left her alternating between anger and deep sadness.

Yet, he'd said he was coming to care for her again. What was the truth?

Oh, it is all too much to contemplate!

And she hadn't thought being told of his betrayal would hurt so much. Now she understood why Gilbert had gone slightly insane when he'd thought she'd done the same to him. There were too many emotions involved, especially now she'd thought they'd reconnected on many levels. Her chest tightened as her heart ached. What did a woman do when infidelity had been introduced into a marriage?

Can I overlook it?

The fact he hadn't groveled for her forgiveness or understanding spoke volumes, yet she'd never cared for women who demanded such from their men. That wasn't what marriage was about, that keeping score or showing mastery over one another or holding an indiscretion over them for the rest of their lives. There shouldn't be such an imbalance of power within a union. Yes, he'd asked her to forgive him and had been a miserable wreck when he'd done so, yet did she have the strength to do so knowing he would have never granted her the same?

Instinctually, she thought to seek Hugh out and ask him for counsel and support as she'd done so many times before when Gilbert had been absent, but that wasn't the wisest course of action now. Yes, he was a close friend and he had accompanied her to Ettesmere Park to help facilitate a reconciliation with her husband, but talking to him now might further inflame Gilbert as well as appear damning enough to make him think she was planning to abandon him.

Why does everyone need be so bloody suspicious?

Of course, if there was another woman here on the property that Gilbert relied on and felt close to, how would she react? *Give him latitude, Madelene. No one is perfect, and you have both been swimming through an emotional morass.* Needing to put distance between them, Madelene ran through the corridors of the manor house, almost blindly, and hoped that he wouldn't follow.

When she was finally outside, she bolted over the well-manicured lawn, still uncertain as to her direction, but the longer she ran, the more she headed toward the hedge maze. It seemed as good a place as any to hide and sort out the jumbled feelings currently trying to pull her apart.

There were no easy answers.

To any of it.

By the time she reached the heart of the maze, her face was

wet with tears and her heart felt all too bruised, but she stumbled to an abrupt halt, for Sophia was there as well, and though she was tending to the roses in the center bed, she was also crying.

Should she intrude? Curiosity won out as well as the urge to assist the other woman if she could. Scrubbing at her own tears, Madelene slowly approached. "Sophia? Is all well with you?"

The ambassador's wife startled. As she glanced over her shoulder, she wiped at the moisture on her cheeks with the back of her gloved hand. "Oh, dear. I was counting on the fact that no one would come here at this time of day."

"I can leave if you would rather be alone." It seemed there was no end of emotional outbursts hidden within the Winterbourne family. Perhaps they were all people who felt things too deeply. When she turned to leave, a rueful chuckle from Sophia stayed her steps.

"Please don't. I don't mind the company." She dusted her hands together and offered a smile. "Perhaps you should tell me why you are here and in some distress yourself."

"Only if you explain why you've become a watering pot over your roses, which are beautiful, I might add," Madelene countered. It would give her time to sort through her thoughts before sharing with Gilbert's sister.

"I suppose it *is* a bit silly." Slowly, Sophia peeled off her gloves and let them drop to the ground beside the mat where she kneeled. "However, I cannot help what I feel." She rose to her feet with all the elegance of a duchess. "I've always been an emotional sort, especially at this time of my life."

"But why? Is all well with your family?"

"Yes, of course." Her smile was as bright as the noon sun. "I was crying because I am so grateful for the turn my life has taken in recent weeks." She offered a wry shrug. "Sometimes, I cannot believe I have Oliver's love, and that I am madly in love with him." A giggle escaped. "And my daughter simply adores him."

So she had cause to witness. "You will remove to France soon, yes?" At least that was what she'd gleaned from listening to snatches of conversation since she'd been in residence.

"Oh, yes! We decided to take a wedding trip there, and Hannah will accompany us, to prepare her for traveling later."

"That sounds lovely." And certainly cause for a celebration. "But, I am confused. All of this makes you cry?"

"Yes." Her smile was a bit wobbly around the edges. "It is sometimes too much for me to contemplate, and still manages to boggle my mind." Slowly, she shook her head. "To think I found love again so late in my life… And after I thought I would die due to health concerns…"

The penchant for trailing off within sentences was slightly maddening, but Madelene allowed her lenience since she understood the confusion. "You are certainly fortunate." A stab of envy went through her chest. "I am happy for you."

"Thank you." The other woman sobered. "When my feelings grow too big and overwhelming and I'm swamped with gratitude, I have no recourse but to cry. It's cathartic at times and a release of tension I don't realize I'm carrying." Another giggle escaped, and her smile returned. "Besides, I have privacy when I come here. In this way, Hannah won't make jest of me."

Despite her own worries, Madelene grinned. "Such is the way of twelve-year-olds."

"So I'm coming to see. Now you know why I am here today." Then Sophia arched an eyebrow. "However, I believe that you have come here to cry for a different reason altogether."

Heat slapped at her cheeks. "Oh, I really shouldn't say. It makes me look like a hysterical woman."

"Ha!" The other woman shook her head. "Not if you are figuring out your life along the way." As she approached, she raked her gaze up and down Madelene's person. "The older we grow—especially as women—the more different life becomes because our existence means so much more and time is limited. Perhaps being labeled hysterical has some merit."

"Perhaps this is true." When the bodice of her dress slipped down one shoulder, she hiked it back up again.

"You are here due to your husband?"

"Yes." She fought off the tears that prickled the backs of her eyes.

"It cannot be all bad if you're here in a scandalous state of undress," Sophia said softly as she slipped behind Madelene. "What happened?" Without censure or lecture, the older woman swiftly did up the buttons on the back of her gown then patted her shoulder. "Have you argued again after doing something very delicious?"

Another round of heat suffused Madelene's cheeks. "We didn't exactly argue. More like there was a discussion where emotions were out of hand. I ended up walking out on him, and now I doubt the wisdom in that, for he was quite upset."

"Come." Sophia took her hand and tugged her over to one of the stone benches. After sitting, she brought Madelene down with her. "Tell me."

"It's too embarrassing."

The other woman huffed. "More embarrassing than running over the property with your dress ready to come off at any moment?"

"True." She allowed herself a tiny smile. "I was upset this afternoon due to some disturbing news I received from my physician in London." Knots pulled in her belly when she remembered those horrible words, but then a measure of relief followed because Gilbert had dismissed the man's assessment out of hand. Her husband fully believed the doctor had been wrong. "In any event, Gilbert came upon me during that torrent of tears. We had a nice discussion regarding my health, and then one thing led to another…"

"Oh, I do so love it when those *things* happen." Sophia squeezed her fingers. "They make for the more wonderful ways to pass the time."

"They do, but I rather doubt such a scenario will happen between us again." Despite her resolve not to cry, tears welled in her eyes. "Apparently, my husband bedded another woman while he was in India." The admission tightened her throat, and for a few seconds, she cried softly while Sophia patted her shoulder. "He broke our marriage vows."

"I had wondered how long it would take before he came forward with the confession," the other woman said in a quiet voice.

Madelene gasped. "You *knew?*" The heat of embarrassment went through her chest. "Does everyone else know too?"

"I don't believe so. Gilbert told me the morning after your arrival." The ambassador's wife glanced at her, but there was no pity in her gaze. "He was broken up about it, though. And if it's any consolation, I don't believe he meant to do it."

"As if that erases what has been done?" She wiped at the tears on her cheeks. "I needed him here. He left anyway, and at the first opportunity, he went off with a woman who wasn't his wife."

"Stop." Sophia squeezed her hand. "What my brother did was horrid enough. We can both agree on that. Yet, he has reformed since that slip, don't you think? And knowing him, he was properly torn up over it when he told you."

"He was. I'll give him that, but how do I know the performance wasn't a lie?" She blew out a breath of frustration. "You believe I should easily forgive him because he's kept himself away from people since then? Because he hasn't repeated the original sin? Because he is changing." That wasn't a question, for she knew it for a fact. If she sounded like a bitter shrew, she couldn't help it. "He wounded me, Sophia. He betrayed what I thought we had. How can I trust him again?"

"That is your prerogative, of course, but let me ask you this question first." The other woman's eyes twinkled when she smiled. "How do you feel about him if you set his indiscretion aside?"

"You wish for me to ignore what he did?"

"Not exactly. I'm asking you to tell me how you feel about your husband right now, because you must feel *something* for him, else you wouldn't be here, crying in front of my mother's prize-winning roses."

Madelene sighed. For long moments, she rested her gaze on the bush that featured deep pink blooms. "I don't know." The answer was complicated at best.

"Liar." Sophia chuckled. Her eyes sparkled with mischief. "Is the intercourse good at least? I would think that should factor into your decision."

"Yes," she managed to eke out from a tight throat, but she couldn't help the smile or the giggle that escaped her despite the maudlin subject matter. "Better, perhaps, than before." Distracted, her thoughts drifted to what they'd shared not a half hour prior. How he'd made absolutely certain she'd found pleasure more than once, how he'd let her see into his soul during that coupling, how he'd said he was coming to care for her.

"Well, that *is* something." Sophia's grin was this side of cheeky. "And hasn't he made great inroads into courting you, into repairing the rifts in your relationship? Do remember the bees, my dear."

He had been a dear to suffer all those stings merely for flowers. "Yes, but in the process, he's opened up a new tear, possibly greater than all the rest." Hadn't he?

"I understand why you would be upset with that, and because you are, it leads me to my next question." She glanced at her. "Do you love my brother?"

Did she?

Madelene traced abstract patterns on her skirt with her free hand. "If you had asked me that question this morning, my answer would have been yes. Despite everything that should have torn us apart, we have never been closer." She moistened her lips. "However, after what he told me not half an hour past... How am I supposed to feel?"

"What does your heart tell you?" When Madelene remained silent, Sophia sighed. "Sometimes, when we think only with our heads, matters are black and white. We tend to overthink things, make them bigger and more desperate than they truly are. We jump at shadows, build problems and walls when there is no need for either." Her eyes were kind and underscored with the infectious merriment she always had about her. "But when we think with our hearts, sometimes that is where our greatest truths lie."

She frowned at the rosebush that featured brilliant red flowers. "My heart tells me I love him still, but it's wary he'll take that love and pitch it away when he's bored or lonely or going through something he fails to tell me about."

"No, not Gilbert." Sophia shook her head. "I know my brother. When he makes a decision and a commitment, he sticks to it. Yet, men are still men." When Madelene would have protested, she lifted an eyebrow. "Unless there is an extenuating circumstance, or he's knocked on his arse by emotions he doesn't know how to face, Gilbert is truly like the North Star."

Perhaps he was in that. "That's not an excuse."

"Of course not. I am merely saying Gilbert isn't a womanizer. He loved you once upon a time, and unless I miss my guess, he will come around to that again, if he's honest with himself." Sophia shrugged. "Everyone makes mistakes, Madelene."

"I know." That cheered her a bit. "Though he has mentioned it once in passing, he refuses to talk about the loss of our babes, refuses to let loose his grief and anger." She swallowed hard in an attempt to dislodge the wad of tears from her throat. "How can we move forward if he continues to deny the things that initially tore us apart?"

"*Is* he denying these things though?" Sophia released her hand in order to stand and pace in front of the bench. "It seems to me that Gilbert grows closer and closer into showing his emotions, bringing them out into the open with each passing day. Never have I seen a more devoted suitor. In fact, he's doing a better job of it now than he did before he married you. It's quite endearing."

"I suppose that's true." Her husband certainly made her feel wanted. "He comes close to sharing what he's feeling, but I think he's afraid."

"We all are that at various times. It's part of the human condition." Sophia sighed. She touched a fingertip to a rose. "Perhaps he needs a catalyst to prod him into showing you how he feels. I certainly needed one to figure out exactly how I felt about Oliver."

"Your romance is inspiring." Madelene rubbed her eyes. "Would you forgive the ambassador if he bedded another woman?"

"Oh, no, at least not right away." Remarkably, Sophia laughed. "I would cheerfully make his life miserable. I do not suffer fools gladly. I'm older than him and I have no qualms in teaching him a lesson, so I would probably exist in high dudgeon until he groveled sufficiently or went through several challenges to show me he was doubly devoted to me."

"Ugh." Madelene shook her head. "I detest when men grovel. It's not attractive for anyone, and quite embarrassing."

"Then good thing your situation is different. I believe Gilbert is truly contrite, and he certainly regrets his actions. If you don't forgive him, he'll mope about the manor for days." She snorted. "He used to be a champion moper when he was a young man."

"I would have liked to have known him then," Madelene said in a soft voice. She glanced at the grass, watched the progress of a butterfly as it flitted from bloom to bloom, then sighed. "I don't want to lose him again, so if forgiving him this transgression is the only way to keep him…"

The scuff of a sole against the crushed shell path betrayed the fact that someone else was in the maze. Perhaps a servant or one of Gilbert's nieces, but as of yet, no one had made an appearance.

"No, dear, it is *not* the only way. There is love at play as well. Don't discount that." Sophia shook out her skirts. Her face had paled. Exhaustion lined her countenance. "I beg your pardon, but I am suddenly quite tired. It's been happening frequently of late, and I really should find out what Hannah is up to. She has been entirely too interested in Major Pritchard right now."

That cheered her considerably. "Hugh is too handsome for his own good, and he's charming and considerate besides. That's what makes him an instant favorite among the ladies." She released another sigh. "I am glad to call him friend."

"Yes, well, I don't need my daughter having her first crush quite yet. I simply don't have the fortitude for that so early. Also, perhaps you shouldn't be *quite* so close a friend to the major just now when the stakes are high, hmm?" She flashed a wan smile. "If you will excuse me?"

Madelene rose to her feet. "Of course. I hope you have a lie down before tea."

"I plan to do exactly that." Then she quickly vanished into one of the hedge-lined paths on the opposite side of how Madelene had entered.

Seconds later, Gilbert came into the heart of the maze, and she gasped. No wonder Sophia had exited so quickly. She must have seen him.

"May I talk to you?" His words were as tentative as his posture, almost as if he assumed she would either yell at him or leave. When she nodded, a sigh shuddered from him. "Why did you run away from me?" Apprehension reflected in his dark eyes.

That she understood, and he appeared so vulnerable her heart trembled. "For the same reason as you did three years ago, I suppose."

"Fear." It wasn't a question.

"Yes. It is an insurmountable prison at times I cannot manage to break out of no matter how many times I try." He came toward her with the same skittish expression. "What now, Mad?"

"You tell me." *Fight for me! Beat back my fears, show me you are stronger.*

When she thought he might reach for that goal, he hung his head instead. "I can never apologize enough times—"

"—actually, you haven't apologized even once." That had slipped her notice after everything else.

"Of course you are correct." His voice was ragged with emotion. "I am so, so sorry. I never meant to hurt you, and now, thanks to one drunken decision I have destroyed everything good that is between us." With a soft sob, Gilbert fell to his knees before her. Never had she seen him so broken or upset, or as repentant as he was now. "If you want your freedom, I will grant it. I'll leave for London tomorrow at first light to meet with my solicitor in an effort to try and secure a divorce."

"But—"

"—if it means emptying my account at the Bank of London and throwing my reputation and yours to the wolves, I'll do so." When he raised his gaze to hers, tears pooled in his eyes and moisture wet his cheeks. "I only want your happiness. I've only always wanted that."

"Oh!" Why did he have to say that? She lost another piece of her heart to him, and despite the damage to her dress, Madelene kneeled in front of him and cupped his cheek. His actions and words spoke to growth, but her eyes welled. It was a start, and he was so brave to say it. "I don't want a divorce or even to be separated from you. I don't want anyone else."

"No?" Relief reflected in his face. "But after what I did—"

"Hush." In that moment, she knew that her decision had already been made. "While I am furious at what you did, it is in the past, and you're quite sorry for it. We have both made mistakes, but I can see how much you have changed. You are no longer that angry, bitter man I met upon my return to Ettesmere Park." That in itself was a minor miracle.

"I don't know about that."

"You are. It's been reflected in many different ways even if you don't believe it." She appreciated that more than anything else." Hope lit his eyes, and Madelene sighed, brushed that stubborn shock of hair from his forehead. They were just broken pieces that required specialized care to mend. "I need *all* of you now, Gilbert. I need you to acknowledge why you really departed for India, why you refuse to grieve, and if you truly believe that we can come to a place in our marriage where we'll be able to make a serious go of it again despite all we might face in the future."

"I…" His composure began to fray at the edges. A muscle twitched in his cheek. Red rimmed his eyes as he struggled to keep tears at bay. "I am so afraid if I do that, I will lose myself. I'll break beyond fixing, and in the process, I will lose you to someone honorable and noble like Hugh. If that happens, I will have indeed lost… everything."

"Never." She took his hands, noted they shook in hers. "I am not going anywhere."

"How can you know that?" Panic twisted through his words. A red flush mottled his neck and cheeks. "*I* wouldn't want to be with me."

"Then continue to change until you become the man you can be proud of." Madelene brought his hands to her lips and kissed his fingers. "Don't stop growing, and certainly don't give up."

His chin trembled. It was the dearest thing she'd ever seen. "I don't want to be alone, Mad. I need you, in so many ways." Then he truly broke and dissolved into quiet sobs. "Please say you'll forgive me and that you won't leave. I cannot bear that after we lost the babes," he added in a graveled whisper.

"I have no plans to go anywhere." With a soft cry, she surged close to him and wrapped her arms around him. When he clung to her, shaking, she buried her face into the crook of his neck. Perhaps it was as Sophia had said, and Gilbert was just now finding his catalyst to discover who he truly was. "I'll be by your side, walking with you, meeting these challenges step by step, for I want you to find happiness as well." She pressed her lips to the skin above the edge of his cravat. "I love you, have never stopped."

It was a risk to open her heart fully to him, but she couldn't hold back the words.

Not anymore.

Though he didn't return the sentiment or try to deny it, he merely held her as she did to him and continued to cry in her arms. For the moment, it was enough, and certainly more than she'd had two days ago. For a man who had spent the bulk of his life denying his emotions, it would be a slow process as they all came bubbling to the surface after years of being stifled, but once he'd cleansed his soul, his potential was limitless.

She wanted to see the fruition of that hope more than anything.

CHAPTER FOURTEEN

August 10, 1819

IT WAS THE night of his mother's last summer ball, and though Gilbert didn't truly wish to do the pretty in country society, those fears were easily enough allayed because the only thing he could think about was his wife.

Four days ago, he'd reached a breaking point of sorts after he'd confessed to his indiscretion. And wonder of wonders, she had forgiven him. He didn't take that gift lightly. They had lingered in the heart of the maze for a couple of hours after that critical juncture, where they'd done nothing except talk, truly, deeply, honestly, about the things that worried them both the most, which is what they should have done all along before everything had gotten out of hand.

During that discussion, he and Madelene had bonded even closer. He had come out with a new understanding of his wife and what her dreams for the future were. Additionally, he'd told her of some of his, how he wished to travel, how he wanted to open a tea shop in London to share his knowledge of teas with the general public. They had both agreed they would meet life as it came, take the opportunities where they could, and ride the highs and lows with hands clasped.

No more hiding behind fear for either of them.

And over the course of those four days, they had spent copious amounts of time in each other's company, both in and out of the bedroom. It was indeed lovely to rediscover the joy of spending hours in Madelene's company for no other reason than he couldn't wait to do so.

Perhaps a man can change after all.

Now, as he prowled the perimeter of the ballroom while the couples on the floor performing a popular country reel, he allowed himself a small smile. Perhaps life had finally turned a corner and he could look forward to the possible good things. It was all so very different this time with Madelene. There was depth and growth to their union that hadn't been present before. Beyond that, he was such a fortunate bastard. He could scarcely believe he'd been granted such good fortune.

The lively music flooded his ears. Excited chatter and laughter echoed through the room. Candles blazed, the grand chandelier was lit and sparkling. The three sets of French-paned terrace doors on one side of the room had all been thrown open to encourage the summer breeze into the overly crowded room. The scents of candle wax, perfume, powders, and pomades competed for dominance in the air, but the energy in the room was undeniable.

I cannot wait to take Madelene out tonight.

"You look like the cat who ate the proverbial canary," Sophia said as she joined him at the far corner of the room. She was resplendent in a gold gown that shimmered with her every movement. "I don't know that I've ever seen you quite so… content."

Was that what he was, then? How interesting. Gilbert nodded. "It has been a difficult few weeks, but I believe I'm finally finding my niche. Or rather, my place in life."

"I'm happy for you." When she held his gaze, this time he didn't try to shy away from her scrutiny. "But the question is, are you happy with yourself?"

For long moments he considered. Then he slowly nodded. "I

am coming to be. At least now I understand it is a process and won't happen overnight, but I am in a better place than I was before." Another grin tugged at the corners of his mouth. "None of this would have been possible without Madelene coming back into my life."

She linked her arm with his. "Are you besotted, then?"

Heat crept up the back of his neck. "I don't know if I'd go that far."

"Oh, Gil, just let yourself fall. There is no shame in it." Sophia's eyes sparkled when she caught sight of her husband across the crowded ballroom. "Once I told myself it was all right and that I needn't be afraid or worry over the future, that transition was so easy."

"I am still wary." He patted his sister's hand. "That is something I cannot seem to break, but I will take your words under advisement. However, I am feeling hopeful, and that is a surprise unto itself." When they came to a halt, he adjusted his hold on the silver head of his cane. "Did you let Hannah stay up to witness the ball?"

"Actually, I did give her permission. However, she has apparently run herself ragged this week and she fell asleep a couple of hours ago. I didn't have the heart to wake her; she'll have enough excitement in her life soon enough."

"Truly, I'll miss all of you when you go to France." The admission was difficult, for over the past few months, he really had enjoyed being around his siblings and extended family. "Who will I talk to?"

"Why can you not talk to your brother?"

They both turned at the sound of Arthur's voice as he came toward them with a wide grin.

"Arthur!" Sophia detached herself from Gilbert's arm in order to close the distance and throw herself into their older brother's arms. "We weren't expecting you until tomorrow."

He bussed her cheek. "Julianna was too worried about her father, so we traveled back a day early. And frankly, I've missed this old pile of stones, as well as my family." Arthur held her away and grinned. "You look the very picture of health."

"Thank you. I am doing well just exhausted at times."

"I trust the ambassador is taking great care of you?"

"Of course." A blush stained her cheeks. "*Very* good care. He insists I take to my bed often."

Oh, bother. Gilbert rolled his eyes to the heavens. "Must you *always* refer to scandalous things?"

"Where is the fun if I don't?" She glanced at Arthur. "I trust you had just as much delicious fun while on your honeymoon?"

A flush rushed up his brother's neck over his cravat. "Ah, that is quite personal. And we are in public!"

"Then that means yes!" A gay giggle escaped Sophia. "I'm so glad. Intercourse is such a lovely expression of love." When both of them gave strangled protests, Sophia ignored them. She tugged Arthur over to where Gilbert stood. "Our little brother has been steadily working out his problems in your absence. I think perhaps soon we shall see a whole new side to Gil."

The heat on his nape renewed itself. "Patience and under-standing, and trust." He glanced over Arthur's shoulder. "Where is your lovely bride?"

"She wished to check on her father and see him settled back at the cottage. As much as the man enjoyed himself here at the park, he was anxious to return home." Concern clouded Arthur's eyes. "Depending on how she feels about leaving him, she might attend the ball, or she might not. Regardless, I'll check in on her in a couple of hours."

"Meanwhile, I believe your daughter would like a few mo-ments of your time," Gilbert said with a smirk as he gestured across the room with his chin at Emily, who had made a concentrated effort to scatter dancing couples in her goal to reach them.

"I *have* missed her." Arthur grinned, and again Gilbert smiled. This was the grand thing about being included in a tightly knit family. "I assume she's behaved herself?"

He snorted. "More or less, but I'm glad you have returned. It seems she and Hannah have taken an inordinate interest in Major Pritchard." Though there was the faintest stab of jealousy that went through his chest, by and large, the mention of his friend didn't bother him.

I really should go the extra step and repair that relationship as well. He didn't want to lose a friend over a misunderstanding.

Sophia giggled. "So has every eligible woman in attendance." She waved to someone across the room. "Oh, by the by, Cousin Louisa has finally made an appearance. And she's quite the managing baggage, if you ask me."

"As much as I want to disagree with you on that, Miss Atherby is quite… efficient, let's say."

"That only means she'll set the village on its ear if we let her… or London for that matter if she's planning on going back with us." Mischief twinkled in Sophia's eyes, and Gilbert didn't quite trust that look. "Only time will tell."

He nodded. "Perhaps, but she *is* good with Mr. Quill, and I believe she gave young John a dressing down when she caught him kissing one of the maids near an outbuilding on the property two days ago."

Both Arthur and Sophia gawked at him.

Gilbert shrugged. "The boy is wily, as we all were at that age, but perhaps it would be in your bests interests, Arthur, to take him back to London before he does something foolish."

"I think you are correct." Worry shadowed his expression, gone as soon as Emily reached their group. The girl hugged him, and he lifted her feet off the floor and spun her about as he'd done when she was a little girl. Her pale blue skirting flared. "Ah, my girl, I'm so happy to be home."

"I'm glad you're back, Papa. I have so much to tell you!" Once she was set onto her feet, Emily linked her arm through Arthur's and tugged him onto the dance floor, where another country reel was setting up.

"It looks like everything is as right as rain here at Ettesmere

Park," he told Sophia. "Somehow, I'm rather pleased with that."

"Oh, it's so lovely to see this change in you! I have a feeling you will be surprised on how differently your marriage will go this time around." She bussed his cheek and squeezed his arm. "Do you promise to save me a dance?"

"Of course. In fact, we can have this next one…" He happened to glance across the room, and he completely forgot how to breathe. Even though he'd seen Madelene not an hour prior, she hadn't yet dressed for the ball, and now that he stared at her in the gown she'd chosen, he wondered if he'd ever truly seen her before.

The gown of royal purple silk rippled with every step she took, but the sheer lace overskirt of lavender gave her almost an ethereal appearance. All that dark hair, piled atop her head and kept in place with glittering combs, practically begged for him to make it tumble down about her shoulders. When she lifted her left hand and waved at Emily, the candlelight winked off the amethyst ring he'd given her at their engagement all those years ago, and as she turned as she caught sight of him, a matching stone glimmered from a white velvet choker at her throat.

I gave her that necklace when our son was born.

He'd meant to present it to her personally on what was to be a joyful occasion, but in the aftermath of the stillbirth, it had been forgotten and then probably tucked away. The fact she'd found it as well as the note he'd secreted inside the jewel box and was now wearing it caused his heart to tremble.

"Dear God," he breathed with his free hand clutched to his chest. "She's incredible."

Beside him, Sophia snorted with laughter. "Oh, no. You're not besotted with your wife. At all." She nudged his ribs with her elbow. "You are so far gone over her it's adorable."

He eyed her askance. "I have nothing to say to you."

With a giggle, she put her lips to his ear. "I somehow think this next dance will belong to Madelene, and that's as it should be." She patted his arm. "I'll claim mine later tonight. For now,

I'm going track pull Oliver away from that group of men no doubt bending his ear with politics and trade talk. Tonight is not for such things." Then she winked. "I would say, if you can arrange it, take your wife out into the gardens. The evening is splendid. And get up to wicked things, Gil. Life is often too short."

There was no use in chastising his sister on her penchant for scandalous talk because there was a grain of truth in it. He would indeed like to have Madelene all to himself in those darkened gardens.

No sooner had Sophia left him than his wife joined him, and he was as tongue-tied around her as a green boy just out of school. "I..." He forced a swallow into his suddenly dry throat. "You are beautiful in purple. Always have been."

A smile curved her kissable mouth. Pleasure sparkled in her eyes. "What a dear you are. Thank you."

"And you wore the amethyst choker." His gaze dropped to her throat. God, he wished he'd been able to give that to her in person, to watch her reaction. "When did you find it?"

A blush stained her cheeks. "Several weeks after you left."

"And the note I included?"

"It was exquisitely romantic." The smile she gave him heated his blood. "'Despite our disappointments, our love is stronger than ever. If you should forget, merely look upon this stone and know that I would choose you over and over, because I love you.'" One of her eyebrows lifted. "Wasn't that what it said?"

"Yes." He cleared his throat. "I had wracked my brain to give you a gift that would show you how I felt since I couldn't think up the appropriate words, but then the babe was stillborn, and there was the burial and service..." At the last second, he stifled the sob rising in this throat. "I didn't know how to act around you and the depth the grief you'd fallen into. I couldn't give you the necklace, didn't seem appropriate somehow, and then I forgot all about it..."

"Hush, Gilbert. It matters not now." She touched a hand to

the stone. "It is a piece I will always cherish merely for the sentiment behind it." As she drew her gaze up and down his person, a shiver moved through him. "That emerald waistcoat is quite dashing on you. I think it's my favorite color on you." Then she frowned slightly. "Why are you not wearing evening dress tonight?"

With a touch of nervousness, he tugged on the hem of the brown jacket of superfine he'd chosen to wear. "The last time I wore the evening rig—the night you came back—it would seem that not only did I retch all over the trousers, but I somehow ripped a hole in one of the sleeves. My poor valet couldn't take the stain out, and I hadn't given thought into ordering another formal set of clothing."

"This suits you." She brushed a speck of lint from his lapel. "Come out to the terrace with me for a few minutes. I want to enjoy the night air before everyone else has the same idea."

"I thought to have this dance with you." Finally, his brain resumed function and he wasn't so puzzled for words.

"I would like that as well but would adore it even more if you'll wait until a waltz." There was so much unspoken emotion in her eyes more green than brown now, that he dumbly nodded.

"Then by all means, let us remove to the terrace. There should be a waltz coming up soon." He offered her his arm as he readjusted his grip on the cane, and as she slipped her fingers into the crook of his elbow, he couldn't help smiling at her. How had he ever managed to spend those years apart from her? She was as vital to him as breathing.

Outside, the slight coolness to the summer night cooled his overheated skin. The soft buzz of insects droned and blended with the gaiety in the ballroom behind him. Madelene's faint scent of lilies of the valley teased his nose. He escorted her to the stone railing that rested just outside the reach of the golden squares of light formed by the open doors.

"There are times when I truly appreciate coming to Ettesmere Park, especially when I can see the wealth of stars in the sky without having them dimmed by the gaslights of London, when there is no noise from carriages on cobbled streets, no mad rush to go hither and yon."

"It is quite a different world out here from Town." Madelene rested a gloved hand on the railing as she tipped her face to the sky. "However, I must tell you, I almost prefer living in London." When she glanced at him, some of the stars reflected in her eyes. "There is an energy in the city you can feel underlying everything you do. It's almost as if it's a lifeblood that connects everyone, and in that I don't feel so much alone."

"That's exactly how I feel when I travel. There is always something that connects me to other people, and once I find that common theme, the trip is more enjoyable." He stood at her side, and unexpectedly, the magic of the night—of her—wrapped around him. It was all too easy to remember why he'd married her to begin with. Madelene made him feel as if he could conquer the world, as if he could do anything he dreamed, and that he was more when she was with him. Suddenly, he wanted to take her all over the world, to discover new varieties of tea together, show her all the incredible things life could hold that didn't need be tied to having children. "Mad?"

"Hmm?" She turned toward him, and with a soft smile flirting with her lips and in that lovely shade of purple while standing in the shadows, she was the most gorgeous woman he'd ever seen.

"Will you please travel to the Orient with me for the wedding trip we never had years ago?" It would be another way to bind them closer, and hopefully, when they returned to England at the conclusion of the trip, every obstacle that they'd encounter would have been overcome. "We had married in haste and then fell directly into the business of living as a married couple, but we never took a wedding trip, and I would really like to have that with you."

Would she think him insane?

Surprise flickered over her face. "Truly?"

"I wouldn't have asked if I didn't mean it."

"I would adore that. Perhaps, in the process, I can discover what I'm passionate about that will guide my steps once we return home." She took his hand. "And it will allow me to see more in depth why you love tea."

Then, he apparently lost his mind, for he easily tugged her into his arms and whispered, "And why I love you."

Her swift intake of breath and the sheen of luminous tears in her eyes further worked to capture his heart. "Do you mean it?"

"Of course I do. My one regret is that I didn't see it before, or all along." Gilbert put a hand beneath her chin, lifted it, and fit his mouth to hers in a gentle kiss that he hoped help to convey all that he felt—was coming to feel—about her again. When she twined her hands behind his neck, he settled her more comfortably into his embrace, and set out to kiss her senseless.

With each pass of his lips over hers, every nip and nibble, he wanted her all the more, wished to make up for lost time, needed to discover his future in her. Without a care for where they were in the moment, he methodically removed the combs from her hair and didn't stop until the tresses hung free about her shoulders and back.

The second chance with his wife stretched ahead of him with nothing except possibilities and hope. It was intoxicating and heady, and he couldn't wait to plunge ahead.

"Gilbert." She laid a palm against his chest and gave a gentle shove. "Gilbert." But she kissed him again before pulling back and finding his gaze with hers. "Stop. We are in public, after all, and your mother's ball for heaven's sake. There is no need to cause a scandal."

The logic of that slowly filtered into his desire-clouded brain. "Perhaps you are correct."

Madelene began the task of putting her hair back into some semblance of a bun. "We can finish what you started later tonight once you've done your duty to your mother and your female family members." One by one, she took the combs from his hand and put them into her hair, securing those wayward strands. The result wasn't nearly as good as what her maid had done, but the relaxed updo made her even more attractive with teasing wisps that clung to her slender neck.

"I look forward to it." He could resist taking one more kiss from his wife. Perhaps it was insanity how hard and how far he'd fallen for her this second time. "But you will do me the honor of dancing a waltz with me before I let you go to other partners tonight?"

"Of course." Concern lined her face in the faint illumination from the ballroom. "Unless your ankle will pain you too much."

"Pish posh. I shall gladly suffer through the pain for a waltz."

"Cheeky." She slipped her hand into the crook of his elbow. "The only other man I have promised a set to is Hugh." As a growl rose in his throat, she clicked her tongue. "No need for jealousy. I am with you, remember, married to *you*."

"I am trying." The possessiveness that filled his chest took him by surprise, but he couldn't help it. "Having you back, falling for you again… it has all taken me by surprise, and it's much more overwhelming this time around." Why he felt the need to once more admit that to her, he didn't know, but it was right on his tongue, right that he told her, right that she would know. "I'm discovering I'm not inclined to share your attentions just now."

"Silly Gilbert. Haven't you discerned by now there is no one else for me except you?" Her smile could have rivaled the light of the sun had it been daylight hours. "You are adorable." Ever so slightly, she tugged him toward the open terrace doors. "Come. Let us procure some champagne then we'll dance."

If she'd asked him to pluck half a dozen stars from the sky merely because she wished for a bouquet of them, he would endeavor to do that with his last breath. That was how far gone he was over his wife.

He was in danger of making a cake of himself tonight, but he didn't care.

I am actually enjoying this… being happy.

How curious, indeed.

CHAPTER FIFTEEN

MADELENE'S FEET SCARCELY touched the ground as she stood at Gilbert's side while they sipped champagne and chatted with the ambassador. All she could think about was the kisses they'd exchanged on the terrace, the way she'd felt so protected and safe in his arms, the way her heart had taken wing when he said he'd loved her.

Now, as the bubbles in the wine tickled her nose, she tried her best to concentrate on what Ambassador Mattingly was saying.

"Now that the earl has returned to Ettesmere Park, do you think he will tarry through summer's end?"

Gilbert shrugged. "I haven't had the opportunity to talk at length to my brother since he came back from his honeymoon, but I don't imagine he'll be keen to leave so soon until they can make arrangements for Julianna's father."

"Ah, yes. This is true." The ambassador nodded. "What are *your* plans after this summer, Lord Yeardly?" As the man spoke to them, he kept roving his gaze over the crowd in the ballroom. "Sophia and I will take Hannah to France in a couple of weeks. Will you return to London?"

"Perhaps briefly." He glanced at her with a grin that loosed hundreds of butterflies in her belly. "After that, I'm fairly certain Madelene and I will travel to India. There are always new teas to discover and pursue, and I would like to show her all the places that spoke to my soul when I was there last." A waver entered his voice. "When I had hoped she would have been there that first time." He choked and covered it with a swallow of champagne. "When I should have come back and brought her with me."

"Oh, Gilbert." She squeezed her fingers on his arm. "That is in the past, and we both know better now. Please don't feel badly about that anymore." The poor thing had suffered so much already. Why couldn't he move on from what had happened? Did he not think her forgiveness genuine?

The ambassador's grin was wide as he bounced his regard between them. "It warms my heart to see the two of you have reconciled, and I know Sophia is grateful for that as well." Again, he looked about the room, presumably searching for his wife. "She worries much about her family. It is one of the reasons she has reservations about going away."

"Please tell her there is no need. Things between my husband and I are going quite well." Madelene smiled at Gilbert. What a fool she was to wish for a waltz when she could drag him upstairs right now and indulge in a different sort of dancing. "I hope she knows we are both happy."

Mr. Mattingly nodded. "She does. In fact, she told me so herself yesterday during our evening walk."

"Good." When the four-piece string quartet returned from a quick break and experimenting with chords for a waltz, Madelene's heartbeat quickened. "I hate to end our conversation early, Ambassador, but my husband did promise me he would dance this set with me."

"Of course." The other man beamed. "I intend to do the same with my wife." His face lit, for he must have seen her on the floor. "In fact, there she is now. If you will excuse me?"

Madelene waved. She quickly finished her champagne and then set the empty flute on the silver tray of a passing footman. "Shall we take a turn about the room?"

"Yes." Gilbert swallowed the remainder of his wine in one

gulp and added his glass to the others on the tray before nodding at the footman. "My apologies in advance if I stumble. I can never ascertain how my ankle will work during exercise."

"I care not if you last the full dance or merely one turn of the room." She drew him onto the parquet floor. "The point is to be in your presence, to show everyone that all is well between us, and that we are finally happy after five years."

Wonder reflected in his eyes for a brief second. "I don't deserve you," he murmured as he leaned his cane against one of the chairs with gilt-painted legs on the side of the ballroom.

"Do hush. I refuse to allow you to entertain such thoughts again." When they gained a free spot and he slipped a hand to the small of her back, a tiny sigh escaped her. "I so enjoy the moments leading up to the first steps of a waltz. Such anticipation, such excitement!"

Worry creased his brow while he took her hand in his and she laid her other hand on his shoulder. Did he fear he would make a fool of himself due to the old injury? "I shall try my best not to disappoint you."

Then the musicians played the opening notes and Gilbert set them into the first steps.

Immediately, the magic of the evening wrapped around her. In his arms, there was nothing she couldn't do. With each step, with every dip, the impression she had from her husband—she could barely discern his limp as well—that her failures and disappointments didn't matter any longer. That just as he'd said, her value as a person and her self-worth was not tied to her ability to reproduce. She held his gaze, and her hand trembled in his. The soft swirl of her skirts about her ankles added a touch of elegance, but it was the heat he imparted as he tugged her closer with each turn of the room that had a smile pulling at the corners of her mouth.

With very little effort, she could finally envision their future. Excitement buzzed at the base of her spine, and she couldn't wait to see where it would lead.

Their bodies touched, brushed together; her fingers tightened in his, on his shoulder. What she wouldn't give to glide her lips along the underside of his jaw, just there where the beginnings of evening stubble was forming, to feel the contrast between smooth skin and that rugged shadow.

"I would caution you to hide your emotions, sweeting," he whispered against the shell of her ear as the waltz concluded. "Else everyone will see the heat in your eyes."

"What if I don't care about any of that?" Though they had stopped moving with every other couple on the floor, she didn't release him.

Answering desire clouded his eyes, and for one thrilling moment, she thought he might sweep her into his arms and carry her upstairs, but he merely stepped away and swallowed heavily. "Go out and take in the air. I must dance with Sophia and my mother, but after that, my time belongs to you."

She nodded. "I'll be sure to wait for you on the terrace."

"I would like that." Gilbert brought her hand up and placed a kiss upon the back. Her hand trembled in his. "I cannot wait to claim your body, to renew my promise to you, to start our live together anew. We shall find maps of where you would like to travel and make plans." Then he released her hand. "Until then."

To say she was bemused for the next hour was an understatement. Once, she met Sophia's gaze across the room. Her sister-in-law gave her a knowing wink that sent heat into her cheeks. A dance with the earl gave her a humorous story about Gilbert from his childhood that she couldn't wait to mention to him, especially when her husband kept shooting her curious glances. And finally, she danced a Viennese waltz with Hugh that made her smile at the polite familiarity of it all. He was every bit the gentleman, but during the dance, she never felt the exciting rush or the need to drag him off the floor like she did with her husband.

That was a good thing.

Then, before she knew it, he'd escorted her out to the terrace where she'd been not an hour before with Gilbert. Such a semi-private venue was ideal, for she had much to say to him that she'd not been able to tell him in recent days. In the shadows, he was more handsome than he'd ever been in the dark evening clothes requisite for such a function. Moonlight winked off the silver-lined pearl buttons of his jacket.

"Thank you for prodding me to come back to Ettesmere Park and to attempt reconciling with my husband," she said as they wandered to the railing. There were a few other couples enjoying the night air on the terrace, but no one glanced their way. "You were the catalyst for the change I needed, for the strength at overcoming certain things Gilbert needed."

"I trust negotiations between you two are going well?" He didn't look at her but kept his gaze on the darkened gardens where a handful of other couples strolled the paths. Cloaked in the shadows beyond was the hedge maze. Had a few gone in there to perhaps give themselves over to kissing and other delicious things?

"It's been lovely these past handful of days." She couldn't help the dreamy sigh that escaped her, for truly, being courted by her husband this second time held more poignancy than the last. "Gilbert has depth to him now that he didn't have before." They were two broken pieces of the same puzzle, but somehow, they fit together despite their jagged edges.

"Though I am truly happy for you and that was the purpose of the trip, I almost do not want you to fall for him again," he said in a whispered voice she had to lean closer to hear.

Shock filtered through her chest. "Why? You were the first person to champion that."

"Yes, I was." Hugh turned toward her and took her gloved hands in his. Intense emotion gleamed in his blue eyes, but it was largely unreadable in the shadows. "If you were with me, I could show you how cherished you could be, how treasured you should feel."

Oh, dear. "While I appreciate the passion in your sentiment and the need you feel to protect me, I believe Gilbert has realized those same things now." For the space of a few heartbeats, she peered upward into his eyes. "I do feel cherished with him. These past weeks, ever since he's applied himself to this courtship…" She shook her head. "It has been wonderful rediscovering why I chose him."

"That is what I figured." His expression settled into glum lines, but he hadn't released her hands. "Would that I never introduced you to him."

Madelene frowned. "You are jealous." It wasn't a question.

"Of course I am." He shook his head. "Gil is my best friend and has everything I have ever wanted in you, but he's too blind to see that."

"Perhaps he was at first, but he's changed. In so many ways, and surely you know that what is between you and I is nothing more than close friendship." There had been one insane moment when Gilbert had been in India and she was fighting her way through grief and loneliness when she might have considered giving into Hugh's subtle advances, of giving herself over to his steadfast strength, but she could never fully betray her husband's trust. "Without you and Dinah in my life, I shudder to think what would have become of me during those horrid years."

He nodded. "Close friendship is apparently what I excel in." A trace of bitterness went through his voice. "Would that I could find someone like you."

"Like me?" She snorted softly. "I have been broken in so many ways, Hugh. Don't look to me for your ideal when there is no shortage of women who are clamoring to be in your company." With a squeeze to his fingers, she gently pulled her hands from his. "I am not the model of feminine perfection you need."

"Perhaps, but I am tired of being alone, tired of seeing life go on around me, tired of needing to plaster on a smile and pretend I am happy, when I desperately want what everyone else has—love and acceptance."

"Oh, Hugh." Her heart broke for him. It was maddening that

he hadn't yet found someone to spend the rest of his life with. "If you apply yourself to the problem, I am certain the answers will come, but you must cease this foolish notion I will leave Gilbert for you." With all of his attention on her, he was rendered blind to any other woman. On impulse, she laid a hand on his arm. His muscles tensed beneath her fingers. "You *will* find a lady who wants you for *you*. And not someone you think you must rescue from life's ills." For that's what she was to him, really. He couldn't help but play the hero, and though she'd suffered much at fate's hand, she didn't require rescuing.

"I hope you are right."

"I am." She gave him a smile. "Why not ask Miss Atherby for a dance? She's a distant cousin of Gilbert's and is quite attractive."

"Perhaps." The major glanced toward the ballroom where a lively country reel was in progress. "I happened to speak with her last night at dinner and found her clever and with a sense of humor."

"You should follow through before the house party breaks and everyone returns to London."

For long moments, he frowned at the ballroom before returning his gaze to her face. "You are certain you're happy with your husband? The last thing I want is to see you devastated again. Then I would know guilt for bringing the two of you back together."

"Stop." She squeezed her fingers on his arm. "I am exquisitely happy with Gilbert."

Hugh cleared his throat. "He could hurt you again."

For one moment, her confidence faltered. "Of course he could, but then so could you if I were with you."

"No, I—"

Madelene shook her head. "However, Gilbert will not do that." She held Hugh's gaze. "He has grown as a person. Truly, he has changed, and…" A giggle escaped her. "I love him, Hugh. It might be folly or perhaps a mistake, but our history binds us, and he has made an extraordinary effort to win me back."

Another smile pulled at the corners of her mouth. "We have shared grief, shared loss."

"Yet he hasn't truly allowed himself to feel any of it," he was quick to remind her.

"Give me time. Slowly, he is talking about those things. There is much healing to accomplish for us both, and these things cannot be rushed."

"Perhaps." Hugh nodded. "I am in awe of you, Madelene," he admitted in a whispered voice. "I hope you come to visit Dinah when you are in London before Gilbert whisks you off to ports unknown. She misses you."

"I will, of course."

"And if it will make it easier for you to visit often, I shall be scarce when those times come." His voice broke slightly on the last word. If she didn't know him quite so well, she would never have noticed the emotion he labored under.

"Pish posh. As I said before, you are a good friend, and it would upset me terribly if you took to avoiding me."

"Very well."

She nodded, but an awkward silence brewed between them. "Gilbert has promised to take me to India and teach me about tea, to show me the country he fell in love with. It's all so fascinating, and in seeing it, I will learn more about him." With a tiny shrug, she let her hand fall to her side. "I cannot wait to see that side of his life and help him with it if I can. To discover who I will be in the future."

"Truly, I am glad for you, Madelene." Yet his face reflected the same sadness in his voice. "I have only ever wanted your happiness."

"Without you, I wouldn't have rediscovered that it is Gilbert who has helped me find that inside me again. He is everything I have wanted in a husband." When he uttered a pained sound, she closed the short distance between them, slipped her arms about his shoulders, and then hugged him. "In that way, you have done exactly what you have promised."

"I am glad to have been in service to you. Thank you for your steadfast friendship." Hugh held tight to her for a few seconds, and just when he had released her, he uttered a soft, "Damnation."

"What the devil is going on out here?" Anger and incredulity rang in Gilbert's voice as he strode across the terrace as much as his limp would allow, and with his free hand wrenched her away from Hugh. "The two of you couldn't wait to return to illicit activities while I was otherwise occupied?"

"No!" Madelene laid a palm on her husband's chest, but he stepped away from her reach. The tip of his cane banged on the ground. "I was merely hugging him in friendship, thanking him for bringing you and I together so we could reconcile."

Anger rolled off him in waves as he bounced his gaze between them. The knuckles of his hand stood out even beneath the gloves as he clutched the head of his cane. "Why don't I believe you?" He strode over to Hugh and then shoved at his shoulder. "You are halfway in love with her, so it would signify that you'd try one last attempt to steal her away from me."

"While this is partially true, and I did try to sway her, your wife is madly in love with *you*, you fool." Hugh stood his ground, but his eyes glittered dangerously in the illumination from the ballroom. "It would behoove you to act appropriately."

"Do not think to tell me what to do." Gilbert shoved again at the major's shoulder. "I have told you to stay away from my wife, but once more, you've shown you don't respect me by putting yourself into a situation exactly like this." His voice rose with each sentence. "Why can you not see we are doing well together?"

"Of course, I apologize. I wanted to make certain you would care for Madelene, that you would love her as she needs to be loved this time around." He held out his hands in supplication. "I respect her too much to let her go back into a marriage where she'll be ignored."

"How dare you assume I am that same man!" Gilbert took a

quick punch at Hugh that caught him on the chin. His cane clattered to the flagstones. "Leave her alone."

"Gilbert, stop!" Madelene rushed over and held onto his arm before he could throw another. "There is nothing between the major and I except friendship."

He shook off her touch, then went and retrieved his cane. "I trusted you, Mad." So much pain and devastation lingered in those four words that her breath caught. "After tonight, when I told you of my feelings, when I couldn't wait to come back to you after doing my duty to my family, I find you in *his* arms! How the hell do you think that makes me feel?"

At least he was freely talking about his emotions. She only wished it wasn't in this capacity, but she could see his point. "I haven't betrayed that trust." Again, she tried to calm him by reaching for his hand, but he moved away. "You saw me hug Hugh. Nothing more. It wasn't borne out of a romantic urge." She met his seething gaze, held it, willed him to understand. "*You* are the one I want, Gilbert, the one I have *always* wanted. That has never changed."

For a moment, she thought he might have believed her, but as each frantic heartbeat passed, hurt and anger warred for dominance in his expression. "I wish I could believe that. The history between you speaks to the lie, though."

Tears stung the backs of her eyelids. "There is no cause to think otherwise."

He shook his head. "Of course you would go to him, seek solace with him." Gilbert fairly spat out the words as he glared at Hugh. "Perhaps you *should* take her from me."

"What?" The exclamation was uttered by both the major and her.

His gaze, terrible in its anger and despair, landed back on Madelene. "He can give you the babies you want."

"This is madness," she whispered. Of course the words were borne of hurt and the emotions he could never let himself release. "Surely you know how much I care for you, that we've already talked of the future. Haven't I told you I would meet whatever comes and not worry over it?"

Had he not been honest about that?

Hugh came toward them, his expression wary in the dim illumination. "I am speaking to you as your best friend, please don't misunderstand what occurred tonight on this terrace. She wished me well. Nothing more, and it was only ever my intention to bring the two of you back together, because I remembered how good you two were for each other in the beginning."

For long moments, Madelene thought that perhaps they would call a truce, but apparently the powder keg of emotions—both inside her husband and what was simmering between him and Hugh—exploded. "Enough!" He wrapped his free hand around her upper arm and pulled her away from the major. "It is quite obvious you are both lying to me, and I suppose I'm the fool for thinking otherwise." A tiny waver in his voice stabbed through her chest. "I'll apply for the damned divorce you want so much, because I refuse to be with a woman who only pays me lip service."

"Gilbert, no!" Why was he letting his insecurities come back and control him? She tried to reason with him, to put her body between him and Hugh, to plead for calm, but he wouldn't listen. "You don't want that and neither do I."

"Agreed," Hugh said. "This is jealousy and fear speaking, not commonsense."

A growl emanated from her husband. "I *will* have the petition put through, but I refuse to go through the rest of my life knowing that you will be with my wife," he told Hugh in a voice that rang with authority and rage. "For I intend to put a ball through your lying, cheating heart this night." He wrenched off one of his gloves and threw it at Hugh's feet, more symbolic than anything else. "Meet me on the back lawn at midnight. I demand you answer for undermining my efforts to win back Madelene's love."

Both she and Hugh protested at the same time.

"This is madness, Yeardly! Think about what you're doing."

"My love has never wavered from you, you great nodcock!" she told Gilbert, but he was clearly beyond listening. Perhaps if emotions caught him up before this stupid duel could be formed, everyone could settle, and he could begin the healing he desperately needed.

"I don't know what is real and what is a lie any longer, and perhaps this will prevent further heartbreak for me." Gilbert shook his head. When he caught her gaze, she cried out at the hurt and grief that filled his eyes. "I am tired of saying goodbye to those I care about."

"Yet you intend to kill your best friend," she said in a voice that shook. "How do you think you'll feel once he's lying dead in a pool of blood?" The likelihood of Gilbert killing the major before he got off a shot was slim. Hugh had been a skilled infantry officer who had won many accolades in the war, and there was every possibility that Gilbert would be the one lying injured or worse.

That terrified her beyond measure.

"At least I'll know he will never have you," he said in a voice graveled with emotion. As he moved back to toward the ballroom doors with her in tow, he said over his shoulder, "Find a second, Pritchard. I will not waver in my intent." He thumped the tip of his cane on the ground for emphasis.

"Then know I will defend not only myself, but Madelene, for I cannot in good conscience let her return to London with a man so unhinged." That note of finality in Hugh's voice sent a chill through her blood.

The night would end in someone's death and the collapse of her marriage if she couldn't think of something to diffuse the situation. The urge to retch grew strong in her throat. "Gil, please reconsider this," she said as they entered the house and endured half a dozen curious stares.

"I am done." His hand on her arm shook. "I can physically take no more of this, for I am going to shatter, and I need to put an end to all of this torment. My mind is so cluttered I will surely go mad soon."

Oh, dear. He had hit his breaking point, but instead of wishing to talk it out, he would take them all down with him. "At least tap the earl as your second. You can depend upon his honor." And she hoped to God his brother could talk sense into him before all of this spun out of control, and she lost him for good.

Never had she been so frightened.

Chapter Sixteen

Gilbert refused to be soothed. He didn't *want* to be soothed, for the anger that shot through his veins and filled his chest with heat was comfortable and familiar.

And safe.

Because if he allowed himself to calm, to think logically about what he was about to do, then his control on the emotions he never let himself feel would snap and they would all come pouring forth to break him.

If that happened, Madelene would hate him more than she probably already did, but at this point, he couldn't see through the red haze of anger, couldn't care any longer, and above all, he didn't want her with Hugh.

At some point, she'd broken away from him presumably to find Arthur. He had to believe that, for if he thought she'd gone to be with Hugh, he would completely lose the rest of his composure, and he needed those nerves to steady so his hand wouldn't shake when he collected his pistol.

Still, his heart ached so badly it stole his breath. Of course, he had assumed the worst when he'd seen her embracing Hugh and the dratted man had his arms around her too. *I have been a fool.* His wife had toyed with his emotions, his heart, the whole time he'd been courting her, proclaiming his love for her. *How could I have let this happen to me?*

Ignoring the guests still milling about the corridors for the ball, ignoring the looks of alarm his mother and sister shot his way, Gilbert marched toward the entrance hall as quickly as his damned ankle would let him. It was half-past eleven, so that gave him thirty minutes to locate his pistol and leave the house for the back lawn. Mama's guests could witness the illegal duel, or they could not; he didn't care, but he would put a halt to Hugh's interference.

At his bedchamber, Arthur caught up to him. "What the hell is this gammon that you've challenged Major Pritchard to a duel?"

"This is none of your concern." He moved to a tall bureau, yanked out the third slim drawer and then retrieved his pistol.

"It is if you mean to murder someone on my property."

"I did give him a warning. He disregarded it. This is the consequence." Gilbert spent the next few moments in silence as he carefully loaded the pistol. The fact his hands shook was ignored.

"You are a fool." Arthur waved off the valet, who'd poked his head into the room. Then he sat heavily in a winged-back chair, leaned forward with his forearms resting on his knees. "You are too blinded by jealousy or stupidity to see what's directly in front of you."

"Ah, you must mean betrayal." Satisfied with his work, he shoved everything else back into the drawer and rested the pistol atop the bureau. Turning about, he regarded his brother as he adjusted his grip on the cane. "Did Madelene inform you of the duel?"

"She did, and she's beside herself with upset."

"I suppose a woman would be when her paramour is minutes away from being killed." The ache in his heart grew, and again, it stole his breath. Lifting a hand, he rubbed his fingers over that faulty organ, but the pain didn't fade.

Damn it, Arthur, help me! I don't want to kill my best friend.

"You are acting like a fool."

"Because I *am* one." He stripped off his remaining glove then threw it to the floor. "I believed Hugh when he told me he wouldn't make a move on Madelene; I believed her when she told me she didn't want him for a lover or husband. Yet here we are. I caught them both in an embrace, and I cannot live like this any longer."

"But you're not thinking clearly." Arthur shook his head. "At some point you are going to have to trust the people around you who love you. When you don't, you disrespect them—us—and do yourself a grave disservice."

"It's easy for you to give me a lecture when your relationship with Julianna has been nothing except lovely." Did either of his siblings understand how much of a struggle it had been for him to reach this point only to find yet another one yawning before him?

"If that is what you think, then you haven't been listening." For long moments, Arthur looked at him with sadness and speculation. "Every relationship has challenges; every couple has the same, but what separates the successes from the failures is persistence. And trust." His brother rubbed a hand along the side of his face. "If I had given up, if I had insisted to dwell in fear because it was the more comfortable emotion, I wouldn't have married Julianna, and that would have been a shame, for she is quite wonderful."

Gilbert rolled his gaze to the ceiling. "Spare me the accolades of romance."

"Don't you dare fall back on bitterness and defeat," Arthur hissed with fire in his eyes. "That man isn't who you are now. For the last couple of weeks, you allowed the man you truly are to shine through, according to Sophia. You were authentic in your feelings and how you cared for Madelene. I was so encouraged when I returned from London to find you a new man, secure in his marriage. Nothing has changed now except your penchant for digging up those past insecurities and drawing them about you like a cloak. Because it's easier than fighting through the last few barriers to your happily ever after."

Damnation. How did Arthur know him so well? "As if I'm

some damned prince in a fairy story?" He didn't want to acknowledge that his brother might be correct or that most of this mess, once again, lay at his feet.

"No, but you *are* the hero of your own story." Arthur shook his head. "Is this how you wish for yours to end? In shame, violence, bitterness, and regret?"

Did he? "Two hours ago, I was blissfully happy." His voice broke on the last word. "I was making plans in my head to take Madelene with me to tour the world, to discover secrets we never knew, but perhaps I should just travel to India by myself, for England holds nothing but disappointment and horrid memories now."

"Why must you insist on cocking this up?" Arthur shoved to his feet. He crossed the floor, dropped his hands on Gilbert's shoulders, and gave him a hard shake. "Open your damned eyes and stop living in fear. Mama is beside herself wondering what she should do about the remainder of her last ball of the summer season. Your nieces are fearful you'll harm yourself or others. Your wife is downstairs crying her eyes out on Sophia's shoulder because she cannot understand why you are doing this, and the poor major—as honorable as they come—is even now readying himself for this insane duel. Why? He'll do anything for you and Madelene, but he is resolved to end this conflict before it grows any more out of hand."

A shiver of unease went don't his spine. "Do you think he'll get off his shot first?" He'd known Hugh for many years and was well aware of the other man's skill.

"No doubt he will, and quite honestly, I don't wish to lose my only brother tonight due to his hotheadedness." Worry clouded Arthur's eyes. "Please give this more thought before plunging ahead. I'd rather Madelene not have to bury a husband beside her son in the churchyard."

Oh, God. What would his death do to her?

Thoughts circled through Gilbert's brain without stop, and once more they came back to the original problem. If he died at

Hugh's hand, Madelene would merely marry the major once her year of mourning was up. Wasn't that what she'd wanted deep down after all? *How could I have been so stupid?* He forced a swallow into his suddenly dry throat. "And run the risk of being cuckholded again?" Slowly, he shook his head. "It must end. *All* of it must end, for I cannot survive more heartbreak." Without letting his brother respond, he retrieved his pistol and moved across the floor. "Either be my second or don't, but Hugh must understand that Madelene does not belong to him."

"Yet you told the poor woman you plan to divorce her." Arthur followed him into the corridor. "What the devil are you afraid of?"

Gilbert rounded on him. "Being alone and unloved."

"Well, you're certainly going down the right path for that!" Arthur's shout echoed off the walls. Rarely did his brother grow this upset, so he must be truly worried.

"I cannot help it!" The admission slipped out before he could recall it. "Not being enough, and obviously that is happening if Madelene is continuing to seek solace and attention from Hugh." Gilbert swallowed around a wad of emotions in his throat that kept growing. "Of being a disappointment to everyone."

Like I am now.

"Then stop this nonsense."

"Nonsense is exactly what I'm planning to put down in the duel."

"You are a nodcock, Gil, and I *am* disappointed in you if you follow through on this action. You are not this man. Do you honestly think your nieces would have helped you in courting your wife if they thought you were beyond redemption?" At his gasp, Arthur nodded. "Oh, yes. I've already heard that tale, and I thought it lovely, but you will hurt them terribly if you go through with it."

"But, I…" He'd not thought about how far the consequences would go, but it would further break his heart to see the major with his wife… if he even survived rendering their marriage ripped asunder by a divorce. With her reputation in tatters, would the honorable Hugh even wish to link their names? *Oh, God.* "You don't understand I *must* do this." Without another word, he left the room and continued along the corridor as fast as he could with the limp before plunging down the stairs.

Every step he took echoed back his heartbeat. The urge to retch rose in his throat while foreboding pulled knots in his belly. This was a nodcock idea, but both Hugh and Madelene had to understand he was dead serious. He was done being cast aside as if his feelings didn't matter, as if he was supposed to look the other way or ignore their affection.

Did neither of them care that he had fallen so hard into love for her this time around he could barely think straight? Or that love had been yanked away like a toy in a bully's hands?

And if the two of them truly were lovers? Well, he wanted Madelene to hurt as much as he was. Bugger the costs.

The steady thud of his brother's footfalls behind him gave him little comfort. Not even Arthur understood what drove him. He didn't have the enormous weight of grief weighing down his shoulders due to infant loss and feeling less than a man. He'd never had to win back his wife for a second time only to have betrayal explode in his face.

I cannot take any more.

A few couples meandered over the grounds, but the bulk of the guests remained inside the ballroom or were contained on the terrace. Of course, those outside would be able to see everything that happened on the back lawn. He shoved the realization to the rear of his mind. There was no backing out now; he was in too much pain to call off the duel.

By the time he reached the expanse of the back lawn where he'd demanded Hugh meet him, the major was there. The ambassador stood beside him. Madelene, Sophia, and Emily were on the lawn as well. Thank God Hannah hadn't been allowed to attend this rapidly growing debacle.

"Bloody hell." His ankle throbbed like the devil, but he hadn't expected an audience.

From behind him, Arthur snorted. "Did you think your family would let you continue this bit of stupidity?"

"You only wish to gawk at my continued misfortune." At least that was what his brain was telling him. His insecurities whispered all the ways he'd failed and magnified them.

"We want to help you, damn it." Arthur reached for him, but Gilbert slipped out of reach.

"No. Everyone is judging. Waiting for me to stumble again." He looked from face to face, and though it was difficult to see in the darkness and shadows, he knew there would be pity in their eyes.

Well, I don't need any of them!

Gilbert trained his gaze on Hugh. "Of course you would choose the ambassador for your second." His own damned brother-in-law.

The major adjusted his grip on his own pistol. "I didn't choose a second. When Ambassador Mattingly discovered what would occur tonight, he accompanied me here in an effort to broker a truce between us." He shook his head. "I believe you aren't thinking clearly, and so therefore refuse to go through with this insane duel."

"Yet you brought a pistol."

Hugh shrugged. "It needed to look believable, but I have yet to load it." So saying, he tossed the weapon away, where it landed with a heavy thud on the grass. Because, of course, he was that damned honorable. Always wanting to show him up. "Besides, what is the point when you refuse to listen to what I have to say?"

"Or me?" Madelene approached them. The purple gown he'd admired earlier the evening seemed almost as if she were readying for mourning in this new setting. Tension brewed in the air between him and his wife, between him and Hugh, between him and his family.

Obviously, the problem stemmed from him.

I don't know how to fix that.

And now it was too late.

Her eyes were dark, and if there was enough light to see them, he would wager the contents of his coffers that there would be disappointment in those hazel depths. Had she ever truly loved him? Had it been an act out of pity? His chest tightened even as the ache in his heart renewed itself. Did she think him such a lost cause that she couldn't imagine a future with him? If he was fortunate enough to be granted a divorce, she would be alone, and with Hugh's death, she would know the exquisite hurt that he did.

"Gilbert, put down the weapon." The plea in her dulcet tones nearly brought him to his knees. "I have already lost too many people who are dear to me. I couldn't bear to lose you too."

"That is the best course of action, Lord Yeardly," the ambassador said with a nod. "I should be happy to help broker peace between the three of you or offer counseling should you need it."

"Please, Gil," Sophia asked in a quiet voice. "We know you are not this man. The brother I love is not violent. He would never take another man's life." She paused to brush tears from her cheeks. "You are merely a man who has been so wracked by grief and disappointment you are near a breaking point, but this isn't the outlet you need. We have all been there, I promise."

Pain tightened his chest to the point that it hurt to breathe. "What would you have me do, Sophia? For far too long, I've shoved it all down... Ignored it. I don't know how to let go..." The tenuous grip on those emotions was rapidly slipping. What would happen when he finally broke?

Will they laugh at me?

Before his sister could answer, Madelene spoke again. "Darling, there is no need for this tonight. Or at all. If you will but trust me..." Her swallow was audible. "If you will dive deep and allow yourself to feel all the things you've denied over the years, you will see that I love you, and only you." Tears trailed through her voice. "That everything which was meant to tear us apart has been defeated and we are stronger than ever, but we need to be together."

"Truly?" The muscles in his body were taut with strain. He kept adjusting his grip on the cane with his opposite hand, for he couldn't hold it and the pistol together.

"Yes." She reached out a hand as Arthur came to stand at his side. "Please, Gil. Give your brother the pistol. Let us go inside, or even into the heart of the maze if you'd prefer, and we can talk about everything until it no long holds you captive."

"I think…" He almost let himself fall for it, almost would have forgiven her, but then Hugh moved to stand behind her, dared to lay a hand at the small of her back, whether for support or to prod her forward he couldn't say, but a wall of annoyance roared through him once more. Gilbert raised his pistol. "Stop hiding behind a woman, Pritchard. I demand you meet me on this field."

The ladies gasped.

"Hold." Arthur dropped a hand on his shoulder. "Don't do this. You'll go to Newgate for cold-blooded murder," he said in a barely audible whisper. "The man isn't armed. You don't even have the sliver of an excuse for self-defense."

"I don't care." In that moment, he truly didn't, but the hand holding the pistol shook. "Move away from my wife, Hugh."

"Easy, Yeardly." The major slowly came forward, but Madelene, being the most stubborn creature he'd ever encountered, stood at his side. Of course she did. That was how she was, for she cared about everyone around her. "No one needs to be hurt tonight."

"I already am! Can you not see that?" He needed help, a guide of some sort, to show him how to navigate the waves of emotion that kept roiling through him, bashing against the wall he kept them behind, battering, splintering, nearly crashing through. "And you need to feel this too since a big chunk of it is your fault, Pritchard."

"I can understand that, so let us talk about it." Hugh's voice was steady and even. "If it will further convince you, I will remove to London tomorrow to show you I am not the threat to your marriage you think. I am merely your best friend as well as Madelene's friend. I care what happens to you both, which is why I brought her here in the first place, because I know how much she loves you."

"But I…" It sounded reasonable enough. He had almost convinced himself to lower his pistol, but then Madelene turned her head and gave the major what looked like a dazzling smile with obvious affection in her expression.

"He is quite sincere, Gil. Please, come take tea with us."

Us. As if she were the major's wife inviting him to their home. *Damn it all to hell.*

"No." As he cocked the pistol, another round of gasps went up from the female members of his family. "For whatever reason, you continue to defend him instead of me, and I cannot go through any more of that pain." Then, his finger slipped on the trigger due to nerves and sweat, and there was no going back.

Bang!

The report of the pistol surprised him, but even more frightening was the blur of movement in the seconds following the blast.

"Hugh!" Madelene darted in front of the major. Then a scream of pain left her throat, for the ball had found its mark in the upper part of her left shoulder, but Hugh grunted as well. He wrapped his arms about her as they tumbled to the ground. The dark stain of blood seeped through the short sleeve of her gown and streaked across her bodice when she landed on her side. Hugh sprawled beside her with a red bloom of blood making its presence known on the white of his formal shirt.

"Oh, God." Gilbert's whole life flashed before his eyes as he stood there with a shaking hand and screams issued from his relatives.

"I didn't think you could cock things up further, but here we are." Annoyance hung heavy in Arthur's voice as he rushed over to the fallen pair.

Sophia and Emily surged forward, both in tears. They joined Arthur and the ambassador to help Hugh into a sitting position, but Madelene remained crumpled on the dark grass.

"What have I done?" In the confusion his mind had become, had he killed his wife? Gilbert dropped the pistol. Transferring his cane to the other hand, he moved with stiff limbs toward the frantic scene, his chest tight and his lungs scarcely drawing in air. "Is she...?" No matter that he wanted to, he couldn't finish the sentence.

"She still breathes." Sophia had dropped to her knees at Madelene's side. His wife hadn't moved since she'd fallen. Gingerly, she pulled the sleeve away from the wound. Blood stained her glove. "I am not a physician by any means, but it seems the ball went through the side of the shoulder, for it embedded itself into the major."

His gaze went to Hugh, who held the ambassador's folded cravat to a wound in his chest on the left side. Pain etched his face. His eyes glittered with annoyance. "Near the heart?"

God, what sort of a man shot his own wife and then put his best friend in mortal danger?

"I would have no idea," Sophia snapped as she accepted Arthur's cravat. "Emily, help me wrap this around Madelene's arm. We need to tie it off tight to help stem the blood." She spared a glance to Gilbert. "She must have passed out from the shock, but you should pray to God that ball didn't sever a vital artery or vein. Or that she doesn't develop an infection."

None of his family members paid him attention while they ministered to the wounded. In the space of a heartbeat, so much had been destroyed, and it had been his fault.

"Will she live?" He hovered on the edge of terror and self-loathing. Would they both die this night thanks to his stupidity? Then he truly would be alone, and in Newgate besides, awaiting hanging by death. To say nothing of how the Winterbourne name would be plunged into horrific scandal.

None of them deserve this.

Sophia huffed. "I cannot divine the future, but Madelene is losing too much blood. See how quickly it is soaking through the fabric?"

He ventured a bit closer. Emily and the ambassador moved out of the way so that he could fit in the tight circle. "I am so sorry." With a cry of horror, Gilbert fell to his knees at the sight of the dark blood stark against the white cravat. His cane hit the grass with a dull thud. Over the years he'd lost his father, the one man whose counsel he trusted. He'd lost his children; had to bury too many people he'd loved. Now, because of his anger and the bottled-up emotions raging through him, he would lose his wife too, the woman who held his heart, the woman he'd never loved more. He would lose his best friend, the man who had been by his side for years, the man who'd introduced him to her in the first place. "Madelene." When he would have stretched out a hand to touch her, he held back suddenly afraid.

At her head, Hugh began barking orders in a graveled voice. "She will need a physician immediately. As will I." A wince of pain crossed his face. "Lady Emily, you know the area well. Run to the house and find your brother. Ask him to ride for the nearest physician."

"No need," Arthur inserted as Emily scrambled to her feet. "I believe there is a Doctor Avery at the party. I saw him last in the card room." He nodded at his daughter. "Find him and tell him what has occurred. We will bring both the major and Madelene to the house as soon as we can. And then tell your grandmother we will need towels and hot water. Once that is done, locate Julianna. She is the most levelheaded of us all."

"Of course, Papa." Emily ran past without a second glance at Gilbert, but the silvery tracks of tears were evident on her cheeks. The cut direct worked to further bash down the lid on the emotions running rampant inside him.

"Can you stand, Major?" The ambassador assisted Hugh to his feet.

"I believe so. I have taken worse injuries in the war." But

there was pain in his voice and blood on his gloved fingers. He, too, refused to look at Gilbert.

I deserve this. It's my fault.

"That may be so, but if that ball has lodged in your chest, it'll need to come out before it shifts and does permanent damage," Ambassador Mattingly continued.

"Or enters my heart. Yes, I am fully aware of the situation, Ambassador," the major said with both humor and annoyance mixed in his tones. "I wouldn't say no to a healthy dose of brandy either."

The other man nodded. "You'll no doubt need it, for the removal won't be pleasant."

"Go to the manor. I'll be there shortly." Arthur glanced at Sophia. "I'm going to take Madelene back to the house. Will you stay with him?" He sent his gaze to Gilbert.

Hot shame went up his neck and into his cheeks. *I deserve their ire.*

"If I must." Clearly, his sister wanted nothing to do with them. "Honestly, I only wish to slap sense into him."

Remarkably, the ambassador chuckled. "I shall remain behind as well. We will join you as soon as we can, but I have a feeling our presence will be needed here for a bit."

His brother didn't answer. Instead, he put his arms beneath Madelene's still form and hefted her up as gently as he could. Blood seeped through the cravat wrapped about her shoulder. So much blood! When he would have moved, Gilbert struggled to his feet.

"I'm so sorry, Mad," he said in a broken whisper as he touched a hand to her cold face. Her eyelids never even fluttered. Tears he hadn't been aware he'd shed wet his cheeks. "Please don't leave me. Not now." A ball of emotion stuck in his throat, tightening it. "I am nothing without you."

Sophia snorted. She nudged him out of the way. "You certainly have an odd way of showing your affection. What made you think that every woman desires being shot as a sign of never-ending love?" Heavy sarcasm threaded through her inquiry. With a nod at Arthur, she held Gilbert back when he would have blocked the path once more. "Get her settled. Hopefully by the time we join you, the physician will have already examined her."

"Of course." He exchanged a speaking glance with her. "As a precaution, shall I have Vicar Parkinson summoned?"

"Oh, God." Gilbert put a hand to his aching heart. That was the clergyman who'd conducted their father's graveside service. "Surely, he's not needed…"

Sophia ignored him. "It wouldn't hurt to be ready for all available outcomes. We just don't know what the next twenty-four hours will hold."

Finally, Arthur moved away from the scene of the most horrible incident of Gilbert's life.

"I need to be with her." When he would have followed, Sophia stepped in front of him with a hand on his arm. "Let me go, damn it! I have to know if she'll live. I need to be with her!"

"While I understand that, you are a sorry mess right now." She laid her hands on his shoulders, gave him a bit of a shake until he met her gaze. "Whatever demons you are holding back, now is the time to set them free. Release your grip on things, Gil. You've held onto them long enough. It's time to let them go." Though her expression softened, worry added lines to the corners of her mouth and eyes. "You cannot help your wife until you have sorted yourself. Surely you realize that."

The metallic scent of blood permeated the air to blend with the lingering sent of gunpowder. While the ambassador quietly gathered the dropped pistols, Gilbert stared at his sister. "I have to be strong. That is what is required of men." A muscle in his cheek twitched. "It is what Papa did."

"Oh, you poor thing." She gathered him into her embrace, and he clung to her as if he were a small boy afraid of a thunderstorm and she would come to his side of the nursery and comfort him. "You are wrong. Papa was a strong man, yes, but he never said it was wrong to let your emotions show. He just meant that you shouldn't let them consume you. There were plenty of times when he was overwhelmed, but he dealt with that so he could move forward."

"He would be so disappointed in me now." Once his tears began, there was no way to stop them. "Why can I not be like you and Arthur?" His siblings seemed to always land on their feet after difficulties.

"Oh, I rather doubt that's true. Papa had his fair share of disappointments in life, but his children were not one of them. He was always proud of you and your sense of adventure." She ran a hand up and down his back. "But he had Mama, and their bond was unbreakable. They talked about everything, faced both good news and bad together. And if you think that Arthur and I are both always strong and confident, you are wrong." Her grin was rueful. "We both have a tendency to be messy as well. Perhaps it's a hidden Winterbourne trait."

"I don't know." He sighed. "In this I have failed Madelene." Gilbert pulled away as the ambassador joined them. "I have done everything wrong. I should have been there for her from the start. Why would she ever want me back?"

"I won't argue with you." Then she sighed and looked at her husband. "Perhaps you should take over from here, Oliver. I am worried about Madelene and wish to be with her. Need to prepare the girls for the worst if..." A tiny sob swallowed her words. "To say nothing of the major's health. They have both doted on him, and it would crush them if—"

"I know. Do not further trouble your mind." He bussed her cheek. "I will stay with your brother for as long as he needs the company. To keep an eye on him."

"Thank you. I love you."

As she fled over the darkened ground, Gilbert's shoulders drooped. "Even she cannot abide me, and I cannot fault her for that decision."

"Sophia is the strongest, most stubborn woman I've ever met, but there is nothing she won't do for her family." Ambassador

Mattingly clapped a hand to his shoulder. "She is upset, obviously. None of us expected the night to end like it has. You certainly caused a sensation."

Hot guilt and shame collided inside his chest, but he didn't care if the other man saw the beginnings of his emotional break. "I didn't want to shoot anyone. I was nearly out of my mind with jealousy and everything else... I love Madelene so much..." He shook his head. "My finger slipped on the trigger..."

"I think we can all agree you didn't mean it. However, you *have* injured two people. Their future is left to fate." A hard note had entered the other man's voice. "There will be a reckoning of sorts, you know."

Gilbert nodded. "What should I do? Pack my bags and go back to London? Take myself off to India and live out my days there? Perhaps everyone would be better off if I quietly left their lives."

"And take the coward's way out?" The ambassador chuckled. The annoyance had vanished from his expression. "I think not. I rather suspect that is not the type of man you are."

"It is who I have been in recent years."

"Only because you are hiding from who you truly are. Out of fear. Out of disappointment, yes?"

When that eyebrow cocked in question, Gilbert slowly nodded. "Yes. I have become a burden even to myself, don't know how to change."

"I don't know if that is quite true, but there is always room for improvement in every aspect of life. Whether you believe it not, every single member of your family loves you—prickles and all. They are cheering you on hoping you'll finally have happiness and peace." His gaze bore into Gilbert's, but despite the heavy subject matter, the ambassador's eyes were kind, as was his slight smile. "It is what every member of the human race searches for. None of that is beyond your reach, Lord Yeardly."

"But—"

"But unless you square with everything you are, everything

you have been through, you cannot make amends or walk unencumbered into a future, for all the baggage you take with you will weigh you down." The other man shook his head. "Drag it all out, no matter how ugly or unpleasant. Let it have at you. Feel what you feel, but then toss it away. Do not return to the manor until you have examined every detail, until you can come back to your wife after forgiving yourself. Trust me on this."

"If she'll have me." His swallow was audible. "If she lives…" *God, what will I do without Madelene?*

"One step at a time, Lord Yeardly." He gave Gilbert's shoulder a little nudge. "Best place for contemplation and clearing one's soul is the heart of the maze where Sophia's roses are. We have all utilized it to find clarity at one time or another."

"Perhaps you are correct." He scrubbed at the moisture on his cheeks. "This won't be pleasant."

"Oh, goodness, no it won't, but it's necessary. You have two people back at the house who are counting on you to puzzle this out, to fully examine your existence, and a whole handful of family who cares for you. Remember that. If you're not back by breakfast, I'll come find you."

"Thank you." He forced a swallow around the ball of emotions in his throat. "And if Madelene… Er, if she isn't going to pull through?"

"I'll come grab you all the same. Despite everything, you should be there in her last moments." Then, with an encouraging nod, the ambassador left him alone.

There was nothing else to do except head for the hedge maze. On the way, he retrieved his forgotten cane. His limp was more pronounced now that he was under severe duress, and the old break had begun to hurt, but he ignored the discomfort. *Please, God, keep Madelene and Hugh safe, and forgive me for what I did in anger.*

Perhaps it was time to be brutally honest with himself and figure out what he wanted most from this life.

CHAPTER SEVENTEEN

August 13, 1819

MADELENE CAME AWAKE to the soft purple shadows of twilight filling her bedchamber. Consistent pain throbbed through her left shoulder, and what was more, the arm had been fitted into a sling made from a heavy sort of fabric and secured around the ribcage on the opposite side with a set of ties. No doubt the physician didn't wish for her to move her shoulder.

From the direction of the corridor beyond, the sound of muffled voices reached her ears through the half-open door.

"…you realize this decision won't just be in effect for days or months, and you will need to stick with it?" Was that the earl's voice, or was her mind playing tricks on her again, for she thought she'd dreamed of him when she'd been in and out of a laudanum-induced haze. Possibly due to being carried back to the house by him after being shot.

She couldn't hear the beginning of the response. "…it's best for all of us…" That sounded like Gilbert's voice. A tiny shudder of relief went down her spine. Ever since she'd been seen by the physician, she hadn't been sure her husband would be there when she came back to herself. Not once had he visited her room, or at least not that she remembered while in the drugged cloud. But then, she'd been in a temper with him for putting everyone into danger.

"…avoiding London because of the major…"

"That is one aspect."

"…best friend. Don't discount that."

"I will talk with him before departure."

Madelene frowned. What did any of it mean?

"Are you certain you have sorted yourself? I refuse to agree to this if you will land right back where you started." A note of authority rang in the earl's voice. "I will not stand idly by…" The remainder of his words were lost. He must have moved away from the door.

"Quite certain. I didn't come out of that maze until I'd purged everything holding me back." She could just imagine Gilbert shoving a hand through his hair like he always did when nervous. "…push her too hard by going directly on a sea voyage."

"…Brighton isn't India…"

"But it's a start… need time alone… as many times as it takes for forgiveness…"

Were they talking about her? And if so, why? In the attempt to push herself up against the pillows, pain shot through her shoulder. She uttered a soft moan; it was a good reminder that she still had healing to do.

Immediately, the voices in the corridor broke off. Then the door opened wide and both men came into the room. Where the earl was elegantly dressed in evening clothes with his hair dressed just so—no doubt he had just finished dinner with the family—Gilbert's appearance put her in mind of a country gentleman who had fallen asleep in a hayloft. His golden hair stuck up at all angles, his buff-colored breeches were slightly dirty at the knees, and his jacket of bottle-green superfine had more than a few wrinkles.

What exactly had he been doing with himself?

At the last second, she tugged the sheet up her chest to hide her breasts, for she only wore a thin lawn shift.

The earl spoke first. "Nice to see you awake again, Madelene.

Should I ring for your maid? Or Sophia, to administer another dose of laudanum?"

"No." Slowly, she shook her head, and when the room didn't spin as it had before, she sighed. "I don't wish for drugs right now." There were things she needed to say to her husband, questions she had to ask, for the last thing she remembered was that shot and then terrible pain afterward. "But thank you for the concern." When her stomach rumbled, she allowed a small smile. "Tea would be nice though."

"I shall see to it myself." With a speaking glance at Gilbert, Arthur departed.

For long moments, she stared at him, and he looked back with varying degrees of guilt and concern running through his expression. Finally, he softly cleared his throat and advanced further into the room, his hand clenched tight around the silver head of his cane.

"How are you feeling?"

Oh, that familiar rumble of his voice was heavenly. *I thought I should never hear it again.* "Well enough I suppose." Why didn't he come closer?

"Does your arm pain you?"

"Like the devil, actually." She didn't feel the vulgarity to be out of place. As a wave of sadness mixed with anger swept over her, she frowned at him. "You shot me."

He snorted as he took another few steps toward her bed. "To be fair, I shot at Hugh. You were the one who put yourself into the line of fire." All too quickly, his expression and attitude sobered, which left her reeling. "But none of that matters. I should never have taken the shot to begin with, should never have challenged Hugh to a duel, should never have let my temper get away with me that night."

Her lower jaw dropped. "Are *you* quite well?"

Another chuckle escaped him as he sat in the hard-backed wooden chair at the right side of the bed and rested his cane against the edge of the mattress. "I am, and it's the best I have been in a very long time." When he took her hand in his, a few butterflies released in her lower belly. "Please know I didn't mean to hurt you that night or any other."

"Of course I know that." Yet the ever-present pain in her shoulder reminded her that it had happened, and he hadn't listened to reason from any of them. Gently, she pulled her hand from his. "We cannot continue in this vein, Gilbert. It is much too hard on my spirit to go about with you in romance and congeniality one minute and then be subjected to your mercurial moods and constant anger or jealousy."

"I cannot imagine what sort of emotional morass I've subjected you to." The response was as surprising as everything else he'd done since entering the room. Where there had been haunted shadows in his eyes before, now they were clear, free from the emotions he'd battled with before. "For that, I sincerely apologize."

Again, she gawked at him, unable to understand the transformation he'd apparently undergone while she'd been recovering. "Ah, what exactly happened to you after I was shot?"

"No doubt it's been murky at best for you." The grin he flashed instantly took years from his face, and he was once more the man she'd married five years ago. "If I had been married to me, I would have kicked my arse out of London."

Heat infused her cheeks. "You *have* been especially trying."

"I know that now." He heaved a sigh. "My siblings weren't happy with me after what happened." When he attempted to put some semblance of order to his hair, she offered a small smile. "Arthur took charge; Sophia took me to task." His swallow was audible. "Right after it happened, I was stunned and shocked. When you were unconscious on the ground, and there was so much blood, I didn't know what to do." The tiny little waver in his voice went straight to her heart.

"You needn't continue on if it's too much for you." How well did she know of his distaste for sharing emotional things.

"It will always be overwhelming, but I am learning—slowly—

that holding such things inside without confronting them is a terrible way to live… and will lead to nights like the one where I could have lost the person I love the most in this world."

Tears sprang to her eyes, but she said nothing for fear it would interrupt the courage it must take for him to admit his truths to her.

"After Arthur removed you to the manor house, I spoke with the ambassador and then went into the hedge maze to be alone with my thoughts." His eyes took on a faraway look. "It was time for a change, so I stopped trying to control my emotions or having them rise to the surface. I let them all come at me in the terrible storm that had been brewing for far too many years, and I had no choice but to face every disappointment, everything that made me angry and jealous, everything I didn't like about myself which led to either expectations of others or hard feelings from them."

"Oh, Gilbert." She extended her right hand, and when he grasped her fingers, warmth slowly licked up her arm. "How long were you there?"

"A few hours." His gaze flicked to hers. "But I was determined I wouldn't emerge until I had come to terms with everything that had happened to me in my life. As I returned to the house, I vowed to myself I would never again run away in fear or hide behind it in an effort to ignore anything unpleasant."

Such unexpected progress took her by surprise. "I would imagine that new resolve was sorely tested when you returned to the house with worry for both me and Hugh." Would he revert to his old ways at the mention of the major?

Instead of the jealousy he'd previously had, a touch of regret clouded his eyes. "I was beside myself, still couldn't believe that such a rash action on my part had torn into two people I care about." The catch in his voice tightened her chest. "The physician said the ball had gone clean through the side of your shoulder but that you would have a decent scar, for he'd had to stitch together the flesh in order to quell the bleeding. You had also developed a fever, which he said was expected after something like that. Helps the body heal, or some such."

Well, that explained some of the pain and the bizarre dreams she'd had. "And Hugh?"

His Adam's apple bobbed with a hard swallow. "Since the ball went through you, it lodged in his upper chest near his heart and had to be extracted immediately lest it work its way into that organ." Moisture filled his eyes. "The choice of which of you the doctor needed to attend to first was agonizing, but Sophia took control of the situation marvelously. Julianna did what she could to make Hugh comfortable. And damn the major for sitting there, watching the man stitch you up while he was in immense pain. He refused to go down the hall until your bleeding stopped."

"Oh, poor Hugh." The man was honorable to a fault. She wished he would drop the ridiculous notion of being in love with her and turn his attention to finding a woman who would appropriate him for all that he was. "He didn't deserve any of this. All he did was bring me to Ettesmere Park because he believed that you and I could reconcile and repair our union." Though she wanted to cry, that effort would take too much of her energy, and already exhaustion was pressing in on her.

"Indeed. I owe him a debt I'm afraid I'll never be able to repay, yet I've treated him horribly."

"Surely he knows you didn't mean to shoot him—or me."

"I haven't had the opportunity to speak with him, for he refused to discuss it that night." Gilbert squeezed her fingers. "In any event, once you were taken care of, the physician worked on Hugh. From what Sophia told me, he had to dig about a bit with forceps into order to locate the ball, but eventually he found it. Hugh had long since gone unconscious from the pain of that operation, which probably was more of a blessing than anything else, for there was much blood and then stiches followed."

"And your sister witnessed the whole thing." Truly, the Winterbournes were a wonderful family, both together and individually. Stubborn to the point of willfulness, yet they were all so brave, and had met futures with their chins held high when such things were probably terrifying.

"She did, as did Emily. In fact, my niece was a brick of a girl, and I wouldn't be surprised if she doesn't badger Arthur into letting her study nursing or perhaps with an apothecary, for she has a talent there."

A snort sounded at the door as the earl returned to the room with a tea tray in hand. "We shall need to discuss that before I let my daughter go haring off to chase such a profession. She is, after all, an earl's daughter and has a bright future ahead."

"Yet you will support her in whatever endeavor she chooses, I would imagine," Madelene said softly. "England needs more women to take the helm and guide her away from the old ways that no longer serve her."

"Perhaps. No doubt there will be many discussions as she grows older." He rested the tray on a nearby occasional table. "Gilbert can pour out for you. I trust he isn't proving a hinderance for your recovery?" A blond eyebrow lifted in inquiry.

Madelene smiled. "He has been relating events of that night for me."

"Ah." Arthur nodded. "I will say, though, my brother has truly been transformed. Whatever happened to him that night after he fired that pistol has changed him from the inside out. In fact, he sat outside this room much of the time to the point that a maid had been dispatched to bring him tea and food, for he refused to budge until the physician declared your fever had broken and you were away from death's door."

"Oh." She felt both small but cherished as she regarded her husband. A flush of red crept over his loosened cravat and into his cheeks. "You were so concerned? After everything you said to me on that horrible night?"

"Yes." A tear fell to his unshaven cheek. "I was a mess, I'll admit, but I've never stopped loving you, Mad. I have been out of my mind with jealousy thinking after everything you might have preferred Hugh, because he is the man I wish I could have been all along, knew I should have been but couldn't due to my inability to live with my emotions." Another few tears fell to his cheeks.

Her heart skipped a beat. "None of that matters now. You are here and I believe your words are genuine."

The earl cleared his throat. "She has a point, little brother."

They both ignored him.

"But I caused you pain, and for that I'm truly sorry." Gilbert lowered his head to the bed, and for a few moments, silent sobs wracked his shoulders. "I never wished to hurt you that night… or ever."

"I know." She combed her fingers through his disheveled hair. "Sometimes we never know just how powerful an emotional storm will be until it finally comes upon us and tosses us about without provocation."

"And you've weathered yours alone. I should have been there." His words were muffled by the bedclothes. "I should have grieved with you and perhaps in the doing we wouldn't have reached this pass."

"Perhaps we both needed to go through this in order to know exactly what we wanted from life." She encouraged his head up, peered into his tearful eyes, and then smiled. "Until you challenged Hugh to that duel, until you shot me, we were in a good place indeed."

"I once again ruined that progress." He shook his head. "When I was forced to contemplate a life without you in it, knew everything was my fault, it was as if I was coming out of a dark place and into the light. Hoping that you would still want me after you survived this ordeal. Changing permanently because I knew I had to in order to keep you in my life."

"I'll leave you to the conversation." With a soft grin, Arthur winked at her then quietly left the room, closing the door quietly behind him.

She barely acknowledged his defection, for the whole of her attention was on Gilbert. Never had he been as honest or willing to talk about what was on his mind and heart. A week ago, this sort of conversation would have terrified him, and he would have removed himself from the situation to avoid it, would have run in fear.

"Does this mean you will be a different man in the future?"

"I will do my best to try, but I must warn you it will be a constant struggle not to fall back into old habits." Though his grin was a bit wobbly around the edges, it was the most beautiful thing she'd ever seen.

As she attempted to shift into a more comfortable position, she winced, for the pain in her shoulder was strong. "When you were in the corridor, talking about Brighton, what did *that* mean?"

For a few minutes, Gilbert busied himself with pouring out a cup of tea, fixing it just the way she liked, and then gave it to her. "You and I need time alone to make certain the changes to our marriage will be able to hold."

"Fair enough." While the time with him at Ettesmere Park had been lovely, there was always a member of his family around.

"Also, I am afraid that as long as Hugh is hanging about, I won't be able to completely be the man you truly need." He took a tiny honey cake from the tray and gave it to her; it was one of her most favorite pastries the cook made. "Though I *am* changing, learning how to be a better man for us both, knowing he is here and that he is halfway in love with you will make all the good going forward a challenge."

"But—"

He eyed her askance. "I am only so strong, Madelene. Hugh is my best friend—or was until I shot him—and while I need to repair that relationship again, I also want to keep my marriage." Once more, his voice broke. "You are the most important person to me right now, and we need to be allowed that time to discover what we want—both together and singularly. No matter how fond we both are of the major, his presence complicates things and is perhaps hindering us breaking through the last of these obstacles."

For long moments she looked at him as she gobbled down the cake. It had felt like days since she'd eaten anything substantial. "I can understand and appreciate that, but why Brighton?" Though she would miss Hugh terribly, their friendship would endure, and perhaps she *had* allowed him too close. It was something she needed to own up to, for the problems weren't all laid at her husband's feet.

Gilbert sighed as he gave her a piece of dry toast. "Arthur has a townhouse there. Rarely has the family used it; it hasn't been opened since Papa died, and that's a shame, for it truly is a picturesque property. Mama prefers this one while Arthur has an affinity for the London townhouse." He shrugged and a wry grin crept across his face. "I thought we should use it for our honeymoon period while we make additional plans. India can wait until we are both certain that remaining married is what we want."

The taste of the bread turned to sawdust in her mouth. Quickly, she swallowed and followed it with a swig of tea. "Of course it's what I want."

He nodded. "As do I, but I want to make absolutely certain." The look in his dark eyes sent tremors of anticipation down her spine. "I am not strong enough to go through another set of hazards to win you, Mad. But I love you and will spend the remainder of my life hoping you'll forgive me for causing you anguish over the years, and especially for shooting you."

"Oh, Gilbert." The poor thing must have berated himself terribly over the last few days. "I won't lie. Being shot was especially traumatic and it hurts like fire, and I still am a bit cross with you about it, for no one should know this sort of pain."

"I—"

"Please, let me finish." She took another sip of tea to fortify herself then rested the cup on the bedside table. "However, I understand some of what you were struggling with that night. You put years' worth of anguish into but a few hours, and that would catch anyone off guard."

"That's not an excuse," he said with such a mournful tone her heart trembled for him.

"No, it's not, but it's an explanation." She took his hand and brought it to her cheek, nuzzled into his palm. The heat of him, the feel of him, the way his breath hitched all worked to bring her closer to him. "I hear it in your words and see it in your eyes that you are indeed a changed man. A trip to Brighton will be just the thing we need so I can see this new attitude in your actions as well, but you must promise me, with everything you are, that you will meet the future together with me and not allow your emotions to push you away into fear."

"I promise." He shifted positions on the chair so he could properly cup her cheek. The pad of his thumb skated along her bottom lip. "Dear God, how I promise to be the man you need going forward."

"Good." She could barely breathe with him so close. "Above everything, please say that you will chase happiness, find it for yourself. You need that, Gilbert. For you, so you can see that living under fear is no life at all."

"I will, and you are a large part of that." When he surged forward to kiss her, she laid her palm against his chest.

"No. Don't rest that responsibility on me. If something were to happen that took me from you, I refuse to know you'll be plunged into the dark again."

"But, sweeting, you *are* my light. I have been too much of a nodcock to take the blinders off my own vision to see that. If I lose you, there will of course be pain, but that is the payment for loving someone, and perhaps that is how it should be."

"Oh." Tears gathered in her eyes, but she quickly blinked them away. Madelene fussed with the folds of his messy cravat. "When I said my vows to you five years ago, I meant every word. Though good or bad, richer or poorer, in sickness or in health, I shall still have you until there is no breath left in my body." Needing to touch him, to reassure him, she slipped her hand to his cheek. The rough stubble there tickled her palm and lit tiny fires in her blood. "I love you, Gilbert, and I cannot wait to see where this next phase of life takes us."

"Me neither."

Then he *did* kiss her, and she surrendered to it with a tiny sigh. Soon after that, frustration welled, for having the use of only one arm put quite the damper on an embrace with any sort of authority. To say nothing of the fact that throbbing pain quite cooled her ardor. But there was plenty of time for all of that.

With a soft sound of regret, Madelene gently pushed him away. "I must rest. My arm hurts too dreadfully to continue this." When an expression of self-recrimination lined his face, she shook her head. "Please do not continue to blame yourself. I don't wish to have a hangdog for a husband."

"It is difficult, for seeing you in pain and knowing I put you there—"

"Stop. What is done is done. We are moving forward, not backward." With a sigh, she nestled into the mound of pillows at her back. "When will be remove to Brighton?"

"As soon as you are able to travel comfortably."

"You will patch things up with Hugh before we go?" She raised an eyebrow in inquiry.

"Yes." He released a sigh of resignation. "If that is what you wish."

"It is. His sister is still my best friend; he will always be a fond acquaintance as well as *your* best friend. You need each other." Wanting another sip of tea but not having the strength to reach for the cup, she gave him a weak smile instead. "Friends are difficult to come by in this world. Keep those you love close."

"Very well."

With a wave of her hand, Madelene sank deeper into the pillows. "I am quite fatigued just now, but will you visit again later? Perhaps lay beside me until I fall asleep?"

"Of course." He scrambled to his feet, scooped up her hand, and then brought it to his lips. "In the event that you wished to know, I did apologize to every member of my family regarding my past behavior. That's a start, yes?"

"It is, and I'm proud of you for it." She squeezed his fingers before releasing him. "I think this time will be different between us. Come what may, I will have you, and truly, that is all I need."

"I don't deserve you," he whispered as he leaned over her and brushed his lips over hers.

"You don't, I quite agree, but have me you do, so you'd best gird yourself. We have much living to do between us." She closed her eyes, for suddenly the lids felt too heavy.

His chuckle reverberated in her chest with delicious tingles. "That we do." Then his footsteps echoed on the hardwood floor, accompanied by the rhythmic thud of the tip of his cane. The sound of the door opening then closing met her ears, and she sighed again.

They had been given another chance, and this time, neither of them would take it for granted. *I have my husband back.* Nothing made her happier than that, for she had waited a long time indeed for him to discover she'd only wanted him to begin with.

CHAPTER EIGHTEEN

October 1, 1819
Brighton, England

GILBERT INHALED THE sea- and salt-scented air, and once more, he thanked God his life had been turned topsy-turvy and inside out since the end of July.

An hour before twilight, he'd come down to the shore to walk in the surf and spend a few moments to himself, for it was a practice he'd started when he'd kept vigil outside Madelene's sick room following the shooting. Over the weeks, he'd discovered that either starting or ending his day with a few words or thoughts of gratitude truly made a difference on the direction his thoughts—as well as his decisions—took. It also helped keep fear in the background.

Damn, but I've been such a fool. Yet as his wife continually told him, each day was a new beginning, and it was never too late to become the man he always wanted to be.

They had been in Brighton for a month, and those days had been some of the most glorious he'd ever spent in his adult life. Her wound had healed sufficiently enough that her physician had let her travel to Brighton for further recuperation. Every day she was obliged to move the arm and encourage the muscles to regain their strength, but overall, she seemed to have no adverse effects.

The stay at the seaside had been all too lovely having Madelene to himself without being interrupted by family obligations or running the risk of old jealousy flaring, and in the process, he'd discovered he adored the unhurried lifestyle that Brighton offered. There were still society events thrown by members of the *ton*, but he didn't feel anxiety to attend or to portray himself as something he wasn't. Every once in a while, she would push him to accept an invitation here and there, for his wife loved dressing in pretty clothes and being taken out to mingle, but by and large, she was at her happiest when they walked the shore hand in hand or spent quiet evenings by the fire in the drawing room.

And he loved her even more for that.

Beyond that, he adored the woman his wife had become while he'd been in India. She was bold and courageous, had a determined spirit, had learned how to gain strength and compassion out of the ashes of her losses. The way she looked at life now pulled him along with her, and with each day that went by, she quietly taught him that dwelling in the darkness of the past wasn't what he needed.

And each evening, they sat in the library to make plans for their upcoming trip to Bombay. Dear God, how was he so fortunate that she still wanted a future with him?

As the sea breeze ruffled through his hair that was a tad longer than current fashion demanded, he pulled himself out of his ruminations to attend to the letter from Hugh clutched in his hand. After leaning a shoulder against one of the large breakers, he carefully unfolded the missive that had arrived with the post just that afternoon.

Dated a month after the shooting, it had taken two weeks to arrive in Brighton, but it was still a welcome connection. Even though Gilbert had made amends with his friend, Hugh had left Ettesmere Park the same time he and Madelene had traveled to the seaside town. They hadn't talked since.

Dear Yeardly,

I trust this letter will find you well, and that you are content and happy in whatever form your life has taken. Before you wonder, my wound has fully healed. I retain another scar to add to my collection, but otherwise, I am no worse for wear, though the damned wound hurts when rain is coming. At least it gives me something to look forward to as I once more take up the reins of my existence in London during this dismal time of the year when it rains more often than not.

Additionally, if you wonder about this as well, I have not heard from your wife since we all left Ettesmere Park. While I miss my friend—and my sister misses her acutely, I might add—I understand that now is not the time to complain about such an insignificant thing. Letters have come from both your brother and sister, as well as Miss Atherby—who, from all accounts is slightly eccentric and a touch compelling—and while I appreciate expanding my circle of friends and acquaintances, I can honestly say I miss your friendship the most.

We both made mistakes in the past, and I can finally see how my presence and perhaps pointed meddling has caused you grief, for which I am heartily sorry. It was never my intention to prove a hinderance for either of you, and my own stupid pride was very much at play leading up to the night things changed for all of us.

What had it taken for Hugh to write those words? Now more than ever Gilbert appreciated the man's strength, honesty, and nobility. Though his chest tightened with remembered anger when the man had stepped too close, that wasn't his future now, and the feeling passed without incident.

It was quite an extraordinary concept to feel something and then not allow himself to dwell on it.

It has taken me many days to ponder the words I wished to convey to you, for it seems our friendship has been charged with underlying emotion ever since the advent of Madelene. While I will admit I once thought she would make the perfect helpmeet for me, after seeing the two of you together, I have been convinced I was right in the beginning when I'd hoped you would make a go of it with her.

If fate is kind, I will find a woman like her, but if I don't, I shall continue on as I have been… without the jealousy, though. I am happy for you and for her. If any two people have ever belonged in a marriage, it is you and Madelene.

Gilbert laid his free hand over his heart. From Hugh, those words were extremely freeing and the best endorsement he could have ever hoped for. In his own way, Hugh had let the dream of Madelene go, and that took so much worry from his mind.

In the meanwhile, I will content myself with my position at the Home Office, and though it will most likely entail executing paperwork and filing the same for a bit, I am grateful for this chance where many former soldiers still struggle.

That being said, I have no plans to travel, and if you find it in your heart to forgive me in the space of the next few months, please consider spending a portion of the Christmastide season with me and Dinah—as well as Mother before you hie off to India. She has been asking after you, and it would be a welcome diversion for both my sister and me from her bloody matchmaking. Consider bringing some of your family if you feel uncomfortable or ask Miss Atherby to accompany you.

In fact, perhaps just bring your cousin. As I said, she is… intriguing.

I promise to interact with Madelene as a gentleman. Already, I miss the close friendship we used to have, and I regret that my actions were partially responsible for driving a wedge between us. After everything, I'd rather not lose my best friend over my stupidity.

God, he missed Hugh. They had both squandered their time together while at Ettesmere Park when they should have been riding or hunting or going into the village to drink or encourage the major to chase a pretty tavern maid. Vowing to make further repairs to the friendship, Gilbert glanced away from the letter to watch a gull cavort through the air.

And what the devil did his apparent fascination with Miss Atherby mean? He would need to ask Madelene's advice on that as well as a visit for the holidays. It would mean a delay to their plans, but since he'd yet to book passage…

With a sigh, he returned to the letter.

> *I suppose I've written all of this to say I wish you the best of luck in your life, Gilbert. You have terrific potential, and I cannot wait to see how you will change the English viewpoint of tea. I am honestly expecting you to announce the news of you opening a tea café in London before too long, and I will be the first guest you let through the door.*
>
> *Please write back at your earliest conveyance. I hope we are both at a point now that the mistakes of the past can remain buried so they will not haunt our future.*
>
> *Yours respectfully,*
> *Hugh*

With care, Gilbert folded the letter and tucked it into the interior pocket of his jacket of bottle green superfine. Then he began the trek over the beach toward the Winterbourne townhouse.

Not finding Madelene in any of the usual places she'd taken to haunting since their residence had begun, he entered their shared bedchamber. "Mad? Are you in here?" Then stopped abruptly, for his wife, clad only in a thin lawn shift, stood in front of a full-length cheval glass while holding up two colorful gowns. *Dear God.* All the windows in the suite had been thrown open to encourage the cooler air inside. The breeze caught at her loose hair and tossed it about her shoulders. "Uh… what are you doing?"

"Trying to decide which gown I wish to wear to the Hoffmans' rout tomorrow evening. These new gowns were delivered an hour ago." She held up a frock of rust-colored taffeta. "This one is lovely and makes my eyes look really green, but this one," she held up a gown of deep purple, "is in my favorite color. The bodices are slightly different, but I wish to choose based on color alone this time."

Gilbert closed the door that led to the corridor. "Where is your maid?"

"It is her afternoon off. I hope she's meeting with a certain groomsman she's had her eye on for the last two weeks." With a sigh, she draped the gowns over the high-backed sofa done in blue and gold brocade. "I think perhaps I'll choose the purple." When she turned to face him, the pink outlines of her hardened nipples were clearly visible through the nearly sheer fabric. "What are you doing back already? You usually spend a few hours at the beach when you go out."

"I wished to request your company." Where he'd thought to ask her to walk in the surf with him, seeing her clad thusly had other, more wicked ideas bouncing through his brain. "Would you be interested if I were to do unspeakable things to you?"

Her eyes rounded, more green than brown as her arousal bloomed. "What sort of things?" she asked, and her inquiry was a breathless sort of affair.

"Need you ask?" After leaning his cane against a nearby table, Gilbert quickly struggled out of his jacket and once he'd fought with the laces at the back of his waistcoat, he fairly ripped the piece from his person. The garments were tossed to the floor.

"Well, a woman does wish to know what she is agreeing to." She raked her gaze up and down his person as he divested himself of cuffs, collar, and cravat. "Perhaps I had earmarked the afternoon for reading in the drawing room."

"Ha!" Over the past couple of weeks, they had taken to coupling in whatever room they happened to be in, but this flirty side of her only enhanced their play. "Would you rather pass the next hour lost in a book or being sent flying?"

"Hmm." Madelene closed the distance between them while

he toed off his boots. She walked her fingers up his chest, and the heat of her seeped through the lawn of his shirt. "I am torn, for both activities are quite stimulating."

"Are you certain you have no preference?" It took next to no time to whip the shirt up and off his body, where it joined the growing trail of clothes.

"Or there is a trip to India to plan…" With a quirk of her eyebrow, slowly retreated.

He, of course, followed. How could he not? This erotic game of cat and mouse made him even more randy. "I'm told planning after being thoroughly pleasured is even more rewarding."

"I wonder." The wall between two windows halted her faux-flight, and she waited with glittering eyes for him to catch up. "However will I decide?"

"Hmm, perhaps I can help with that." With little effort, he leaned into her, trapping her with a palm against the wall on either side of her head, and when he claimed her lips, she kissed him back with a fervor that equaled his own. As with every time he was with Madelene in this capacity, things went from innocent to heated all too quickly. By the time she plucked at the waist of his breeches, he was already terribly hard and ready.

"Surely, Lord Yeardly, you know what I like," she purred and ran her hands up his bare chest. Every grouping of muscles she passed clenched or twitched.

"Mmm. Shall we put that to the test?" At her nod, he divested her of the shift. Damn, but he never tired of seeing her nude with her hair wild and down and need sparkling in her eyes.

"Are you that good?"

"You tell me." With a carefree laugh—when was the last time he'd felt thusly?—Gilbert kissed a path beneath her jaw, followed the length of her slender throat, licked and nibbled at her breasts and nipples a bit before going further south. Down, down, down he went, letting his fingertips trail over the sides of her body as he kneeled before her.

That satiny skin captured his imagination and kept his lips

busy as he explored the soft swell of her belly then moved on to place a kiss at her mons. Up and down, he glided his fingers along the outside of her thighs and when she widened her stance, he did the same to the quivering skin of the inside of them.

Gooseflesh followed everywhere he touched, and when she delved her fingers into his hair, he grinned. Oh, his Madelene enjoyed each time they were together, and that was why he always sought to be inventive in their play.

"Don't keep me in suspense," she practically purred while she lifted a leg, hooked her knee over his shoulder, and urged him closer with her heel into his back.

"Vixen." Yet he didn't wish to draw this out. Despite being with her all these months, his hand shook as he parted her flesh and urged that tiny bundle of nerves out of hiding. Then, when a shiver careened through her body, he grinned and buried his face in the heated heaven that was his wife.

With every sweep and pass of his tongue to that nubbin, his shaft hardened. As he teased the swollen button, and tiny cries were pulled from her throat, he explored further, wishing to bring her to a crashing release before he claimed her body. Up and down, Gilbert caressed her legs, both the inside and outside, and as trembles played over her skin, he worked that all-important nubbin at her center. Tiny moans left her throat, and she tightened her fingers in his hair. The gentle pinpricks of pain spurred him onward. He increased his friction: sucking, nipping, flicking, and then soothing the bud with his tongue before repeating the cycle.

"Ah… Gilbert!" A low keening cry broke from her throat. Her legs shook; her thighs trembled. "So quickly this time."

"Well, I suppose you were primed before now."

"Yes, but…" She sighed and her leg slipped from his shoulder. Her knees wobbled.

"I adore seeing you undone." With a smug chuckle, he stood and wrapped his arms around her, kissed her mouth, told her with his tongue exactly what he would do to her mere moments.

She maneuvered a hand between their bodies to cup his erection through the breeches. "Is that all you'll give this afternoon?"

"Have I ever disappointed you in this?" Before she could answer, he released her long enough to shuck out of his breeches and kicked them away. Thank God for the impressive arousal he sported; he had wished to make a good showing for her.

"You have not." As she swept her gaze over his manhood, he swore he felt that hot glance as if she'd caressed him. "And I couldn't be happier." With a laugh that promised wicked things, Madelene took his hardened length in her hand, stroked her curled fingers down his shaft, and at his stones, she cupped them and gave them a gentle squeeze.

"Damn." A sigh shuddered from his throat, but wanting to give tit for tat, Gilbert slid a hand along the silky expanse of her back to pinch a buttock.

"Cheeky." But that didn't deter his wife. She merely grinned, teased one of his nipples with her fingernail, laughed at his surprised inhalation, then tormented that bud with her teeth and tongue. All the while, she pumped her hand up and down his straining shaft. So much so that his stones tingled from an excess of desire, and he thrust into her hand.

"Sweeting, I'm primed enough. I will explode soon."

"Good. I like keeping you on that edge." Yet she didn't leave off with her brand of exquisite torture. Twisting her curled fingers as she worked him over, she laughed when he gasped. "Shall I take you into my mouth?" she whispered, and the warmth of her breath skated over the nipple she'd already tormented, bringing it to a hardened tip once more.

"No." The word was garbled, choked. He would barely last while standing there. "Tonight, you may play all you wish if you still have the urge."

She frowned. "Spoil sport." But she released his shaft, and he breathed a sigh of relief. Then she caught up his hand. "Bed me, Yeardly. I want to feel you moving inside me."

God, he adored when she was forceful. "Shouldn't we close

the windows?"

The look she pinned him with as she gently propelled him over the floor toward the bed sent molten need surging through his veins in place of blood. "If the neighbors are that nosy, let them listen. Perhaps it will inspire them."

"You are amazing." There was truly nothing else to say, for every day that went by, he was more and more surprised by her and determination to live a good life despite what she'd been through.

"So are you." With a tiny shove, she smiled as he toppled backward onto the mattress. "However, that doesn't give you leave to do a piss-poor job of it right now." When she joined him on the bed, she straddled his waist, and he died a thousand deaths when his engorged shaft rubbed against her bottom.

"I need you, Mad." The words came out more breathless than he'd intended, and for the first time in a long while it wasn't due to fear. None of that held him captive any longer; he'd conquered most of it, and what remained he wouldn't feed its power.

"There's nothing stopping you. In fact, I highly encourage it." Amusement mixed with desire in her eyes.

"Ride me. Start us off at your command." Gilbert drew her down so he could kiss her lips. "Give me all of you so that I might do the same."

"Ah, aren't you full of surprises?" When she wriggled her hips, he nearly went out of his mind with need.

"Yes, but soon you will be full of me, so please don't tarry."

"So needy." Madelene lightly bit his bottom lip, but then easily lifted onto her knees, and once more her fingers were on his length, guiding him along her flesh until his tip paused at her opening.

"Argh!" He gripped her hips, moving her body as he met her gaze. "Are you—Ah!" The hold on his control snapped when she slammed her body downward onto his shaft, never stopping until she was fully impaled. "You, my dear, will surely kill me." White light strewn with sparkles erupted behind his eyelids. Wild sensation raced through his length, and if he didn't calm, this coupling would soon be over.

"I absolutely adore this position." Madelene glanced her fingertips along his abdomen, his chest, his shoulders. Each touch sent him crashing toward the point of no return. Then she moved, sliding up and down his shaft, gyrating her hips at times, and he thought he might expire right there, for with every quick penetration, he went impossibly deep. Pleasure lined her expression. "Never will I tire of doing this with you." As she bounced, her breasts swayed, and her head went back. In that moment, when she claimed ultimate pleasure—claimed *him*—she was the most gorgeous woman he'd ever seen.

"I'll go over too soon." And he knew they both didn't want that. When her movements slowed, he gripped her waist while his body tensed. The brief reprieve bought him some time, so he flipped them both over and covered her body with his. "Let me give you all of me now."

"I was hoping you'd say that." She lifted her head, gave him a hard kiss, and then fell backward into the bedding.

"You have no idea how much I adore you." For long moments, he kissed and licked seemingly inch of her soft skin that he could reach in a bid to stave off spending. With fingers, tongue and teeth, he brought her, shaking and gasping, to the edge of release as he tormented her nipples and teased between her thighs to torture that swollen bud. She retaliated, of course she did, by nipping the underside of his jaw then slipping a hand between them to once more cup his stones. When she squeezed, he nearly bit through the inside of his cheek to stop the inevitable.

"Enough. I won't last like this."

"That is the point, is it not?" Such affection gleamed in her eyes, he wanted to cry from the sheer joy of it.

How much did he love her? Gilbert settled himself comfortably between her bent, raised knees, and with one flex of his hips, he penetrated her as deep as he could go. Her honeyed heat surrounded him, pulled at him, and he sighed. "Ah, Mad, you are heaven."

"Mmm, perhaps." She drew him closer, twined her arms about his shoulders. "Let me feel you. Give me everything."

"You already have it." Over and over, he moved into her with slow, gentle strokes while he held his weight on his forearms. She clutched his shoulders, lifted her hips, and matched his rhythm, easily finding the style they both liked. It was so easy with her—his wife—for they moved together as if dancing on a ballroom floor; their bodies glided together in perfect harmony as their moans mingled and they exchanged breath. All too soon, Madelene's eyes shuttered closed. She wrapped a leg about his waist, urging him onward while he speared into her tight passage.

Making love with the proper emotions behind it made the act all the sweeter. Swift need tingled at the base of his spine. Urgency roiled through his stones, pulling them tight to his body. Finally, his control shattered. There was no time to make the coupling last. Faster and faster, he stroked into her, and she met him every time. Deeper and deeper he went, and each time, she cried out her pleasure. As her vocal encouragement continued, he worked harder to send her over the edge before he went too.

"I'm nearly gone." Heated need consumed him, and he shifted his angle. His length rubbed again her button, and he knew it was one of her favorite things.

"Gilbert!" A cry left her throat.

That was all he needed, for he fractured. Frenzied cries came from her as she dug her fingernails into his shoulders. The leg about his waist tightened and she pulled him closer to her body. Then she shattered in his arms, and his wife ushered in her release. As her keening cries continued, her body greedily fluttered around his member. A strangled moan escaped him. And still he worked in an effort to join her. On one last deep thrust, he was gone. White light broke around him, catching him up in a swirling vortex, and then he dissolved into bliss.

"Well, damn." With a sigh, he collapsed and wrapped his arms around her. His racing heartbeat pounded in time with hers.

For several seconds, the sound of their ragged breathing filled the air. "You, madam, are a marvel." When he rolled onto his back, he threw an arm up over his head. "And you have tired me out."

"I am sorry to hear that." A happy sigh interrupted a giggle, but when she layered herself to his side, renewed awareness stirred through his length. "This session wasn't nearly enough."

Dear Lord, she would put him into an early grave, but at least he would die a happy, loved man. "I'll show you later tonight why you should cry enough." He shot her a grin, and when she returned the gesture, he wanted to shout his good fortune from the rooftops. "Thank you for never giving up on me. I would have been lost without you."

"Thank you for finally coming to your senses and returning to me." She brushed a shock of hair from his forehead, and the lovelight shining in her eyes was stunning. "For loving me through the disappointments." Her eyes were luminous with unshed tears. "You have no idea how much that acceptance means."

"You are my wife, Mad. I love you no matter what." He claimed her lips and spent the next few minutes leisurely kissing her. After, when she laid her head on his shoulder, he sighed. "I rather enjoy Brighton."

"So do I, but I will enjoy anywhere we go because we'll do it together." When she drew abstract circles on his hip, he sucked in a sharp breath, for every pass sent awareness dancing over his skin.

"I had a letter from Hugh today. He's invited us to London for Christmastide."

She rose up on an elbow with surprise in her eyes. "Do you think that's wise? I don't want to introduce problems again."

"Honestly? I think it would be a lovely gesture to take a meal with him and Dinah. We have both made mistakes, treated each other horribly, but we have made our peace and apologized. New beginnings will be welcomed. Besides, he's said we could bring some of our family, and he wishes to see my cousin Louisa especially."

"What?" Then a knowing light appeared in her eyes. "Do you think he is interested in her romantically? Oh, she would lead him a merry chase, I'll wager."

"It's anyone's guess at this point, but if he is distracted by her, all the better." He tugged her down and pressed a kiss to her forehead. "If you would rather not delay our passage to India, I will go along with that plan too."

She laid a palm to his chest. "Let's stay here until Christmastide begins. Then we shall go up to London and be with your family as well as Hugh's, but by Twelfth Night, I wish to be finished with visiting. For whatever reason, I do not believe our future lies in England for a bit."

"That is my feeling as well." He tucked her against his body once more. "We are going to have such fun together. I cannot wait to show you some of my favorite places in the world."

"And I cannot wait to discover where I fit into that world." She kissed his chest. "I am exceedingly thrilled with how our marriage is growing."

"As am I." Whether the future held the birth of a live child, the opening of a tea café, or whether it held more heartache, it didn't matter. Madelene was the true treasure of his heart, and as long as she was with him, as long as he continued to keep himself sorted, he required nothing else in order to be content.

She had taught him that.

And that was perhaps the most valuable lesson of all.

The End

About the Author

Sandra Sookoo is a *USA Today* bestselling author who firmly believes every person deserves acceptance and a happy ending. Most days you can find her creating scandal and mischief in the Regency-era, serendipity and happenstance in Victorian America or snarky, sweet humor in the contemporary world. Most recently she's moved into infusing her books with mystery and intrigue. Reading is a lot like eating fine chocolates—you can't just have one. Good thing books don't have calories!

When she's not wearing out computer keyboards, Sandra spends time with her real-life Prince Charming in central Indiana where she's been known to goof off and make moments count because the key to life is laughter. A Disney fan since the age of ten, when her soul gets bogged down and her imagination flags, a trip to Walt Disney World is in order. Nothing fuels her dreams more than the land of eternal happy endings, hope and love stories.

Stay in Touch

Sign up for Sandra's bi-monthly newsletter and you'll be given exclusive excerpts, cover reveals before the general public as well as opportunities to enter contests you won't find anywhere else.

Just send an email to sandrasookoo@yahoo.com with SUB-SCRIBE in the subject line.

Or follow/friend her on social media:
Facebook: facebook.com/sandra.sookoo
Facebook Author Page: facebook.com/sandrasookooauthor
Pinterest: pinterest.com/sandrasookoo
Instagram: instagram.com/sandrasookoo
BookBub Page: bookbub.com/authors/sandra-sookoo